"We are friends, are we not?"

Reese nodded. "We are."

"Wouldn't you also agree that friends help friends?"

He ran a hand along his jaw. "I would."

"I don't mind if this puts us in close proximity." Callie's bow-shaped lips curved upward. "I enjoy your company."

"I enjoy yours, too." A little too much. And therein lay the problem. Reese really liked Callie. He especially liked this new Callie, the one who dressed in rich, bold colors that made her skin glow and her eyes sparkle.

Her transformation awed him. Her beauty stole his breath.

"If you will give me a chance—" she pulled her hand away from his arm "—I believe I can be of great assistance in your search."

Hadn't he already arrived at that same conclusion? "That is not the point."

"What is the point?"

He couldn't remember.

"I need a day or two to think this through," he said, grasping for any reason to make his exit before he said or did something he couldn't take back.

Books by Renee Ryan

Love Inspired Historical

*The Marshal Takes a Bride
*Hannah's Beau
  Heartland Wedding
*Loving Bella
  Dangerous Allies
*The Lawman Claims His Bride
  Courting the Enemy
  Mistaken Bride
*Charity House Courtship
*The Outlaw's Redemption
*Finally a Bride
*His Most Suitable Bride

Love Inspired

  Homecoming Hero
†Claiming the Doctor's Heart

*Charity House
†Village Green

RENEE RYAN

grew up in a Florida beach town where she learned
to surf very poorly. Armed with a degree in econom-
ics and religion from Florida State University, she ex-
plored various career opportunities, including stints at
a Florida theme park, a modeling agency and a cosmet-
ics conglomerate. She also taught high school econom-
ics, American government and Latin while coaching
award-winning cheerleading teams. She currently lives
in Nebraska with her husband and a large, fluffy cat
many have mistaken for a small bear. Renee's website
is www.reneeryan.com. You can also find her on Facebook and Twitter, @ReneeRyanBooks.

His Most Suitable Bride

RENEE RYAN

⟨H⟩ **HARLEQUIN**® LOVE INSPIRED® HISTORICAL

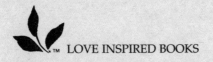

LOVE INSPIRED BOOKS

Recycling programs
for this product may
not exist in your area.

ISBN-13: 978-0-373-28278-4

HIS MOST SUITABLE BRIDE

www.Harlequin.com

Printed in U.S.A.

For the Lord does not see as man sees;
for man looks at the outward appearance,
but the Lord looks at the heart.
—1 Samuel 16:7

To my amazing, handsome, fabulous husband, Mark.
Because of the love and grace you show me
on a daily basis, writing romance is easy for me.
I just have to look at you and know happily-ever-after
is real. Love you, always and forever.

Chapter One

Denver, Colorado—1895
The Tabor Grand Opera House

Tonight should have ranked among the finest of Callie Mitchell's life. Certainly all the elements were in place. She sat in a box seat, on a plush velvet chair, watching a world-class performance of *Roméo et Juliette*.

Based on William Shakespeare's play, the popular opera consisted of five drama-filled acts with four—*four!*—duets between the main characters.

Callie was supposed be happy.

She *was* happy. Almost. But not quite.

Stifling a sigh, she took her gaze off the drama unfolding on the stage and glanced around. Horace A. W. Tabor had spared no expense in the construction of his opera house. The expert woodwork, elaborate chandelier and vibrant frescos made for a luxurious decor unrivaled by any other theater in Denver.

Perhaps therein lay the problem. Too many sights assaulted Callie, begging her to gawk in openmouthed wonder.

She was entirely too sensible for such a vulgar reaction. After all, she was the more levelheaded of the two Mitchell sisters, the boring one. Everyone said so.

Another sigh worked its way up her throat. Callie only

had herself to blame for what people thought of her. She'd deliberately cultivated her uninteresting persona after her shameless act all those years ago when she'd attended school in Boston.

Fortunately, no one in Denver knew just how close she'd come to ruin. God may have forgiven her sin. Callie could not. Nor could she forget and thereby risk repeating the same mistake twice.

She closed her eyes for a moment—just one—and lost herself in the music. The heart-wrenching melody washed over her, each note more superb than the last. An urge to hum told her she was inches away from losing control.

She whipped open her eyes and focused on the woman perched on the chair beside her. A renowned beauty in her day, Beatrix Singletary's golden brown hair held not a speck of gray. And her face barely showed that nearly two decades had passed since Mr. Singletary, now deceased, had won her hand in marriage.

Serving as the widow's companion had come at a time in Callie's life when she'd needed a change and a reason to focus on someone other than herself.

The music hit a crescendo.

Callie turned her attention back to the stage. This time, she did give into a sigh. The doomed Juliette had no idea the pain she would soon suffer because of love.

Callie knew. Oh, how she knew. Not only because of the incident in Boston, but also because of...*him.*

She didn't dare glance in his direction, though he sat directly across the theater, in a box seat mirroring Mrs. Singletary's. *Don't look,* Callie ordered herself.

Do. Not. Look.

She looked.

The breath clogged in her throat. Her heart slammed against her ribs. Reese Bennett Jr. She knew every facet of that strong, handsome face. The full breadth of those wide, muscular shoulders. The dark, intense eyes that were the same rich color as his hair, a shade nearly as black as a raven's feather.

He sat with his father and seemed a little too content for a man recently jilted. Not by Callie. She would never reject an offer of marriage from him. He'd proposed to someone else, and would have married that someone else had the stubborn girl not left town.

The fact that the person in question was Callie's younger, prettier sister was a source of intense distress. Fanny had made a terrible mistake. And the longer she stayed away the harder it would be to rectify her rash decision.

Reese would not stay single for long. Not only was he a successful attorney, but he was also very masculine, so utterly appealing. Any number of women would happily take Fanny's place.

Callie could not allow that to happen. He must remain free of any entanglement until Fanny came to her senses.

Stubborn, headstrong girl. How could she have rejected Reese? He was…so very…wonderful. Callie swallowed. Restrained another sigh. Felt her eyelashes flutter.

As if sensing her watching him, Reese turned his head in her direction.

Their gazes met. Held.

Callie nearly choked on her own breath.

Floodgates of emotion burst open, giving her no time to brace for impact. Sensation after sensation rolled over her. There was something else in the storm of feelings running through her, something truly terrible, a scorching pain in her heart. *He can never be mine.*

The thought itself was beyond inappropriate, perhaps even a betrayal to the sister she adored.

Pressing her lips tightly together, Callie set her hands in her lap and willed away the emotion threatening to take hold of her. A quick, sharp gasp slipped out, anyway.

"Something troubling you, my dear?"

"No, Mrs. Singletary." Callie dragged her gaze away from Reese. Keeping her voice low enough for only the widow to hear, she added, "I...I was simply caught up in the music."

"Ah, yes." The widow swept a glance over the auditorium, stopping a shade too long on the box directly across from them. "Perfectly understandable."

Callie gave her employer a faint smile, praying they were talking about the opera. Surely, she hadn't given herself away.

Thankfully, the widow turned her head back toward the stage and studied the drama unfolding before them. After only a moment, though, she leaned back toward Callie. "I find the music quite lovely, I'd even suggest inspiring. What say you?"

Lovely? Inspiring? Were they watching the same opera? "Not really. The music is haunting and the story is...so very—" she took a quick, hitching breath of air "—tragic."

"My dear, dear girl." The widow patted her arm in a way that made Callie feel both young and ridiculously naive. At twenty-three, and with *the incident* in her past, she was neither. "One must never focus on the ending when the story has yet to fully begin."

Had the widow not been paying attention? "Mrs. Singletary, we have come to the final moments of the third act. Tybalt is dead. Romeo has been banished for murder. Nothing but misfortune and heartache lies ahead."

"Oh, Callie, you are missing my point entirely. No matter the outcome, we must enjoy each moment of every journey as it comes."

The words were entirely too profound for an evening at the opera, alerting Callie that the widow, in her non-too-subtle way, was encouraging her to relax her serious nature.

It wasn't the first time she'd let Callie know her opinion on the matter. Arguing now would be useless.

"Yes, Mrs. Singletary." Callie inclined her head in a polite nod. "I shall try my best to heed your advice."

"That is all I ask." The widow settled back in her chair, but not before Callie caught a speculative gleam in her eyes.

Oh, this was bad. Very, very bad.

As if to confirm her suspicions, Mrs. Singletary ignored the performance and turned her attention back to the box across the auditorium. She held steady for one beat, two, then continued circling her gaze around the auditorium, stopping at seemingly random spots along the way.

Or, perhaps not so random.

If Callie wasn't mistaken, the widow only paused to consider single, unattached men around Callie's own age before moving on to search out the next section of seats.

Callie wanted to smack her hand over her eyes and groan aloud. Mrs. Singletary was hunting out suitable young men to court her.

Oh, Lord, please, no.

It was no secret the widow considered herself a skilled matchmaker. And why not? She'd made several high-profile matches in the past two years. Her most recent success had been her former companion, Molly Taylor Scott. Callie's closest, dearest friend, Molly was now married to one of Callie's older brothers. And—

No. Oh, no.

Mrs. Singletary *was* attempting to find Callie's one true soul mate. It didn't seem to matter that she'd made it abundantly clear she wanted no part in the widow's matchmaking schemes, either as an accomplice or the object of a pairing.

Callie hadn't made this declaration because she didn't believe in love, or want to be happily settled. She did. So very much. But the one man—the only man—she wanted could never be hers.

If only he hadn't asked another woman to marry him. If only that woman hadn't been Callie's sister, a woman who would come to her senses any day now and ask Reese to take her back.

The third act came to an abrupt, dismal close.

Mrs. Singletary enthusiastically applauded the performance. Callie very much doubted that look of joy on the widow's face had anything to do with the spectacular singing and superior acting.

As soon as the lights came up, Mrs. Singletary rose regally to her feet. "Come along, Callie." A cagey smile played across her lips. "It's time we indulge ourselves in conversation and refreshment."

Callie would rather stay behind. Unfortunately, that particular activity was not in her job description.

Giving in as graciously as possible, she squared her shoulders and followed the widow to the curtained exit of their box seating. Against her better judgment, she glanced over her shoulder and allowed her gaze to find Reese once again.

If only...

Reese remained in his seat during intermission, while his father left to work the crowd in the atrium. He knew he was ignoring his duty. As the new managing senior partner of his family's law firm, Reese should be circulating among the other opera patrons, engaging in small talk with current clients and scouting out potential new ones.

At the very least he should make a point to speak with the firm's most important client, Beatrix Singletary.

Reese couldn't drum up the enthusiasm.

He'd already endured three acts of the ghastly *Roméo et Juliette*. He needed this moment alone to gather the fortitude he would need to suffer through the remaining two acts. He didn't especially dislike opera, not in general, just this particular one. The main characters' senseless behavior struck an unpleasant chord.

The impulsive, reckless actions of youth, the unchecked passion that overwhelmed all common sense and eventually led to needless death, it was all so…familiar.

Reese battled against the fourteen-year-old memories always lurking at the edges of his calm nature. They came stronger tonight, momentarily bringing back the fear. The helplessness. The searing pain of grief he'd vowed never to experience again.

Love was a costly proposition best avoided.

Poised between the pull of the past and a need to push toward a predictable, steady future, he looked out over the nearly empty seating below.

The din of conversation and high-pitched laughter grated on him. He kept his reaction hidden behind a blank stare.

To the outside observer he probably appeared to be enjoying this moment alone. If anyone looked closer, would they sense the dark mood beneath? Would they falsely attribute it to his broken engagement with Fanny Mitchell?

He shifted in his seat, fought off a frown.

He regretted losing Fanny, as one might regret the loss of a good friend. Her erratic behavior had given him pause, though. He'd been so careful in his choice of brides, so meticulous. Fanny had seemed a good fit. Until her sudden change of heart had revealed an inconsistency in her character that Reese had missed originally.

Though unexpected, her actions had saved them both a lifetime of regret.

Enough. Enough thinking. Enough pretending he was enjoying himself. There was nothing keeping him from leaving. He would rather spend his time pouring over legal briefs, anyway. The dry, precise language always managed to restore his tranquility.

Decision made, he stood, turned to go and…

Froze midstep.

He was not alone in the box. Two women had joined him. But when? He hadn't heard them enter. How long had they been standing there, watching him?

The older of the two gave him a slow, significant smile, alerting him that he was staring.

He firmed his expression and opened his mouth to speak.

The widow cut him off before he could begin. "Why, Mr. Bennett, I believe we caught you on your way out."

"You did." He hooked his hands together behind his back. "That's not to say your arrival isn't a pleasant turn of events. Good evening, Mrs. Singletary." He inclined his head in the widow's direction. "You are a vision as always."

He didn't need to catalog her attire to know this to be true. She spared no expense when it came to her clothing and made sure her personal style rivaled any woman in Paris, New York or London. As a result, Beatrix Singletary was undoubtedly the best dressed in all of Denver.

"That is very kind of you to say." She swept her hand in a graceful arc. "I believe you know my companion."

"Of course." Reese continued to look into the widow's eyes another two seconds before turning his attention onto Callie Mitchell.

For a moment, they stared at one another with mutual discomfort. Reese felt the muscles in his back stiffen, and knew his reaction had nothing to do with Callie's personal connection with his former fiancée. He always had this disturbing visceral response to the woman, a woman most looked past in order to focus on her more glamorous sister.

Reese suspected that was exactly what Callie wished people to do.

"Miss Mitchell." Her name came out sounding oddly

tortured, even to his own ears. He cleared his throat. "You are looking quite lovely this evening, as well."

"Thank you, Mr. Bennett." Her gaze didn't quite meet his, nor did she make a move to enter the box fully. Shadows still curtained most of her hair and face.

"Mrs. Singletary." He addressed the widow once again, wondering at her sudden arrival. "To what do I owe this honor?"

"The theater is far too full of people milling about, even on the landings between the tiers of box seats." She flicked a wrist in the direction of the curtain behind her. "We thought we might escape the maddening crush and sit with you a moment before the rest of the performance begins."

Odd. The *maddening crush* had never bothered her before. He'd seen her happily mingling amid the largest of crowds. He couldn't help but wonder again at her sudden presence.

"Please, come in and relax, partake in the desserts the Tabor has provided for my father and me tonight."

Gesturing to his right, Reese stepped aside to let the woman pass.

The widow went directly to the small buffet table and studied the offerings. After a moment, she released a weighty sigh. "There are too many choices. Come closer, Callie." She waved the girl forward. "I shall rely on you to fill my plate."

"Yes, Mrs. Singletary." Callie hesitated only a beat before moving, her steps surprisingly graceful for a woman of her height, a mere head shorter than his six feet two inches.

She floated along like a snowflake, slowly, smoothly and icily controlled. Eventually, she emerged from the shadows completely and Reese's heart kicked an extra hard beat.

His stomach knotted with tension.

Did Callie know the way she'd ruthlessly secured her

pale blond hair off her face displayed her arresting features in startling detail?

His stomach rolled again.

This was not a new reaction for Reese, nor was it in any way a pleasant sensation. Callie Mitchell disturbed him.

He shook aside the thought, not wishing to dwell on how she made him...*feel*. Yet he could not look away from those sculpted cheekbones, the perfectly bowed lips and green, green eyes the color of summer-fresh leaves.

What a picture Callie Mitchell made. So pretty. So perfectly upright. Not a hair out of place. Not a wrinkle in her gown. An image that didn't completely ring true. The woman was too controlled, too perfectly put together.

Reese sensed she hid something a little wild beneath that measured calm. He'd sensed it from the start of their acquaintance and thus had made a point of avoiding her more often than not.

"Mr. Bennett, how are you enjoying this evening's performance so far?" Mrs. Singletary asked him the question as she sat on a chair beside him, settling her skirts around her with practiced ease. "Do you not find the music lovely?"

"Lovely, no. I find it extremely haunting."

A soft gasp came from Callie's direction.

He ignored the sound, and the woman. "The story itself is far too tragic to be considered enjoyable," he added.

"Isn't that interesting?" The widow reached out her hand and accepted the plate full of tea cakes and chocolates from her companion, who for some reason looked entirely disconcerted. "Callie made those exact observations not twenty minutes ago."

"Indeed." Uncomfortable hearing that he and Callie shared the same opinion, Reese adjusted his stance and deflected the conversation back to the widow. "I believe you were instrumental in bringing this particular troupe of performers to Denver. What do you think of their efforts so far?"

It was the perfect question to ask. The widow set about telling him her precise opinion. In great detail.

Listening with only half an ear, he nodded at all the appropriate places. Out of the corner of his eye, he watched as Callie returned to the buffet table. She contemplated the offerings once again. A delicate frown of concentration spread across her brow.

She huffed out a small frustrated breath. Though it had taken her no time to decide what to pick out for her employer, she seemed at a loss when it came to filling her own plate.

Reese found himself oddly riveted.

Would she choose a soft, gooey confection? Or something with more substance? Maybe a mixture of both.

He had no idea why it would matter to him. What could her choices possibly mean in the grand scheme of the evening's events?

"Oh, my, Mr. Bennett, that is quite the fierce expression on your face." Mrs. Singletary's voice cut through his thoughts. "I take it you disagree with me."

He silently filed through the widow's last words. "In my opinion, four duets are three too many."

She let out a soft laugh. "You haven't enjoyed one moment of the tonight's production, have you?"

"No."

His brief response seemed to amuse her further. "I see even in matters of entertainment I can count on your candor."

It did not occur to him to be anything less than frank.

"But, truly, are you not pleased with any portion of tonight's performance?"

"Not in the least."

Watching Callie's attempt to make a decision, however, enthralled him to no end.

Mrs. Singletary made a disapproving sound in her throat. "Are you considering leaving the theater early, then?"

"I am."

"I cannot persuade you otherwise?"

He shook his head. "I'm afraid not."

He continued watching Callie hover over the buffet table. She was being so very, very careful and working so very, very hard to pick just the right confections to put on her plate. Her scrupulous process was oddly sweet and utterly adorable and Reese couldn't bear to watch another moment more.

"Pick one of each, Miss Mitchell."

Her responding flinch warned him his suggestion had come out harsher than he'd meant. He softened his voice. "There is no need to be particular. There is plenty to go around."

"I… Yes, thank you."

She began filling her plate with more enthusiasm. Halfway through, though, she looked up and stared briefly into his gaze.

Briefly was enough.

For that single moment, Reese caught a hint of something disturbingly familiar in her eyes, a willingness to push the boundaries when no one was looking. Dangerous, dangerous territory.

He knew he had a split second to make a decision before it was too late, before he forgot who this woman was and that he'd once been engaged to her sister. He could continue staring at Callie, attempting to fight off this unwanted fascination a few seconds more. Or he could turn his back on her.

He turned his back.

There. She was no longer riveting.
Reese was no longer enthralled.
Everything was back as it should be.

Chapter Two

The following morning, Callie woke early, with gritty eyes, a foggy brain and an uneasy heart. The bright August sunlight had yet to filter through the curtains' seams. Considering her gray mood, she preferred the muted dawn light. The events of the previous evening had left her feeling anxious and mildly out of sorts. It was as if her world had been tilted slightly off-kilter and she couldn't seem to regain her balance.

Whenever she found herself in need of comfort, she turned to her Bible. The Psalms especially had a way of putting matters into perspective, her favorite one reminding her to lean on the Lord and not on her own understanding.

Unfortunately, her mind kept wandering back to last night, to Reese. To the time they'd spent in his opera box.

Something had shifted between them, something new and utterly perplexing.

There'd been that awkward moment when he'd leaned forward and urged her to pick one of every dessert on display. His voice had held equal parts kindness and frustration, the odd mix of emotions confusing her even more. So she'd done as he suggested and filled her plate with sweets she had no intention of eating.

After that, he'd turned his back and avoided speaking to her directly for the rest of the intermission.

She'd been relieved. Then filled with despair.

Then relieved all over again.

Sighing, she curled her fingers around her Bible and pressed the book to her heart. Reese was so handsome, and in many ways so familiar, yet she hardly knew him. For all their interactions through the years, they'd never stepped beyond polite pleasantries.

Last night had been no different. Except…

Everything had been different. *Reese* had been different. The way he'd looked her directly in the eyes, as if she mattered, for herself, had left a peculiar feeling in the pit of her stomach.

Had anyone ever told her that she would one day be the center of Reese's attention, even for a few precious moments at the opera, she would have declared them quite mad. He'd barely spared her a glance before last night.

This was getting her nowhere. Callie was reading far too much into his behavior, looking for a hidden meaning where there was none. Now she was running late for breakfast.

She dressed quickly, choosing a basic gray dress and practical, low-heeled ankle boots. She secured her hair with extra pins this morning, smoothing and tugging until every stray curl had been ruthlessly tamed into submission.

Feeling more herself, she went in search of her employer.

She found Mrs. Singletary in the morning room, perusing the *Denver Chronicle,* which was laid out on the table in front of her. Her treasured cat, Lady Macbeth, slumbered in the bright sunbeam at her mistress's feet. A tray with pastries, coffee and two soft-boiled eggs in enameled cups sat untouched beside the newspaper.

"Good morning, Mrs. Singletary."

The widow looked up, frowned. "No, dear, absolutely not."

Callie's feet ground to a halt. "Pardon me?"

"That dress simply will not do." The words were spoken without meanness, but the censure was there all the same.

As if to punctuate her mistress's disapproval, Lady Macbeth cracked open an eye and studied Callie through the narrowed slit. A delicate sniff and she returned to her nap, chin resting lightly on her front paws.

Callie tried not to feel offended. But, really, dismissed by a cat? It was beyond humiliating.

Worse, Mrs. Singletary wasn't through inspecting Callie's attire. "That color is all wrong for you."

Perhaps the dull gray did clash with her skin tone. But no more than it had the other three times she'd worn the dress in Mrs. Singletary's company.

"The fit isn't right, either."

Callie resisted the urge to cinch the black ribbon around her waist tighter. Mrs. Singletary was correct on both points. The color was unflattering and the dress was, indeed, too large. That had rather been the point. Still, the widow's blunt appraisal stung. "I thought you didn't care what I wore."

"Now, see. That is where you went wrong. Of course I care. I care a great deal."

"You've said nothing before." Head down, Callie lowered herself into a chair facing her employer. "I don't understand."

"It's quite simple. You have been in my employ for precisely four weeks since I plucked you out of the Hotel Dupree kitchens where, I might add, your talents were completely underutilized." The widow leaned forward, trapping Callie in her gaze. "You are no longer underpaid kitchen help, but my trusted companion. It's high time you look the part."

Callie carefully placed a napkin in her lap. She should have known this was coming, should have prepared for this eventuality. Mrs. Singletary was the best dressed woman in Denver. Of course she would care what her companion wore.

"We will begin rethinking your wardrobe today."

So soon? "What's the hurry?"

"As I already mentioned, how you dress reflects directly back on me."

Well, yes. Yet Callie couldn't shake the notion that the widow had a different reason for wanting her to dress better.

"Besides—" she smoothed her hand over the newspaper, turned the page with a flick "—one must always be prepared for the unexpected visitor."

Something in the way the woman made this casual remark put Callie immediately on guard. "Are you expecting anyone in particular this morning?"

"No one out of the ordinary, dear." She picked up her spoon and tapped one of the eggs perched in its enameled cup. A perfect series of cracks webbed out in every direction. "Only my attorney."

Callie's heart lurched. "Reese? I mean…Mr. Bennett is coming here?" She swallowed back a gasp of dismay. "Today?"

She wasn't ready to see him again, not yet, not until she could process their odd interaction at the opera last night.

"He will be here this morning, and I should warn you." The widow turned another page of the newspaper. "Now that Mr. Bennett is once again overseeing my business affairs, he will be around quite often, perhaps even daily."

Callie breathed in sharply, the only outward sign of her discomfort. Her brother Garrett had handled the widow's business affairs until he'd married Molly and left town for a position in St. Louis. It stood to reason that Reese, as the senior partner in his firm, would take over in Garrett's absence.

If only her brother hadn't felt the need to strike out on his own, away from family and the prominent Mitchell name. Callie missed him so much. Molly too, nearly as much as she missed Fanny.

Oh, she was still angry at her sister, but this was the first they'd been apart for more than a few days at a time. With only a year separating them in age, they'd done everything together.

Now Fanny was living in Chicago. And Callie was here in Denver working for Mrs. Singletary. Not alone, precisely, but definitely more lonely than she'd ever been in her life.

"Did you hear what I said, dear?"

Callie started. "Er...no."

"I said I want you to change your dress before Mr. Bennett arrives."

Again, she wondered, *why the hurry?* Yet she didn't feel comfortable enough to ask the question a second time. "Yes, Mrs. Singletary, I'll do so immediately following breakfast."

"Very good. Something in blue would be most preferable." The widow went back to reading the newspaper in silence.

Left alone with her thoughts, Callie picked up her spoon and gave the egg in front of her a good hard whack. The shell exploded into a hundred little pieces.

Pushing the ruined egg aside, she selected a pastry off the tray. As she ate, she silently reviewed the contents of her closet. She didn't own anything in blue. In truth, none of her dresses were any more exciting than what she currently wore.

The green one was the most modern in fit and style. However, the color was a sort of drab olive. Better, she supposed, than gray. Decision made, she brought the pastry to her mouth once again.

"Don't even think about putting on your green dress." The widow made this announcement without bothering to glance up. "The color is horrid on you."

Callie dropped the pastry back to her plate. "Surely, it's not...horrid."

"Horrid."

Trying not to feel insulted, Callie pulled her bottom lip between her teeth and thought a moment. "Perhaps the yellow one with the ivory lace collar?"

"No."

"The soft pink—"

"Not that one, either." At last, Mrs. Singletary removed her attention from the newspaper and looked up. Her unwavering gaze bore into Callie's. "You are far too pretty to hide behind pale, lifeless pastels and neutrals."

As those were the only colors in her closet, Callie frowned. "Which dress would you have me wear?"

"None in your current wardrobe." The widow placed her hand atop Callie's. "Those we will donate to charity."

She jerked upright, working for breath. "But if I give away all my dresses what, then, will I wear?"

A robust smile spread across the widow's lips. "Leave that to me."

"I find this conversation so very strange." She pulled her hand free from beneath Mrs. Singletary's and placed it in her lap. "You've never once said a word about the way I dress."

"We were still getting to know one another. Now we are friends."

Callie widened her eyes. Mrs. Singletary considered her a friend?

"And from one friend to another, you need to make smarter choices in your attire. If I didn't know better, I'd say you were deliberately trying to camouflage your natural beauty."

Callie pressed her hands together in her lap and fought off a strong desire to defend herself. Once she'd attracted the wrong man's attention and barely avoided disgrace. Better to be safe than put herself on display and risk another mistake.

"Finish your breakfast." Mrs. Singletary leaned back. "We have much work to do before Mr. Bennett arrives."

What did Reese have to do with—

Oh, no. Mrs. Singletary couldn't be thinking of making Callie more attractive for Reese. A match between them was... Why, it was impossible.

Tongues would wag all over town.

The potential for scandal made the very idea ridiculous. Reese's business would suffer, along with his reputation. And what about Fanny? Callie would never hurt her sister, not for anything in the world. And especially not over a man.

No, Callie wouldn't dare attract Reese's attention. Yet she couldn't allow anyone else to so, either, not before Fanny returned home and made things right with him.

While it wouldn't be easy seeing Reese and Fanny together again, it would be better than seeing him with someone else. Callie really hoped Fanny would come to her senses soon.

"If you are finished eating, we will begin."

"Begin?"

"Populating your wardrobe with more suitable gowns."

Callie could think of no good reason to refuse her employer. She set her napkin on the table and forced a smile. "I'm at your mercy, Mrs. Singletary."

Thirty minutes later, she stood in the widow's private dressing room, facing a full-length mirror. Two maids hustled about her, securing buttons, fluffing material in one spot, smoothing out wrinkles in another.

The dress was supposedly one of Mrs. Singletary's castoffs. Callie had her suspicions. Who could not want this gorgeous silk creation? The color was that of the Colorado sky, a deep, rich blue that somehow brought out the green in Callie's eyes. The fit was perfection. The silver buttons added just enough elegance without being too much for day wear.

Even with her severe hairstyle, Callie looked beautiful. She *felt* beautiful. But the woman staring back at her from the mirror was not Callie Mitchell. Not anymore.

Never, never again.

"Let's have a look at you." The widow paraded around her, considering her from various angles. "Much better." She nodded her head in approval. "You were born to wear jewel tones."

Once her closet had been filled with nothing but vibrant colors, Callie thought wistfully.

The housekeeper entered the room and announced, "Mr. Bennett has arrived for your meeting, Mrs. Singletary."

"Thank you, Jane. Tell Winston to show him to my office."

"Yes, ma'am." The housekeeper turned to go then caught sight of Callie. Her eyes rounded with shock. "Oh, miss. Look at you. Why, you're positively glowing."

Callie sighed at her reflection. She *was* glowing.

She'd never felt more miserable in her life.

Reese gathered up the contracts he'd brought with him and stuffed them in his leather briefcase. "I'll make the changes you requested and send over the revised versions before the end of business today."

"That will be fine." Mrs. Singletary sat back in her chair, eyeing him closely, her hands primly clasped in her lap.

He'd worked with the woman long enough to know she had more to say. Something he probably wasn't going to like.

When she remained silent, he braced himself and said, "Is there something else I can do for you, Mrs. Singletary?"

"On the contrary, it's something *I* can do for *you*."

He stifled a groan. Despite her unconventional reputation, the widow meant well. She had a kind heart. Her charity work spoke for itself. But she was also considered a matchmaker of the first order. A terrible thought occurred to him. Surely she wasn't thinking of making him her latest victim.

"I'm probably going to regret this, but tell me. What is it you believe I need?"

"A wife."

Reese pulled in a sharp breath and resisted the urge to snap back, to tell her he didn't need—or want—her input on such a personal matter.

She is your most important client, he reminded himself. One he knew well. Her meddling was never malicious and, more often than not, had a way of bringing about good rather than harm. Eventually.

Even if he suggested, oh-so-gently, that she mind her own business, all she would say was that he was her business.

From a certain angle, she would be correct. Everyone in town knew he was her personal attorney. His actions reflected on her.

Still. She was dangerously close to crossing a line. "There are many men my age still unattached."

She smiled at this, looking quite pleased with herself, as if his response was exactly what she'd expected from him. "True. But now that your father has stepped away from daily operations of your firm, it is up to you to ensure Bennett, Bennett and Brand remains the finest in town."

"Agreed."

"A wife will help you achieve that goal."

"I had a bride picked out," he said. "She begged off."

"A blessing in disguise. You and Fanny Mitchell did not suit one another in the least."

He gritted his teeth. "I disagree. We were an excellent match on many levels."

"Not on the most important point. You weren't in love."

No, he hadn't been in love with Fanny. And, as it turned out, she hadn't been in love with him, either. But they'd liked one another, found many things on which to converse. They would have had an amiable, comfortable life together. "Love is not a necessity in marriage."

"It is if you want a happy one."

Again, he disagreed. Happiness was fleeting, like a wave driven and tossed by the wind. Companionship. Friendship. Those were the things that lasted. The things Reese desired most. He also wanted children, a family of his own.

He needed a wife first.

"I am not opposed to getting married," he admitted.

"I'm glad to hear it, because your image needs improving."

He tilted his head, fought off a surge of irritation. "I always comport myself in a manner above reproach."

"Yes, yes." She waved this off with a graceful sweep of her hand. "You are the quintessential man of integrity."

"This is a good reputation to have."

"The very best. But, Mr. Bennett, may I speak plainly?"

He doubted he could stop her. "By all means."

"You are also considered stern and overly rigid."

He blinked. "People think I'm…rigid?"

"I'm afraid so."

He blinked again. Valuing lists and adhering to a tight schedule merely meant he knew how to plan ahead.

"I daresay a wife will soften your image."

"Yes, you alluded to that already. I don't have time to court a woman, especially now that Garrett Mitchell has left the firm."

"Ah, now we're getting somewhere. You see, my good boy—"

"Boy?" He let out a humorless laugh. He'd left his youth

behind him a long time ago, the day Miranda had died in his arms. "I'm thirty-two years old and—"

"A very busy man." She beamed at him, as if announcing something he didn't already know. "That, Mr. Bennett, is where I come in. I will assist you in your search for a wife."

He didn't like the idea of this woman meddling in his life. But this was Beatrix Singletary, a determined match-maker. Now that the notion was in her head, she would persist. Perhaps even go behind his back. He shuddered at the thought. "Define...assist."

"I will find your one true soul mate."

He'd already found her, when he was eighteen years old. "I'm not looking for a love match."

"Now, Mr. Bennett—"

"I am firm on this point."

She titled her head at an angle, her thoughts whirling in her gaze. She wasn't going to let the matter drop. "Perhaps if you explained why you don't wish to fall in love—"

"If I allow you to help me..." Was he really considering this? "I will expect you to adhere to my rules."

"That goes without saying."

Nevertheless, it needed to be said. "I mean it. Attempt to do things your way, or act on my behalf without my knowledge, and we're done."

"I understand completely."

Did she? Time would tell.

"I will draw up a list of the most important qualities I want in my future bride." Giving her specific requirements appeared the best way to retain control of the situation. "You will stick to the list."

"Mr. Bennett." She looked up at the ceiling and sighed dramatically. "Finding a suitable woman for you to marry cannot be approached with studied calculation."

He stood. "Then I will bid you good day."

"Now, now." The widow sprang to her feet with less grace than usual. "Let's not be hasty."

He paused, eyebrows lifted.

"Oh, very well." She puffed out her cheeks. "Draw up your list, if you must. I will look it over and see what I can do."

"Very good." He made his way to the door.

The widow joined him halfway across the room. "You will not regret putting me in charge of your bride hunt."

He offered a bland smile. "We shall see."

A tentative knock on the door had him turning at the sound.

"Come in," Mrs. Singletary called out in a cheerful voice.

The doorknob twisted. The hinges creaked. And then…

Callie Mitchell popped her head through the open slit, only her head, not any other part of her body. *Odd.* "You wanted me to let you know when it was noon."

"Yes. Thank you, Callie. But my dear, there is no cause for you to hover in the hallway. Join us."

Giving her no time to argue, the widow reached around the door and pulled her companion into the room. For several beats, the two women stared at one another. It was one of those silences far more eloquent than words. Clearly something had put them at odds.

Finally, Callie floated deeper into the room. She caught sight of him and froze. "G-good afternoon, Mr. Bennett."

He gave her a curt nod. "Miss Mitchell."

Breaking eye contact, she reached down to pick up the large tabby cat threading around her skirts like a black-and-white ribbon. Despite the added weight in her arms, she stood perfectly straight, her spine as unbending as a board, her lips pressed in a flat line.

While she held completely still, and silent, he took the opportunity to study her more closely. She'd pinned back her hair too tightly again. And the dull gray of her dress made her look almost sickly. All she needed was a pair of spectacles perched on the bridge of her nose to complete the masquerade of a spinster twice her age.

Reese's lips twisted in annoyance.

Callie Mitchell was deliberately masking her beauty. A gorgeous swan draped in ugly duckling's clothing. And she was doing so on purpose. But why?

Why did the woman wish to make herself unattractive? What was she hiding?

Chapter Three

Callie held Lady Macbeth tightly against her for two equally important reasons. The first was so the cat could serve as a kind of furry shield between her and Reese. The other was a bit more practical. Holding the overweight animal gave Callie something to do with her hands.

Oh, but she desperately wanted to reach up and smooth her palm over her hair, to tuck away any stray curls. The gesture would only reveal her nervousness.

No one could know how anxious she felt in Reese's company, least of all the man himself.

But, really, why was he watching her so intently?

His unwavering focus made her beyond uncomfortable, slightly breathless. Perhaps a little afraid.

Not of him—never of him—but of herself. Of what she might do if he continued looking at her like…like *that*. His eyes practically bore into her, as though she was a puzzle that needed solving. That if he looked long enough and hard enough he could uncover her secrets.

She shivered at the prospect. He could never know the terrible mistake she'd made in Boston.

If only he wasn't standing so close, Callie might have a better chance of regaining her composure. She could smell his familiar scent, a pleasant mixture of books and leather and some woodsy spice all his own.

The man should not smell so good. The result left her poised in stunned immobility. And badly wanting to fidget.

At least he seemed equally uncomfortable. He was as self-possessed as ever, but also appeared wary. Of her? Possibly.

Probably.

No doubt her being Fanny's sister accounted for Reese's discomfort. But there was something else, too, something much more disquieting than their connection through his ex-fiancée.

"Mr. Bennett." Mrs. Singletary's voice broke through the tension hanging in the air. "Was there anything else you wished to discuss before you depart for your office?"

Jerking slightly at the question, he turned to face the widow directly. "No. Our business is sufficiently concluded."

"I assume I can expect your list by this afternoon."

He pinched the bridge of his nose. "I will work on it later today, as soon as I've revised the contracts."

"That will be acceptable."

Tucking his leather briefcase under his arm, he squared his shoulders. "Good day, Mrs. Singletary." He nodded in Callie's direction. "Miss Mitchell, always a pleasure."

His stilted tone said otherwise.

Callie didn't know whether to laugh or cry as she watched him leave the room. The moment he stepped into the hallway and shut the door behind him with a determined snap, she set Lady Macbeth back on the floor.

The cat waddled over to her mistress, pawing at the widow's skirt. Mrs. Singletary ignored the animal and fixed a scowl on Callie.

She winced. "Is something the matter, Mrs. Singletary?"

Fists jammed on her hips, the widow circled Callie, her gaze narrowing over the dress she wore. "I am waiting for an explanation."

Callie feigned ignorance. "I'm sure I don't know what you mean."

"You are an impertinent, headstrong young woman, Callie Mitchell." Although she attempted a stern tone, the widow's lips twitched, as if fighting back a smile. "If you didn't remind me so much of myself I would be seriously displeased with you right now."

"Your disappointment would be no less than I deserve."

The widow's smile came fully now. "Indeed."

"So you are not angry with me?"

"I should be, but no."

Best not to push the subject, Callie decided.

"Cook has several questions about the menu for Friday evening." Callie moved casually through the room, running her fingers along a stack of books on the shelving to her left. "She seems to be confused as to how many guests will be attending. I told her twelve. She thought it was only ten."

"Cook is right. You are wrong." The widow wagged a finger at her. "And that was a wonderful attempt at distracting me, but it won't work."

"It was worth a try," she muttered.

"You changed back into that ugly gray dress, and I want to know why."

"It's not ugly. It's just—"

"Dismal, drab, *dreary.* All three apply equally."

Yes, she supposed they did. "I was going to say respectable."

"I thought I made myself clear." Mrs. Singletary circled her again, clicking her tongue as she made a second, slower pass. "You were supposed to remain in the blue dress all day."

"It needed several alterations."

"Not even one."

Callie pressed her lips together, but refrained from responding. What could she say, anyway? That she felt too pretty in the dress? That would only encourage the woman in her efforts to update her style.

"At the risk of being redundant, and I do so hate to be redundant, I will say it again. The way you dress reflects directly back on me."

"I know, Mrs. Singletary. But my goal is to blend in with the crowd, not stand out." She attempted a smile. "It would be unseemly of me to attract attention away from you."

"That's utter nonsense. With the right clothing and hairstyle you would, I think, be a great beauty, even more attractive than your sister."

Callie felt panic gnawing at her, tearing at her composure. No one was more beautiful than Fanny. "Please don't say such a thing."

After *the incident* in Boston, Callie had made sure her sister outshone all others, including Callie. Especially Callie. She'd chosen Fanny's dresses and steered her toward the proper hairstyles to set off her unusual amber eyes and doll-like features.

How she missed her sister. As the only two girls in a house full of brothers they'd grown up with a special bond between them. They'd had their share of arguments through the years, the majority following Fanny's broken engagement. Nevertheless, Fanny was Callie's favorite person in the world. She missed her so much she thought she might weep.

As if sensing her fragile state, Mrs. Singletary pulled Callie to a chair and urged her to sit with gentle pressure on her shoulders. "Why do you insist on playing down your assets?" Her gaze softened, her tone warmed. "When there are so many to highlight?"

"Scripture teaches us that we are not to focus on external adornment." Callie lifted her chin. "The Lord doesn't look at outward appearances but what is in our heart."

Could she sound any more pompous, prudish and self-righteous? The moral high ground was a dangerous place for a woman like her...with her sordid past.

"I'll not deny God doesn't look at the things we humans look at. But Scripture also teaches that we are not to hide our light under a bushel. And, Callie, my dear, you are the very essence of light."

Simon had said something similar to Callie when they'd first met at a theater production of *As You Like It*. His leading-man good looks and smooth, practiced words had turned her head. Only when it was too late had she discovered his declarations of love held no substance. He'd been playing a role with her, merely acting a part as he did on the stage.

As a result, she carried the shame of her foolishness with her every minute of every day. "There's nothing special about me. I am a very ordinary woman."

"Now that's just false humility." Mrs. Singletary all but stomped her foot in outrage. "You are anything but ordinary. I never want to hear you say such a thing again."

Callie bristled.

Mrs. Singletary laid a gentle hand on Callie's shoulder, her gaze holding her eyes with deep sincerity. "You are a beautiful child of God, never think otherwise."

What a lovely thing to say. How she adored this woman. Mrs. Singletary had come into Callie's life when she'd been at her lowest, when the three most important people in her life had left her without a backward glance.

She could have returned to her family's ranch. But she couldn't see herself there anymore.

She couldn't see herself anywhere.

Where do I belong, Lord?

"Tell me, dear, why do you hide your true self from the world? What are you afraid of?"

If the widow knew what Callie had done, she would dismiss her on the spot. Mrs. Singletary may have a reputation for being unconventional in business matters. But she was an upright, faithful Christian woman who lived a blameless life. She would expect nothing less of her companion.

"I asked you a question." The words were spoken as gently as if she was speaking to a hurting child.

She knew Mrs. Singletary meant well. The widow only wanted to help, but Callie hesitated still, fearful of relaxing her guard and thereby spilling the entire story.

Her foolishness was not something she wanted to revisit, ever. The gullible belief that she was the most important woman in a man's eyes had nearly been her ruin. How foolish she'd been, falling for the famous actor's ploy. But Simon had only wanted her as a temporary substitute, until he could marry the woman he truly loved.

"I dress this way because it is respectable." *Too late,* an ugly voice in her head whispered. *It is far too late to regain respectability now.*

"What happened to you? What terrible trauma did you suffer that has made you afraid to embrace who you really are?"

"You…you wouldn't understand."

"You might be surprised." The widow closed her hand over Callie's. "I have my share of secrets and I've certainly made mistakes in my day. You'll find no judgment from me, no condemnation. You can tell me anything."

"I…I…wouldn't know where to start." That was certainly true. "It's complicated."

"Now I understand. The cause was a man."

"Yes." The cost of admitting that was so great tears welled in Callie's eyes. She stiffened her spine, refusing to allow even one to fall.

"However he betrayed you—"

"I didn't say he betrayed me."

"You didn't have to."

As if sensing her distress, Lady Macbeth hopped on her

lap. Callie hugged the animal close, burying her nose in the thick, silky fur.

In much the same way she would pet the cat, Mrs. Singletary ran a hand over Callie's hair. "Whoever he was, he didn't deserve you."

Callie lifted her head, felt the burn of tears in her throat and dropped her face back to the cat's neck.

"There is a man out there just for you," the widow said. "He will love you and care for you. Even the most mundane details of your life will matter to him. He is out there, Callie, and I will find him for you. I promise."

"No, Mrs. Singletary." Callie's voice hitched over the words. "Please, don't try to match me with anyone. I—" *Give her a reason. Any will do, even the truth.* "I…I'm not ready."

Crouching in front of her, the widow waited for her to look into her eyes. She studied Callie's face longer than was comfortable, her eyes searching, boring in as if she could read the very secrets of her soul. "No, perhaps you aren't ready," she decided at last. "Not yet. But you will be soon."

Reese went straight to his office after leaving Mrs. Singletary's home and shut the door behind him. He needed privacy, craved it as badly as air.

He laid out the contracts on his mahogany desk and began reviewing the changes he'd scribbled along the margins. He lost himself in the process, managing to focus for several hours before his mind wandered back to his morning meeting across town.

What had he been thinking? Agreeing to allow Beatrix Singletary to help him find a suitable bride?

He blamed the weak moment on the melancholy he'd been unable to shake since his disastrous evening at the opera.

Now he was stuck.

If he cried off from their agreement at this point, Mrs. Singletary would only continue her quest without his assistance. He'd seen her do it before. Several times, in fact. She wouldn't rest until she had him happily married off.

Reese wasn't opposed to getting married again. But he'd already had his chance at happiness. It had slipped away like water through splayed fingers. A split second had been all it took. One unseen root in the ground and Miranda's horse had gone down hard, landing on top of her after the initial tumble, crushing her delicate body.

Reese had spent the next three days at her bedside, holding her in his arms even as it tore at his heart to watch her life slip away one strangled breath at a time.

Shutting his eyes against the memory, Reese drew in a slow breath of air. He would never love again. Not because he didn't want to, but because he didn't know how to go at it half measure. He'd learned during his brief marriage to Miranda that he was a man who felt too much, gave too much, needed too much in return. Unspeakable pain accompanied such uninhibited emotion.

Thus, he would insist the widow keep to their agreement, and only suggest women who met his specific requirements.

With that in mind, he pulled out a fresh piece of paper and began constructing his list. He came up with seven items, the number of completion.

Fitting.

A familiar, rapid *knock, knock, knock* had him folding the list and setting it aside. "Enter."

The door swung open and his father's broad shoulders filled the gap. Other than the graying at the temples and the slightly leaner frame, it was like looking into a mirror and seeing himself twenty-five years from now.

As always, Reese Sr. got straight to the point. "I need to speak with you immediately."

Unsure what he heard in the other man's tone, Reese pushed away from his desk. "Of course."

He started to rise.

His father stopped him with a hand in the air. "Don't stand on my account."

Reese settled back in his chair.

Face pinched, his father strode through the room, then flattened his palms on Reese's desk and leaned forward. "I'm worried about you, son."

"There's no need to be."

"You left the theater abruptly last night." He searched Reese's face. "I need to assure myself you are well."

"I had contracts that required my final review."

"That wasn't the reason you left early." Pushing back, the older man stood tall. "I haven't seen that look on your face since…"

He hesitated, seeming to rethink what he'd been about to say.

"Since when?"

"Since Miranda's accident."

Reese's stomach took a hard roll. They never spoke of Miranda, or the accident that had taken her away from him. Now, after last night at the opera, Reese couldn't stop thinking of her, or how he'd sat at her bedside, willing her to stay alive, begging her to come back to him, praying for God to intervene.

She'd woken but briefly, said his name in a soft, wheezing whisper and then died in his arms.

She'd been eighteen years old. He the same age. They'd had only one month of happiness together. Thirty days.

Not enough.

And yet, far too much. He knew exactly what happiness looked like, felt like and, more important, how quickly it could be taken away.

"I don't wish to speak of Miranda."

"You can't run from the past."

He had every intention of trying. "Was there anything else you wanted to discuss with me? Something important?"

"This is important."

Reese said nothing.

His father came to stand next to him. "You need to get married again. I think it will help you."

Was the man in collusion with Beatrix Singletary? Impossible. Though they were polite with one another on most occasions, the two rarely saw eye-to-eye on most subjects. "I attempted to marry again, but—"

"You chose the wrong girl."

Although he'd come to realize that himself, his father's quick response gave Reese pause. "I believed you liked Fanny. You've been friends with her parents for years. If I remember correctly, which I do, you said you would welcome a match between myself and Cyrus Mitchell's daughter."

"I meant the other one. There is substance to Callie Mitchell, something far more interesting than most see when they first meet her. I thought you agreed."

His heart gave a few thick beats in his chest. Oh, Reese agreed there was much lurking beneath Callie's sensible exterior—a wild, perhaps even passionate streak that, if unleashed, could possibly lead to a life of recklessness.

He knew far too well how that ended.

A tap on the doorjamb heralded Reese's law clerk. A thin young man with regular features and an eager smile, Julian Summers was detail-oriented and thus invaluable to the firm. "Mrs. Singletary's companion is here to see you, Mr. Bennett."

His father lifted an ironic eyebrow.

Ignoring this, Reese stood and circled around his desk. "Send her in, Julian."

"Yes, sir."

A handful of seconds after the clerk disappeared in the hallway, Callie appeared, head high, spine ramrod-stiff, chin at a perfect ninety-degree angle with the floor. At the sight of her, Reese went hot all over, the inexplicable sensation similar to a burst of anger.

She was the same woman she'd always been. Yet, not. The past few hours had produced a remarkable transformation. Her cheeks had gained color. Her eyes sparkled. Her skin glowed.

Simply because she no longer wore that gray shapeless garment from this morning but a blue silk dress that complemented her lean, lithe figure and brought out the green in her eyes.

The effect was devastating. Disconcerting.

Any words of greeting vanished from his mind.

There was something unreal about Callie now, something vulnerable and highly appealing. The impact of her beauty nearly flattened him.

Confounded by his reaction to a simple change of clothes, he blinked at her. "Miss Mitchell, I..." His brain emptied of all thought. Why was she here, looking like a fairy-tale princess? "That is, I wasn't expecting you."

She shifted from one foot to the other, then snapped her shoulders back. Ah, there she was. The Callie Mitchell he knew. "Mrs. Singletary sent me to pick up a package you were to have ready for her this afternoon."

He couldn't think of what package she meant. He remained silent so long his father cleared his throat.

Still, Reese couldn't make his mind work properly.

"Well, if it isn't Callie Mitchell." His father shoved around him. "How are you, my dear?"

"Mr. Bennett." She hurried to him, reaching out her hands to clasp his in greeting. "What a wonderful surprise to see you here today."

He smiled broadly. "You are utterly captivating."

Her face brightened at the compliment. "What a sweet thing to say."

"Only the truth, my dear. Only the truth."

Until this moment, Reese had forgotten how well his father and Callie got along. Watching the two interact so easily, their heads bent at similar angles, he found himself stewing in an unpleasant rush of…

Jealousy?

Absurd. Reese couldn't be jealous of his own father.

And yet, he had to take slow, measured breaths to prevent himself from walking over to the pair, shoving his father aside and insisting Callie pay attention to him. Only him. As if he was some sort of spoiled, selfish child with no manners or common sense.

He managed to avoid stooping quite that low. "Callie." He barked out her name. "A word, please, in private."

One stilted sentence and Reese had crossed several unimaginable lines.

His father's responding grin spoke volumes. As did Callie's reaction. Had she stiffened at the familiar use of her name? Or because of the inappropriate request itself?

Reese wasn't sure he wanted to find out. But he made no attempt to retract his words. This conversation had been coming on for some time.

No turning back now.

Chapter Four

Years of practiced restraint kept Callie from gasping at Reese's request. But…but…*glory.* He'd just asked to speak with her. Alone.

She couldn't think why.

And that, Callie decided, was the primary source of her distress. Her shoulders wanted to bunch. Her knees threatened to give way beneath her. But she remained perfectly still.

Perfectly.

Still.

No easy task. Not with Reese looking at her with all that intensity. He was so focused on her she had a sudden, irrational urge to rush out of his office without a backward glance.

Callie had never been one to run from a difficult conversation. She would not start now.

Still, Reese's command, spoken so abruptly, was out of character. Why would he wish to speak with her, *alone?*

Seeking a clue—any would do—she slid a covert glance over his face. His chin jerked, very faintly, a sure sign that he'd shocked even himself with his words.

"Well, then." A corner of the elder Mr. Bennett's mouth curled upward. "I believe that's my cue to depart."

Callie started. She'd forgotten Reese's father still held her hands. Had he noticed the faint tremor in her fingers?

"There's no need to leave so soon," she said on an exhale. Even to her own ears, her voice sounded exceptionally calm, almost detached, with the emotional depth of a stone. *Perfect.* "I'm sure whatever your son has to say can be expressed in front of you."

She hoped.

"Perhaps. But alas, I have another appointment calling me away." With a fatherly smile, he gave her hands a quick squeeze before releasing her. "It was a pleasure running in to you, my dear. We must make this a more common occurrence."

The kindness in his voice, as much as the sentiment itself, calmed her nerves considerably.

"Oh, yes, Mr. Bennett." She managed to get both sides of her mouth to lift in a responding smile. "That would be lovely, indeed."

She'd always felt comfortable around this man, as though he was a second father. Callie desperately wanted him to stay but couldn't think of a reason why he should, other than to beg him to serve as a shield between her and his son.

Callie Mitchell was made of sterner stuff.

"Reese." Mr. Bennett gave his son a short nod. "We will continue our discussion another time."

A muscle knotted in Reese's jaw as he returned his father's nod with one of his own.

Another smile in Callie's direction and the elder Mr. Bennett quit the room.

She remained precisely where she stood, twisting the handle of her reticule between her fingers. She hated this anxious, almost panicky sensation spreading through her. Unfortunately, it couldn't be helped. Simply standing in the same room with Reese caused her anxiety.

She should not be here, alone with him.

She wanted to be nowhere else.

Time slowed. The moment grew thick with tension, the

silence between them so heavy that Callie could hear their individual breathing.

"I don't think this is a wise idea, Mr. Bennett," she said, mostly to herself, and meaning it with all her heart.

"Callie." His lips flattened in a grim line. "At this juncture in our acquaintance, perhaps it's time you called me Reese."

She looked at him blankly, absently noting the way sunlight from the window emphasized the dark, rich brown of his eyes, the color of freshly brewed coffee. "Oh. But I—"

"I insist." His tone was both gentle and firm.

A dangerous pang snatched at her heart and the rebellious part of her thought, *Well, why not, we've known one another for years?*

"If you insist." She lifted her chin a fraction higher. "Then, yes, I should very much like to call you Reese."

His name came from low in her throat, and sounded really quite wonderful, as if she'd been meant to say his name, just that way, all her life.

She sighed. "Was that all you wished to say to me?"

"No." He rubbed a hand across his forehead. "Forgive me for not getting to the point sooner. I've spent the majority of the afternoon pouring over legal briefs and my mind is still half on the pages."

His confession softened her guard and Callie found herself feeling a moment of deep affection for this man. "My brother is much the same way," she said. "After a long day of pouring over contracts, Garrett is the worst conversationalist imaginable."

Reese visibly relaxed at this. "Then you understand my abruptness earlier."

"Indeed I do."

A shadow of a smile played across his lips.

Callie responded in kind.

For that one moment, everything felt right between them, comfortable even, a solidarity that went beyond words.

But then...

Reese's brow creased in thought. His brow often creased in thought, she realized, rather liking the result. The studious look made him appear half as stern as usual, twice as appealing. And so very, very handsome.

"You mentioned that Mrs. Singletary sent you over to retrieve a package from me." His brows pulled tighter together, making him appear more confused than thoughtful. "Do you know what package she meant?"

"She didn't give me any details." Callie tried to shrug off her own bafflement. "She merely said that you would be expecting me before the end of business today."

Frowning now, he glanced at his desk.

Callie followed the direction of his gaze, but saw no package, only several piles of papers, a cup of writing utensils, countless ledgers of assorted sizes and an ink pot.

"She must have meant the revised contracts." Making a sound deep in his throat, Reese moved around to the other side of his desk. Instead of reaching for one of the larger stacks, he placed his hand over a single piece of paper. Folded from top to bottom, it looked more like a letter than a legal brief.

Shaking his head, he muttered something under his breath. Callie didn't catch all of what he said, but she thought she might have heard something about *meddlesome, interfering woman*.

"Mr. Bennett...I mean, Reese," she amended when he looked up sharply. "Is something the matter?"

He drummed his fingers atop the letter. "No." He drew in a slow, careful breath. "Everything is in order."

His tone said otherwise.

"You are certain?"

For a span of three breaths, he said nothing, merely held her gaze. Then, he gave a single nod of his head. "Yes."

He looked back down at his desk, reached out and stuffed one of the smaller stacks into a leather satchel.

He started to flip over the lid then paused.

His gaze shifted to where the folded piece of paper still sat. A moment's hesitation and, with a swift move, he picked up the letter and placed that inside the satchel, as well.

His lips were twisted at a wry angle as he came back around his desk. "Here you are. The *package* Mrs. Singletary sent you to retrieve."

"Thank you."

Their fingers briefly touched as he transferred the satchel into her care. Callie smothered a gasp as her heartbeat picked up speed. Her mouth went dry.

Every muscle in her body tensed.

Her strong, inexplicable, tangible reaction over a light brush of their hands mortified her.

Hiding her reaction beneath lowered lashes, she turned to go.

Reese's voice stopped her at the threshold of his office. "Callie."

She paused, looked over her shoulder. "Yes?"

"I still have more to say to you."

Glory. That sounded ominous.

His footsteps struck the wood floor as he approached her from behind. Closer. Closer. He reached around her, grabbed the door as if to shut it, then quickly dropped his hand and stepped back.

Callie felt a cold rush of air sweep over her.

"I prefer not to speak to your back."

She turned around to face him.

He leaned toward her, a mere fraction closer. "I wanted

to tell you…" His words trailed off as he considered her through slightly narrowed eyes. "That is, have a nice day."

Have a nice day? Reese had asked her to face him so he could tell her to *have a nice day?*

Perplexed, she gave up all pretense of control and gaped at the confounding man. If she was wise, she would turn around again and walk out the door. After, of course, she issued the same nonsensical platitude he'd just given her.

Or…

She could be a little more daring. She could tap in to the woman she'd been long ago, before a secret scandal had nearly ruined her.

"No, Reese." She took a step toward him. "I will not have a nice day."

A single, winged eyebrow lifted in surprise. "I beg your pardon?"

"I have five brothers," she said in way of explanation. "Three older and two younger."

Now both eyebrows rose.

It was a very intimidating look. Dark, brooding, slightly dangerous. Most women would be cowed. Callie was not. "I know precisely when a man is skirting around the truth."

"Did you just call me out for lying?"

At the sound of his masculine outrage, mutiny swept through her, making her bolder than she'd been in a very long time.

"Take it however you will. But I'm not leaving this office until you tell me exactly why you really asked to speak with me—" she closed the distance between them and pinned him with her gaze "—and why you requested to do so in private."

Reese's chest felt odd. His pulse quickened in his veins. His throat tightened. All because this woman, a woman he'd known for years, had morphed into a completely different creature than the docile, overly polite, levelheaded wallflower she presented to the world.

The transformation had nothing to do with the clothes she wore. And everything to do with the woman herself.

Proud and defiant now, her unwavering gaze locked with his. She was clearly waiting for him to explain himself, to tell her why he'd requested a private word with her.

He couldn't remember why. He could barely organize his thoughts beyond the shocked realization that the woman leaning toward him with a fierce scowl on her face was a total stranger.

Callie Mitchell usually drifted along the edges of most rooms, never drawing attention to herself, never making waves. At the moment, that woman was nowhere to be found.

On the surface, she'd changed nothing but her dress. Yet now, Reese saw the woman beneath the dull facade. A little wilder, a tad more dangerous, exciting and—

"Reese?"

He'd been staring too long.

He opened his mouth, then shut it again as several voices rang out from the hallway. Not wanting an audience, Reese reached to take Callie's arm. He dropped his hand before making contact. Touching her would be a terrible idea.

The worst of all terrible ideas.

He motioned her deeper into the office with a nod of his head. He did not, however, close the door behind her.

There was privacy. And then there was *privacy.*

"Please, Callie, take a seat." He indicated the set of chairs facing his desk.

She nodded, moving through the room with exaggerated dignity, her steps graceful yet carefully monitored.

Always so controlled, he thought, always hiding behind a veil of self-possession and restraint.

How well he understood.

The realization they had that in common left him vaguely disturbed.

Her posture perfectly precise, she lowered into the burgundy wing-back chair facing his desk and placed the leather satchel upon her lap.

After a moment of consideration, Reese chose to sit in the empty chair beside her.

She twisted her hands together. With all emotion stripped from her face, she nearly fooled him into thinking she was completely self-possessed. But her gaze didn't quite meet his, landing instead on a spot just above his right eye.

She was nervous.

Good to know he wasn't the only one feeling uneasy.

Now that he had Callie alone—mostly—Reese wasn't sure how to broach the subject that had been nagging at him for some time now. The direct approach was always best. "We need to discuss the changing nature of our relationship."

Her gaze whipped to his and he noted, somewhat inappropriately, that her eyelashes were long, utterly enchanting and several shades darker than her blond hair.

"I wasn't aware we had a relationship."

He frowned at her stiff tone, oddly irritated. "Of course we do." It was awkward and uncomfortable, to be sure, but existed all the same. "Now that you are Mrs. Singletary's companion and I'm once again in charge of her business affairs, our paths will cross often."

"Mrs. Singletary said the same thing just this morning." She lowered her gaze. "My brother taking that job in St. Louis has brought changes to all our lives."

Before now, Reese hadn't considered what the attorney's departure meant to Callie. "You miss him."

"Very much." She worked her hands together in her lap. "I also miss his wife, Molly."

"You two were close?"

"Oh, yes, but not as close as—" She broke off, drew her bottom lip between her teeth, looked everywhere but at him.

"Not as close as you and Fanny," he finished for her.

She nodded. "I miss her most of all."

"That's understandable. You are sisters. And the only two girls in a large family of boys." As an only child he couldn't imagine what it was like to grow up with that many siblings.

"Fanny has always been my best friend." She met his gaze. "We are only eleven months apart in age."

Reese tried not to show his surprise, even as he did a mental calculation. He'd always thought Callie far older than her sister. Her maturity, her outer calm and, of course, her ability to control her emotions were qualities he attributed to a woman far older than twenty-three.

"Have you heard from your sister recently?"

"No." She shook her head. "She has not answered any of my letters."

"None of them?"

"Not one."

That didn't sound like Fanny. Then again, Reese was quickly discovering how little he knew the woman he'd once asked to marry him. How could she not respond to her only sister's letters?

No wonder Callie appeared upset.

For a shocking moment, he yearned to pull her to him and offer what comfort he could. The urge grew stronger when she wiped secretly at her eyes and snuffled a little. The sound was practically nonexistent, and all the more sorrowful because of the restraint.

"It must be difficult," he said, lowering his voice, "not hearing from your own sister."

"You have no idea." Her expression closed, but not before he'd seen the hint of misery in her eyes. "Have *you* heard from Fanny?"

"Of course not."

"I'm so sorry. Oh, Reese, truly I am." Her hand reached out and touched his forearm, as if she thought he needed comforting. "Do not despair. Fanny will come to her senses."

Surely, Callie didn't think he pined for her sister. For a long, tense moment, he watched her watching him with silent sympathy in her gaze.

This, he realized, was why he'd wanted to speak with her alone. They needed to sort a few things out between them. "I miss your sister, it's true. But not, perhaps, as you may think." He held her gaze, willing her to hear him. "I miss our friendship."

"Your...*friendship?*" She said the word as if tasting something foul. "Surely Fanny was more to you than a friend."

"At the time I issued my proposal I believed your sister and I were well suited." An error in judgment he didn't plan to repeat. Perhaps relying on Mrs. Singletary's help would turn out to be a wise move, after all. What better way to avoid pursuing the wrong woman again? "I'm not what your sister wants."

Callie flinched as though he'd slapped her. "Don't say that. Of course you are. Fanny is going to change her mind, I just know it. And then you and she can—"

"No, we can't."

"But—" she blinked at him "—if she came home, wouldn't you want to—"

"I would not." He touched her hand briefly, once again willing her to hear him. *Really* hear him. "Even if Fanny changed her mind tomorrow, I would not want her back."

Her eyes widened. Then narrowed. "Why are you telling me this?"

"Because I want you to understand that your sister and I will never marry." He waited for her to process his words, then added, "However, just because I'm not engaged to Fanny anymore doesn't mean you and I can't be…"

He paused, not sure how to continue. Even taking into account the personal nature of their discussion, this conversation shouldn't be so difficult. He was a trained lawyer, skilled at putting words together to make his case.

"I don't want there to be any more awkwardness between us," he said, finally coming to the crux of the matter.

Her shoulders relaxed, just a hair, but enough for Reese to know she agreed with him. "I don't want that, either," she said, her eyes shining bright with emotion.

Those eyes, he thought, they were unlike any he'd ever seen. How had he never noticed the various shades of green in them, or the way thin, gold flecks wove through the irises?

He cleared his throat, a gesture he seemed to repeat far too often in this woman's company.

"I believe you and I could be friends." He told himself this was a necessary step if they were going to be in daily contact. But, strangely, conversely, Reese actually wanted to be friends with this woman. "I'm willing to make the attempt."

Pulling her bottom lip between her teeth, she angled her head. "You used the same term to describe your relationship with Fanny. Are you not concerned what she will think when she comes home and discovers we have become…friends?"

"No."

Something flickered in Callie's eyes. A hint of rebellion? Reluctant interest, perhaps? Either way, he had her attention. And now that he did, he decided to change tactics. "Don't tell me you're afraid."

She abruptly straightened in her chair, her spine as stiff

as a fire poker, her face free of expression. "What a ridiculous notion."

Oh, this woman was a true master of control.

Some long-remembered defiant streak of his own wanted to ruffle her calm. Just how far could he push this woman, Reese wondered?

He leaned in closer still. "Are you afraid of me, Callie?"

She sniffed with obvious disdain. *"Never."*

He'd known that would be her response. Somehow, he'd known. "Then we start anew, right now."

"You are very persistent."

She had no idea how persistent he could be when he wanted something. He wanted Callie's friendship. More than he should.

More than was wise.

"What do you say?" Feeling more alive than he had in years, he reached out his hand. "Shall we be friends?"

She took his hand, her smile bolder than before and far too appealing. "I'd like nothing better than to forge a friendship with you...*Reese*."

The way she said his name, low and challenging, filled his chest with dread.

What have I just done?

Chapter Five

Callie exited Reese's office with purposeful strides. She could feel his gaze following her progress down the never-ending hallway that eventually spilled into the law firm's reception area. Was he watching her departure with a smile on her face?

Or did he wear that thoughtful expression she found so appealing? She desperately wanted to glance over her shoulder to discover what was in his eyes.

She kept walking, ensuring each step was precisely placed on the floor, one foot in front of the other. Heel, toe. Heel, toe. No doubt she appeared in complete control of herself.

Not true.

Her emotions, though carefully contained, were in tatters.

Why had she agreed to Reese's suggestion they become friends? It was true, she'd once wished to grow close to the man, perhaps even build something more than a friendship. But that had been before he'd asked Fanny to marry him.

Even if he hadn't offered for her sister's hand, Callie was still, well, Callie. A staid, boring, sensible woman who took no missteps, crossed no lines and certainly never be-friended a man outside her own family.

Feeling confused—and so very much alone—she at-tempted to pray for discernment as she exited Bennett, Bennett and Brand law offices. A cool, gentle breeze caressed her face yet the words wouldn't come, even in the privacy of her own mind. She hunched her shoulders forward and approached the waiting carriage.

"Ready to go, Miss Callie?"

"Yes, Horace." She smiled at Mrs. Singletary's coach driver. "I am more than ready to go home."

Home. Where was home for her now? Mrs. Singletary's massive house? The Mitchell family ranch?

Neither place called to her.

Another reason she felt so alone. *Lord, where do I belong?*

Heavyhearted, she climbed into the carriage. Once settled on the butter-soft calfskin seat, she rapped on the ceiling. The coach jerked into motion. Tightly coiled springs absorbed most of the dips and bumps along the twenty-minute journey across town. So smooth was the ride, in fact, that Callie relaxed her head against the plush squabs.

Her thoughts, however, continued to race.

Why—oh, why—had she reacted to Reese's obvious attempt to bait her? She may be many things, but afraid? Rarely. And yet...

She was afraid now. Afraid of what came next. Afraid of what a friendship between her and Reese really meant, especially with regard to Fanny.

A sob worked its way up her throat. For an instant, just one beat of her heart, she wished her sister would stay away forever. In the most hidden part of Callie's soul the truth rang loud.

She resented Fanny.

The girl had callously walked away from a good man, the best of them all. And now, that same man claimed he wanted to be Callie's friend. *Her friend.*

No good would come from such an arrangement. Friendship often blossomed into something deeper. That was her greatest fear. Because, deep down, it was her greatest hope.

In fresh agony, she pressed her fingertips to her temples and squeezed her eyes closed. She knew the situation was hopeless—truly, she did—yet Callie yearned for something more. Something life-altering.

Something…she had no business wishing for herself.

The carriage drew to an abrupt halt, splintering the rest of her thoughts.

Thankful for the interruption, Callie gathered up the leather briefcase Reese had given her and exited the carriage.

Mrs. Singletary's butler met her just inside the front entryway. Thick threads of silver encroached on the few strands of red left in his hair, but his broad, welcoming smile erased at least ten years from his heavily lined face.

"Mrs. Singletary is waiting for you in her office, Miss Callie."

"Thank you, Winston." She smiled in return. "I'll head right up."

Leather satchel pressed against her heart, she hurried through the cavernous foyer with its mile-high ceiling and expensive chandelier hanging from the center. The sound of her heels striking the imported marble reverberated off the richly decorated walls, where several oil paintings had been strategically placed for optimal effect.

Callie paused at the foot of the winding stairwell to study a portrait of Mrs. Singletary and her now-deceased husband. The two looked beyond happy, yet Callie felt a wave of sadness as she stared into their smiling faces. They'd had so little time together, barely fifteen years.

It should have been a lifetime.

Sighing, she mounted the stairs. At the second-floor landing, she turned left and worked her way through the labyrinth of corridors that led to the back of the house.

As the butler had indicated, she found Mrs. Singletary in her office. The widow sat in an overstuffed chair, her head bent over a book, Lady Macbeth spread out on her lap.

Neither the widow nor the cat noticed Callie's arrival. She took the opportunity to glance around the room. Bold afternoon sunlight spread across the empty stone hearth. Bookshelves lined three of the other four walls. The scent of leather and old book bindings mingled with Mrs. Singletary's perfume, a pleasant mix of lavender and roses and...

Callie was stalling, though she couldn't think why.

Squaring her shoulders, she rapped lightly on the doorjamb to gain the widow's attention.

Mrs. Singletary lifted her head. "Ah, there you are." She closed her book and set it on the small, round table beside her. "I trust everything went according to plan."

What an odd choice of words.

Had Mrs. Singletary sent her to Bennett, Bennett and Brand with a purpose other than business in mind?

That would certainly explain Reese's initial confusion when she'd stepped into his office.

Then again...

He'd been buried in legal briefs prior to her arrival. He'd recovered quickly enough and had given Callie a stack of papers to deliver to her employer. Papers contained in the leather case she now held.

Papers his law clerk could have delivered, as was usually the case.

Realizing her steps had slowed to a halt Callie resumed moving through the room and addressed her suspicions directly. "I must say, Mr. Bennett appeared genuinely surprised to see me in his office this afternoon."

The words had barely left her lips when her foot caught on the fringe of an area rug and she momentarily lost her balance. In her attempt to right herself, the satchel flew from her hands.

Callie rushed forward. Unfortunately, she picked up the briefcase at the wrong end and the contents spilled out.

"Oh, oh, no." She dropped to her knees and began picking up the papers as quickly as possible. "I'm not usually so clumsy."

"Not to worry, dear." Mrs. Singletary set her cat on the ottoman in front of her chair and joined Callie on the floor. "These things happen."

Together, they retrieved the strewn papers, placing them in a neat pile between them.

Lady Macbeth, evidently sensing a new game afoot, leaped on top of the stack and plopped her hindquarters down with regal feline arrogance.

The widow laughed. "Move aside, my lady." She playfully poked the cat in her ribs. "You are in the way."

The animal lowered to her belly, her challenging glint all but daring her mistress to protest.

Wrinkling her nose at the ornery animal, Callie carefully pulled papers out from beneath the furry belly. She managed to free the bulk of them when the cat gazed at the new pile with narrow-eyed intent.

"Oh, no, you don't." Callie snatched the papers off the floor and placed them on the table next to Mrs. Singletary's book.

Not to be deterred, Lady Macbeth went after a lone sheet of paper that had landed farther away than the rest.

Callie moved a shade quicker. "Ha."

Swishing her tail in hard, jerky movements, Lady Macbeth stalked off toward the fireplace and curled up on a rug near the grate.

Disaster averted, Callie glanced down at the paper in her hand. There was a crease in the center of the page, indicating it had once been folded in two. Written in a bold, masculine hand, it looked like a record of some kind, an inventory perhaps.

The third item from the top captured her notice. *Loves children, wants several, at least five but no more than seven.*

Beneath that odd statement, was another equally confusing entry. *Must come from a good family and value strong family ties.*

Callie frowned.

What sort of list had she stumbled upon?

Realizing it was none of her business, she pressed the paper into Mrs. Singletary's hand. "This is clearly meant for your eyes only."

The widow scanned the page in silence then clicked her tongue in obvious disapproval. "That man is going to be my greatest challenge yet."

At the genuine look of concern in the woman's eyes, Callie angled her head. "Is there anything I can do to help?"

"No, dear. Not just yet." The widow refolded the paper at the crease and stowed the list inside a pocket of her skirt. "Later, perhaps, once I consider my options I shall ask for your assistance."

Her tone invited no further questions.

Shrugging, Callie searched the floor around her. She found no more papers. "I think that's all of them." She sat back on her heels. "Would you like me to leave you alone to review the papers Mr. Bennett sent over?"

"Thank you, yes." The widow nodded distractedly. "I would."

"I'll be in my room if you need me." Callie rose to her feet and started for the door.

"Not so fast, dear."

She pivoted back around. "Yes, ma'am?"

"About the dinner party I have planned for Friday evening. I should like for you to attend as one of my guests."

Callie felt her eyes widen in surprise. In the entire month of her employment she'd attended precisely none of Mrs.

Singletary's parties. "You wish for me to attend as...as...a guest?"

"Quite so." The widow moved back to her chair and began spreading the legal papers across her lap. "Now that one of the ladies has declined her invitation there will be too many men at the table. Your presence will even out the numbers."

A hard ball of dread knotted in Callie's stomach. In the span of a single day, her perfectly ordered world was no longer so perfectly ordered. But aside from direct insubordination, Callie saw no other recourse than to agree to her employer's request.

"If you wish for me to attend your party then, of course, Mrs. Singletary, I am happy to oblige."

"Excellent. Most excellent, indeed."

Again, Callie turned to go.

Again, Mrs. Singletary called her back. "One final thing, dear."

Forcing a bright smile, she turned around a second time, preparing herself for the rest. Because, of course, there was more. With Mrs. Singletary, there was always more. "Yes?"

"When Jane and I were cleaning out my closet this afternoon we came across a lovely crimson gown that isn't at all the right color for my complexion. The garment would look far better on, say, a woman with—" the widow pinned Callie with a sly look "—flaxen hair."

Wasn't that convenient? Callie thought miserably, as she smoothed her hand over her light blond *flaxen* hair.

"I should like for you to wear the dress to the party."

Naturally.

Callie suppressed a sigh as yet another piece of her ordered life chipped away.

"Is there anything else?" she dared to ask.

"That is all for now." The widow waved a hand in dismissal. "You may go."

This time, when Callie stepped into the hallway, the widow did not protest her departure. A small victory, to be sure. But with the day she'd had, one she gladly claimed.

Despite a last-minute meeting with a new client, and the onset of a thundershower just as he left the office, Reese arrived at Mrs. Singletary's home a full minute before the designated time on the invitation. He stepped into the foyer at the precise moment a large grandfather clock began chiming the top of the hour.

As he shook off the rain, the widow's butler stepped forward and took his hat. "Good evening, Mr. Bennett."

"Good evening, Winston." Reese handed over his coat and gloves next. "Am I the first to arrive?"

"You are one of the last," the butler informed him. "The other guests are gathered in the blue sitting room."

"Has my father arrived yet?"

"Twenty minutes ago."

Twenty minutes? That seemed pointlessly early. Or had Reese read the invitation incorrectly? There was one way to find out. "Thank you, Winston. I'll see myself to the parlor."

"Very good, sir."

Reese spared a glance at the grandfather clock in the foyer as he passed through. One minute past seven. Certain he'd arrived on time, he nonetheless increased his pace.

Pausing at the threshold of the blue parlor, he took in the scene. He counted eight people in the room already.

His father stood near the fireplace, where a small fire had been lit presumably to offset the damp air created by the rain. A woman in a red dress stood beside Reese Bennett Sr., her back to the entrance. The deep, rich color of her gown offset her pale blond hair. Twisted in one of those complicated modern styles with several tendrils hanging loose, the resulting effect was mesmerizing.

For reasons unknown, Reese could do nothing but stare in muted wonder. Then, the woman turned slightly, presenting her profile.

His stomach rolled in recognition.

His throat burned. His heart pounded. And still he continued staring, unable to look away. With the firelight brazing off her, Callie Mitchell reminded him of a lighthouse beacon calling to him, promising shelter, as if he was a floundering sailor in need of a safe haven.

Reese swallowed.

He should not be this aware of Callie. Nonetheless, a new alertness spread through him, a sublime shift from one state of being to another.

The sensation rocked him to the core.

He looked away, at last searching the large parlor.

Mrs. Singletary held court on the opposite end of the room, conversing with one of Denver's most prominent couples, Alexander and Polly Ferguson.

Their son Marshall, a man Reese considered a friend, was here tonight as well, as were two of his seven sisters. The young women were beautiful, with golden, light brown hair and cornflower-blue eyes. He was certain he'd met them previously but at the moment found it difficult to tell them apart. To further complicate matters, he recalled each of their names started with the letter *P*.

Both were in their early twenties and fit most of his requirements for a bride.

Were they here for his benefit?

If so, the widow had wasted no time in presenting viable candidates for his consideration.

One of the Ferguson daughters turned her big blue eyes in his direction. Reese shoved away from the door.

He'd barely taken two steps when Mrs. Singletary broke away from Mr. and Mrs. Ferguson. "Ah, Mr. Bennett, you have finally arrived."

At the hint of censure in her tone, he wondered again if he'd gotten the time of tonight's gathering wrong. "I hope I haven't kept everyone waiting."

"Not at all." Smiling now, the widow closed the distance between them and captured both of his hands. "There is still one more guest yet to arrive."

On cue, there was a movement in the doorway.

"And here he is now." The widow stepped away from Reese to greet her final guest. "Mr. Hawkins. I'm so glad you could join us this evening."

Jonathon Hawkins was back in town?

This was the first time the new owner of the Hotel Dupree had returned to Denver since he'd offered Fanny a job in his Chicago hotel.

By giving her the position, Hawkins had provided Reese's ex-fiancée a way to start over when the gossip over the broken engagement had become unbearable. Reese held no animosity toward the man. Fanny's departure had been good for everyone.

Callie seemed to have a differing opinion.

Her shoulders stiffened, her chin lifted at a haughty angle. When her gaze locked on Hawkins, the barely banked anger in her eyes gave Reese a moment of hesitation. He'd always sensed Callie had a large capacity for emotion hidden deep within her. But this...

He almost felt sorry for the hotelier.

Then he remembered his last conversation with Callie and her admission to missing her sister greatly.

With this new piece of information, he absorbed her reaction with a wave of sympathy. She and her sister had been close. He wanted to go to Callie, to offer his support, but her expression shuttered closed, as if she'd turned off a switch. A slow blink, a quick steadying breath and she wrenched her attention away from Hawkins.

Her wandering gaze landed on Reese.

A moment of silent understanding passed between them. Everything in him softened, relaxed, urging him to continue in her direction. His father said something and she turned to answer.

The moment was lost. And Reese immediately came to his senses.

Tonight wasn't about Callie Mitchell. The Ferguson daughters had likely been invited here for his benefit as the first candidates in his bride search. Reese would be remiss not to take this opportunity to know them better.

Chapter Six

Bracketed by Reese's father on her left and Marshall Ferguson on her right, Callie would be hard-pressed to find more pleasant dinner companions. Both men held a vast knowledge on a variety of topics and never let the conversation lag.

Under normal circumstances, she would consider tonight's dining experience a pleasant respite from what would have been a solitary supper tray in her room.

These were not normal circumstances.

As evidenced by the unexpected presence of the man sitting diagonally across the table from her.

Jonathon Hawkins.

Why had Mrs. Singletary invited the hotelier to this particular dinner party? True, the widow was in the process of expanding her business association with the man. Did she have to socialize with him, as well? On a night Callie was in attendance?

Swallowing a growl of frustration, she narrowed her gaze over Mr. Hawkins's face. In the flickering light of the wall sconces, his features took on a dark, turbulent, almost-frightening edge. A man with many secrets.

She supposed some women might find his mysterious aura appealing. Not Callie. She didn't like brooding, enigmatic types. Besides, with his glossy brown hair, steel-gray eyes and square jaw, he reminded her entirely too much of the man who'd deceived her and broken her heart.

In fact…

If she narrowed her eyes ever-so-slightly and angled her head a tad to the right, Jonathon Hawkins could pass for Simon.

Was the hotelier as equally duplicitous as the famous actor? Did he spout well-practiced lies to unsuspecting gullible women?

She knew the comparison was unfair, and based solely on her own prejudice, yet Callie felt her hands curl into tight fists. She briefly shut her eyes, battling the remembered shame of her own actions. Before her experience with Simon, she'd lived a life of unshakable faith. She'd lived with boldness, gifted by the Lord with utter confidence in her own worth.

But now, *now,* she had no such confidence. She felt lost, afraid and, worst of all, alone.

She had no one to blame but herself, of course. She'd made her choices and must forever live with the consequences.

Refusing to wallow over a situation of her own making, she willed Mr. Hawkins to look at her. He turned his head in the opposite direction and listened to something Mrs. Singletary said.

His rich laughter filled the air.

Callie battled a mild case of dejection.

How could the man be so blissfully unaware? Had he no shame? Did he not know—or care—about the pain his actions had caused? Were it not for his untimely job offer, Fanny would have stayed in Denver and worked things out with Reese.

Reese.

What must he be suffering? Surely, Jonathon Hawkins's presence here tonight had to be a physical reminder of the woman he'd lost.

Callie shifted her gaze to where Reese sat wedged between the Ferguson sisters. He skillfully divided his attention, speaking to both women at well-timed intervals, taking in every word of their high-pitched chatter. He didn't look upset. In fact, he was smiling. *Smiling!*

"Is the fish not to your liking, Miss Mitchell?"

She dragged her gaze away from Reese and focused on Marshall Ferguson.

"On the contrary," she said, picking up her fork. "It's quite wonderful."

"Such certainty, and yet…" Marshall dropped an amused gaze to her plate. "You haven't taken a single bite."

"Oh. Right." She filled her fork. "I sampled some in the kitchen before everyone arrived."

His mouth quirked up at one corner. "Ah, well, that explains it, then."

She took the bite on her fork, studied his handsome face as she chewed.

Still holding her gaze, Marshall sampled his own fish. Only when Reese's father said his name did he break eye contact and answer a question about railroad stock. Which soon segued into a lengthy discussion on water rights.

With nothing to add to either topic, Callie listened in silence. The brief interlude with Marshall had given her time to recover her equilibrium and she was grateful to the man.

She glanced at him from beneath her lashes.

In temperament and in looks, he reminded her of her brother Garrett. Marshall's tawny hair was a bit more unruly, and his brown eyes were several shades darker, but they could almost pass for brothers.

There was another glaring similarity between the two men. Marshall had once been engaged to Garrett's wife, Molly. Did he pine for his lost love? Callie wondered.

How did one ask such a question?

One *didn't* ask such a question.

Yet she'd practically done so with Reese the other day in his office.

Callie cut a glance across the table, noticed Reese was no longer engaged in conversation with either of the Ferguson sisters. Instead, he was watching her. Closely. Intently.

She looked down at her plate then just as quickly glanced back up. Reese was still watching her, just as closely, just as intently. She wished he would look away. Then, perversely, wished he would continue looking at her all night.

At least he wasn't conversing with either of the Ferguson sisters anymore.

Why not?

They were both very beautiful, educated, came from a good family and…

Callie suddenly remembered the words written in a bold, masculine hand she'd fished out from beneath Lady Macbeth. *Loves children…must come from a good family and… value strong family ties.*

Qualities a man might look for in a wife.

Alarm filled her.

Was Reese actively seeking a woman to take Fanny's place in his heart? Had he enlisted Mrs. Singletary's assistance?

No. It was too soon. Fanny had barely left town.

"I understand your brother is practicing law in St. Louis," Marshall said, the gently spoken question sufficiently breaking through Callie's growing panic.

"Yes." She rummaged up a smile for her dinner companion. "I received a letter from his wife just today."

"You and Molly are still close, I presume?"

"Very. It was hard to say goodbye to her after the wedding, but the ever-faithful postal service keeps us in touch."

If only Fanny would write, as well. One letter. Callie yearned for nothing more than one, short letter from her sister.

"Is Molly…" Marshall hesitated, his smile dropping slightly. "Is she happy living in St. Louis with your brother?"

How best to answer such a loaded question? *The truth,* she told herself. *Stick with the truth.* "She has settled into her new life with Garrett rather nicely. She's even started her own millinery shop."

"I'm pleased for her." The relief in his eyes was more powerful than the words. "And your brother."

"I believe you truly mean that."

He turned thoughtful a moment, lifted a shoulder. "Though Molly is a generous, beautiful woman, she was not the woman for me. We would never have truly happy together. Content, perhaps. But not happy."

Something sad came and went in his eyes.

Wanting to soothe, she reached out and touched her fingers to his forearm. "I'm sorry, Mr. Ferguson."

He placed his hand atop hers and squeezed gently. "Molly and I parted ways amicably. We will always be friends."

Friends?

There was that awful word again, spoken by another man in reference to his former fiancée. Why would anyone propose to a woman he considered nothing more than a friend?

Oh, she knew many marriages were based on far less, and were entered into for a vast array of reasons. But in her family love was the most important foundation to marriage. *And now abide faith, hope, love, these three; but the greatest of these is love.* The Bible verse was practically a family motto.

Realizing she'd been silent too long, Callie drew in a steadying breath. "I'm glad there are no hard feelings between you and Molly."

"You are different tonight, Miss Mitchell. More..." His words trailed off.

When several seconds passed and he didn't continue, she lifted a brow. "More?" she prompted.

"Charming," he said with a smile. "Engaging. Quite wonderful, really. Until tonight, I hadn't realized how..." His gaze fell over her face. "What I mean is, you are a very beautiful woman."

A rather inconvenient surge of pleasure surfaced at the unexpected compliment. Callie had forgotten how lovely it felt to be called beautiful.

She shifted uneasily in her chair.

"I didn't mean to make you uncomfortable."

"You didn't," she assured him. "It's just—" she lifted her chin "—I'm not used to compliments."

"Then I shall make it my mission to pay you several more throughout the night."

"Please," she whispered, absently shoving at her hair, shifting in her seat again. "You really don't have to do that."

"I have made you uncomfortable again." He focused on his plate a moment, then turned back to her. "Did you notice how the rain earlier this evening brought a surprising chill to the night air?"

What a kind, sweet man, changing the subject to the universally innocuous topic of the weather.

For the rest of the meal, they spoke of nothing more substantial. Callie found Marshall Ferguson witty, amiable and handsome. She quite enjoyed his company. And decided to be glad for her position at the table.

As the servers began clearing away empty dishes and

plates, one of the Ferguson sisters, in an overly loud voice, asked Reese if he'd heard from Fanny since she'd left town.

A full five seconds of silence met the question, whereby the girl's father cleared his throat.

"No, I haven't," Reese said without inflection. "Nor would I expect to hear from her since we are no longer engaged."

Though he didn't appear especially agitated, his icy tone said the conversation was over.

The girl missed the obvious cue. "Oh, but surely, after what you meant to one another you would wish to know how she's faring in Chicago?"

"She is faring very well" came a deep, masculine reply.

All heads turned toward Jonathon Hawkins and an expectant hush filled the air.

"You know Fanny?" the Ferguson sisters asked in unison.

He gave a brief nod. "Miss Mitchell is an invaluable member of my Chicago hotel operation, *our* operation," he amended with a nod in deference toward Mrs. Singletary. "With her attention to detail, she's all but running the place on her own."

"Isn't that lovely." Mrs. Singletary set her napkin on the table and stood. "Let us adjourn to the parlor for coffee and dessert."

And that, the widow's turned back communicated to the room, was the end of that.

The rest of the evening went by pleasantly for Callie. Until Jonathon Hawkins approached her.

"Miss Mitchell, it's a pleasure seeing you again."

Everything around her went still. Though she'd once worked at this man's hotel, she'd hardly interacted with him. Once, maybe twice, and only in passing, yet he acted as though they were old friends.

"Thank you, Mr. Hawkins." She gave him a brief nod and a forced smile. "It's nice to see you again, too."

"From what I understand," he continued, his gray eyes smiling, "your absence has left a considerable hole in the Hotel Dupree's kitchen operations."

Emotion threatened to overtake her. Now that she had his attention, there were many things Callie wanted to say to this man. A discussion of her former position in his hotel was not one of them.

"I'm sure you'll find a suitable replacement soon."

"Let us hope you are right." He fished inside the interior of his jacket. "Your sister asked that I give this to you."

Callie stared at him suspiciously. Then realized he was holding a letter in his hand from Fanny, folded in the special way they'd designed back in school. So happy to receive word from her sister, the annoyance she felt toward this man was nearly forgotten.

"Thank you." She plucked the letter from between his fingers and—feeling bold—asked the pressing question running through her mind. "Is Fanny truly well, Mr. Hawkins?"

"She's thriving." His eyes filled with pride and something else, something almost tender, a look that set Callie's teeth on edge.

"I recently promoted your sister to front desk manager."

Callie's heart dipped. No. No, no, no. Fanny would never come home now. She'd been reasonably happy working at the Hotel Dupree. But, Callie admitted to herself, Fanny hadn't *thrived*.

Sighing, she fingered the letter in her hand. She desperately wanted to read the words her sister had penned on the page. She didn't dare exit the party, though, not yet.

As if matters weren't already tense enough, Reese materialized by her side. "Callie? Are you unwell?"

She smiled thinly. "I'm fine."

Reese's eyebrows lifted in silent challenge.

Stuffing the letter from Fanny in her sleeve, she explained further. "Mr. Hawkins has promoted Fanny to front desk manager."

"Ah." Reese turned his attention to the other man. "So she's truly happy living and working in Chicago?"

"Quite."

"That's good to know."

Awkward silence fell over their tiny group.

"I see Mrs. Singletary motioning to me," Hawkins declared. "I should go see what she wants."

"I'll join you," Reese said, deserting Callie without a backward glance.

The two men fell into step with one another, their heads bent in conversation. Both were of an equal height and build, their hair nearly the same color. Callie hadn't noticed the similarities before and wasn't sure what to make of them now.

Were they discussing business as they made their way across the room? Callie would never know.

Soon the guests began to leave, Jonathon Hawkins first, the rest not long after him. Marshall Ferguson made a special effort to approach Callie and assure her he'd enjoyed sitting beside her at dinner.

"I had a lovely time, as well," she said, meaning every word.

"Perhaps we will do it again sometime soon."

"I'd like that."

She watched him depart with his family, wondering why she felt no sense of loss as he exited the room. Because, she realized, there'd been nothing special between them, at least not from her end. No spark, not one ounce of interest.

Had she learned her lesson with Simon? Was she finally safe from making another, impetuous mistake where a man was concerned?

As if to test her theory, Reese came up beside her once again. Her heart skipped two full beats. Her throat tightened. Her knees wobbled.

So much for *that* theory.

Before she could think how to break the silence between them, Reese's father joined them. "My dear, dear, girl, I have come to bid you good evening."

"Good night, Mr. Bennett." She lifted onto her toes and kissed his weathered cheek.

Smiling broadly, he nodded at Reese. "Son."

"Father."

With a strange, satisfied gleam in his eyes, the elder Mr. Bennett approached Mrs. Singletary. They spoke no longer than a minute and then he, too, quit the room.

The widow frowned after him, even as she worked her way over to where Callie and Reese still stood.

"It is my turn to say thank you, Mrs. Singletary." Reese took her hands. "The food was wonderful, the company—" he paused "—interesting and—"

"Before we say good-night, there is a matter of some importance we must discuss."

"Can it not wait until our Monday morning meeting?"

"It cannot."

He released her hands and took a step back. "Carry on, then. Say what you need to say."

"I have concerns about your list."

His eyes cut to Callie and filled with what could only be described as alarm, or perhaps cynicism, or perhaps he was simply looking at her as he always did and she was reading too much into the moment.

"What concerns?" he asked tensely.

Mrs. Singletary made an airy, circular gesture with her hand. "I believe several of your requirements need revising or, at the very least, expanding."

A muscle jerked in his jaw. "Those changes can be addressed on Monday."

By his stiff tone alone, Callie had a bad feeling about this alleged list. Then she caught sight of Reese's thunderous expression.

Oh, yes, a very bad feeling indeed.

Chapter Seven

Reese relaxed his jaw, inch by deliberate inch. All the evening needed was a discussion concerning his requirements for a bride. He'd already endured one of the Ferguson girl's intrusive questions, while fending off her sister's attempts to place her hand on his arm at inappropriate moments.

As if that hadn't been enough, he'd been forced to witness Callie share smiles with Marshall Ferguson. She'd blossomed under the man's attentiveness. Reese didn't fully understand why this bothered him, but it did. Massively. No matter how irrational, he didn't like knowing another man could make her smile.

She wasn't smiling now.

Her eyebrows were pulled together in a sweet, delicate frown. The same expression she'd worn at the opera when she'd agonized over her choice of dessert.

She looked equally adorable this evening, which inexplicably put Reese further on edge.

"This is not an appropriate time to revise my list." He spoke firmly, decisively, as he would in a courtroom, looking meaningfully at the widow in case she missed his meaning.

True to form, the contrary woman refused to give an inch of ground. "There is no better time than the present, while all three of us are together."

The *three* of them? "Callie has no cause to hear—"

"So, it's *Callie* now?"

Reese gritted his teeth.

"Oh, dear." Mrs. Singletary laughed softly. "You look quite put out. Perhaps we should sit down."

"Please, Mr. Bennett." Her tone took on an apologetic air, and her eyes filled with silent appeal. "All I ask is that you hear me out. I promise to be brief and—" her gaze shifted to her companion "—circumspect."

Had the widow continued wrestling for control of the situation, Reese would have left without another word. But she'd switched tactics. Short of being rude, which went against the grain, he was stuck.

He would prefer Callie not be nearby. But if Mrs. Singletary followed through with her promise and chose her words carefully, he had no cause for concern.

"Very well," he said. "I will hear you out."

He narrowed his eyes so the widow would understand that if she pushed too hard or revealed too much he would end the conversation immediately.

Her brief nod indicated she caught his silent warning.

Hands clasped behind his back, Reese waited for the women to choose their seats. Mrs. Singletary sat in a wingback chair, while Callie lowered onto the brocade divan facing her.

After only a moment's consideration, he settled on the divan beside Callie.

He did not look at her. She did not look at him.

Awkwardness had returned to their relationship.

He started to push to his feet. Anticipating the move, Mrs. Singletary held up a hand to stop him.

"Callie." Lowering her hand, she smiled at the younger woman. "Would you be so kind as to retrieve a piece of paper off my desk?"

Callie blinked at her employer. "Which one do you mean?"

"You'll know it when you see it. It is a list of seven items penned in Mr. Bennett's handwriting."

"A list?" Callie's gaze whipped to Reese. "But—"

"Off you go, dear. The man doesn't have all night."

"Yes, Mrs. Singletary." Mouth pressed in a firm line, Callie marched to the door. At the threshold, she looked over her shoulder, sighed and then continued on her way.

The moment she disappeared into the hallway, the widow broke her silence. "I'm sorry to tell you, Mr. Bennett, but I will be unable to help with your bride search."

Reese blinked in stunned silence. This woman, who prided herself for being a consummate matchmaker, was relinquishing her duties? Before she'd even begun?

He should be relieved. He'd only cooperated with the widow's scheme to appease her and to maintain control of the situation.

Yet, now, as she attempted to step away from the project, Reese realized he wanted to find a suitable woman to marry. But with his schedule full and his time limited, Mrs. Singletary's assistance would have greatly expedited the process.

"Why are you begging off?" he asked.

"It's not that I don't wish to see you happily settled. I do, indeed." She picked up her cat and settled the overweight animal atop her voluminous skirt. "At the moment, I am overtaxed and am unable to give the matter my full attention."

It was a flimsy excuse at best. Reese had seen the widow orchestrate matches while simultaneously negotiating highly volatile business deals. Clearly, she was up to something.

"What other commitments are you referring to?"

"Oh, this and that, which will require me to go here and there."

The intentionally vague response had him reaching for

a calm that didn't exist. "Perhaps you could be more specific."

"Of course." She nodded agreeably. "As you know, I am in the process of raising funds for a new wing on the hospital. If we are to break ground before winter, I must move my annual charity ball up by several months. Added to the expansion of my business partnership with Mr. Hawkins, well, my plate is full."

"I will put my search on hold."

"There's no need for such drastic measures." With the faintest trace of amusement shadowing her mouth, the widow leaned forward. "I have no plans to abandon you completely. I propose we put my companion in charge of your search."

"Callie?" Reese hauled in a sharp breath. "You are thinking of putting Callie in charge?"

"I understand your surprise, but if you would take a moment and view this from the proper perspective, you would see the value in my proposal."

He scowled at the ridiculous play on words. "What you suggest is impractical, illogical and completely absurd."

"Now, now, do not give in to skepticism so early in the game." She made a tsking sound with her tongue. "My companion is acquainted with many young women in town. She will know their character personally, as well as their strengths and weakness, perhaps even their hidden shortcomings."

A valid argument, to be sure, but Reese couldn't imagine working with Callie on something as personal as the search for his future bride. Their friendship was still too new, too tentative.

There was another, more glaring concern that could not be ignored. "She is my former fiancée's sister. Her involvement in this could prove awkward."

"My dear Mr. Bennett, life is full of awkward moments."

The widow spoke as if he was a slow-witted child. "How we deal with them ultimately reveals our character."

In the hushed silence of Mrs. Singletary's private office, Callie stared at the list in her hand. Now that she was finally alone, she desperately wanted to read Fanny's letter tucked inside her sleeve. But Callie sensed this piece of paper held equal importance, if not more.

There was no heading on the page, just seven items written in bold masculine strokes beside neatly spaced Roman numerals.

She scanned the list quickly, a hint of alarm crawling up her spine. When the sensation refused to desist, she read each item again, this time out loud.

"'Number one,'" she said, starting at the top of the page. "'Well-educated and articulate. Number two. Have a good moral compass. Number three. Loves children, wants several, at least five but no more than seven.'"

Callie stopped reading as the familiar line sunk in, twisting her insides into knots. What was Reese after?

Oh, but she knew. She knew.

Lord, please, no, let me be wrong.

Battling a wave of panic, she continued reading down the list. "'Must come from a good family and value strong family ties. Be an excellent hostess. A witty conversationalist. Conventional. Steady, absolutely no risk takers.'"

As Callie read the final entry her voice trailed into a hushed whisper. Her heartbeat thickened to a slow, painful thudding. Reese *was* looking for a wife, and he'd secured Mrs. Singletary's assistance in the matter.

The widow was the obvious person to turn to for help in such a matter. Reese was a logical cerebral man, it made sense that he would take the time to draw up a list of his preferred character traits to aid the widow in her search.

Callie couldn't allow her employer to succeed. She had

to think of a way to keep Mrs. Singletary from finding Reese a suitable match or, at the very least, stall the process until Fanny returned home.

Again, Callie read the list, attempting objectivity on this third pass.

She sighed miserably.

What was the man thinking?

The qualities Reese had listed were so common, daresay ordinary. Any number of women in town could fit these characteristics.

With that thought came a surge of hope.

Perhaps there was another reason for this list. Maybe Reese was looking for a housekeeper for himself and his father. Or an assistant in his law firm.

Even as the thought materialized, her gaze landed on the third entry from the top. *Loves children, wants several, at least five but no more than seven.*

No housekeeper or law clerk needed to desire children.

"What am I going to do?"

She needed a plan. But first, she must gather more information. She hurried back to the parlor.

At the same moment she entered, Reese strode across the room and returned to his seat on the divan facing Mrs. Singletary. The widow muttered something Callie couldn't quite make out and then patted his hand as if she was attempting to soothe his concerns.

That didn't bode well.

"Ah, Callie, there you are." The widow motioned her forward. "We were just discussing you."

That *really* didn't bode well, and sparked a kind of awful terror in her, even as excitement sang in her blood. Would Reese consider *her* a likely candidate?

Inappropriate thought. *Inappropriate.*

Reese belonged to Fanny.

Determined to protect her sister's interest, Callie led

with the piece of paper outstretched in front of her. "Here you are, Mrs. Singletary. The list you requested."

She handed over the paper and, against her better judgment, glanced over at Reese. When their gazes connected, the floor seemed to shift beneath her feet. Why did he have to look at her like…*that?* The same way he'd looked at her in his private box at the Grand Tabor, as though she were a puzzle he needed to solve.

On ridiculously shaky legs, Callie moved to stand by the hearth, steadying herself with a hand on the mantelpiece. The heat of the fire penetrated through the thin silk of her gown, yet did nothing to warm her. A cold sweep of foreboding ran through her veins.

She shifted, ever-so-slightly, and caught Reese still looking at her, his gaze tense and unwavering.

Oh, my.

As they stared at one another, silence fell over the room, very awkward and pulsing with all sorts of hidden meaning.

Mrs. Singletary's voice cut through the tension. "Now that you have returned, you will want to know what Mr. Bennett and I have discussed in your absence."

Callie nodded stiffly. "Yes, ma'am."

"Mr. Bennett is in need of your assistance."

"He wants my assistance?" She turned her gaze to meet his. "For what?"

His eyebrows pulled together in that thoughtful expression she found so attractive. For a long, stressful moment he looked undecided, obviously mulling over the best course of action.

Several heartbeats later, he let out a slow breath and reached out his open palm to Mrs. Singletary.

Nodding in satisfaction, the widow handed him the paper Callie had only just retrieved from her office.

He glanced down at the list. "Mrs. Singletary has recently pointed out that my image needs improving."

Callie gasped, a rusty sound that hurt her throat coming out. "That's ridiculous." She spoke without thinking, and straight from her heart. "Forgive me, Mrs. Singletary, but you are wrong."

"Am I, dear?"

"Absolutely." She felt a rush of frustration at her employer's nonchalant response, angered on Reese's behalf. "Reese is a man of unquestionable integrity."

He chuckled softly. "Though I appreciate the sentiment, you don't need to defend me, Callie."

"I'm not defending you." She felt her shoulders bunch, forced herself to relax. "I'm speaking the truth. You are greatly admired throughout all of Denver."

He acknowledged this with a brief nod and a very small smile. "But as Mrs. Singletary pointed out, I am also considered stern and overly rigid."

"Nonsense."

"Nevertheless, Mrs. Singletary has presented a compelling argument. Now that I am the managing senior partner of Bennett, Bennett and Brand, my reputation matters. What I do, how I am perceived by others, reflects on my employees and my clients. Thus, the quickest route to softening my image is to find a suitable woman to marry, who will—"

"No." Callie's voice caught on the word. Oh, but this was terrible. Terrible. "You can't possibly be thinking of replacing Fanny with—" she glared at the list in his hand "—with, well, just anyone."

The smile he gave her was soft and full of silent understanding.

"Fanny is special," Callie declared when he returned his attention to the list. "There is no one like her in all of Denver."

Head bent over the paper, he nodded distractedly. "I don't disagree."

"My sister will be coming home soon." The words tumbled over one another in squeaking desperation. "You must wait for her return."

"Callie, you heard what Mr. Hawkins said." Reese placed the paper face up on the cushions beside him. "Fanny is happy in Chicago. She is not coming home, at least not anytime soon."

"We don't know that for certain."

"Perhaps not, but you and I have had this discussion before. Even if Fanny returns to Denver tomorrow, I won't be renewing my suit."

Why did this proclamation send a surge of joy running through her? And where was her guilt for such a traitorous response? Callie loved her sister, and believed Fanny deserved only the best in life, including a second chance with this wonderful man.

"You won't truly know how you feel until you see her again." Who was she trying to convince? Reese? Or herself? "Please, Reese, just hold off on this until—"

"Fanny and I said everything we needed to say to one another the day she broke our engagement. It's past time I moved on with my life." He picked up the list again, scanned the page. "I want to find a bride, soon, no later than year's end."

His tone held such a lack of passion he could be speaking of any number of pursuits, all business-related. "Why?"

His head snapped up. "Pardon me?"

"*Why* do you want to get married?" She glanced at Mrs. Singletary. The widow gave her an encouraging nod, as if urging her to continue.

Callie drew in a tight breath and forged ahead. "Other than to enhance your image, why do you wish to marry by the end of the year?"

To his credit, Reese didn't answer right away. He considered her question silently, thoughtfully, then said, "I want to get married for the same reason I asked for your sister's hand."

She blinked at him, swallowed back a wave of trepidation and forced herself to say, "Because you want to fall in love again?"

He laughed, the sound abrupt, hard, almost bitter. "I am not seeking a love match."

Puzzled, she cocked her head. "Then what are you seeking?"

"Companionship, friendship and most of all children. I'd like a houseful of them."

He'd answered without hesitation, without even stopping to think about it, as far as she could tell. Admittedly, Callie couldn't fault his answer. Wanting children was a good reason to marry, almost as commendable as love. Almost.

"Now that we have the 'why' settled, let's move on." He passed her the list. "These are the specific qualities I'm looking for in a wife."

Callie pretended to read each entry as if for the first time. "They are terribly vague."

"Not in the least."

Throughout this interchange, Mrs. Singletary had remained silent. Callie looked at her now. Surely she had something to say, some advice to give. The widow ignored her completely as she paid avid attention to a loose thread in her skirt.

Sighing, Callie glanced back down at the list. "Any number of women could fit these requirements."

At last, Mrs. Singletary joined the conversation. "Well, then, your task will be all that much easier."

"*My* task?" Callie gasped. The list slipped from her fingers and fluttered to the floor.

"Yes, dear, I am putting you in charge of finding Mr. Bennett a wife."

Torn between frustration and sheer horror at the prospect, she rounded on Reese. "You have agreed to this?"

He lifted a shoulder. "Mrs. Singletary quite wisely spelled out the value in leaning on you for this particular task. I have weighed the pros and cons, and have decided I agree. You are the perfect choice."

Stunned by both his offhand attitude and his dry tone, Callie stared at him for an entire three seconds. "I don't understand."

"It's simple," he said. "You are acquainted with many eligible young women in town. And have cause to know them in ways neither I nor Mrs. Singletary could hope to achieve, especially considering my deadline."

The backs of Callie's eyes stung. Her breath clogged in her throat. Oh, this was awful, truly awful—a complete disaster in the making. She had to stop this madness.

Then again...

What if she agreed to Mrs. Singletary's scheme? Callie would then have the ability to control this terrible turn of events from a place of strength.

She could stall the process, delay the outcome or even mishandle her duties. If she scrutinized each candidate before introducing her to Reese, Callie could present only the ones he'd find unappealing.

In the meantime, she would contact Fanny and insist the stubborn girl return home. Before it was too late. Before Reese found another woman to marry.

"I'll do it," she declared, smiling sweetly. "I'll help you find a wife."

Chapter Eight

Reese watched in utter fascination as a complicated array of emotions spread across Callie's face. In less than two minutes, she'd gone from a state of shock to gaping outrage to panicked consideration, and ending, finally, with her features settling into a look of female resolve.

It was the resolve that put him immediately on guard.

He'd never seen a woman look quite that determined.

He hadn't misspoken when he'd claimed he'd carefully considered handing over his bride search to Callie. She came from a well-respected ranching family and had an unblemished character. Despite their personal connection through Fanny, Reese trusted Callie without reservation.

And, as the widow had graciously pointed out, Callie was personally acquainted with young women of equally high standing in the community. Relying on her to introduce him to suitable women made sense logically.

Yet Reese couldn't help but wonder. Had he been too hasty in agreeing to Mrs. Singletary's plan?

The widow, Reese could handle. He'd been doing so for years, tackling her business affairs with unprecedented success, regardless of her unconventional requests and thinly veiled personal agendas. That was business.

But Callie?

Callie, a woman he thought he knew, kept surprising him, making him reassess his preconceived notions of her character. Docile one moment, bold the next. Plain one day, jaw-droppingly beautiful the next.

Boring. Then exciting.

Demure and shy. Then confident and determined.

Which woman was the real Callie Mitchell?

The fact that he wanted to know the answer posed too many problems to sort through at the moment.

He'd made a mistake.

"I've changed my mind." He hauled himself to his feet, moving quickly, rolling his shoulders in order to maintain his balance. "I will select my own bride, in my own way."

He'd done so before. Of course, his previous efforts hadn't turned out well. But he knew what to avoid this time around.

"Now, now, Mr. Bennett, I believe you are getting ahead of yourself." With her lips set at an ironic angle, Mrs. Singletary placed her monstrous cat on the floor and pushed to her feet. "There is no need to make a snap decision merely because a few details have changed in our plan."

Technically, only one detail had changed. The sister of his ex-fiancée was now in charge of helping him find the woman to take her place. He'd almost find the situation humorous, if it wasn't so unspeakably bizarre.

"There has been nothing but haste in this entire process."

Reese only had himself to blame. He'd pursued the easiest route, pawning off the task of finding his future bride because he hadn't wanted to take the time to court another woman.

Yet, he didn't want to take another misstep, either, hence his original agreement to pass off the duty to the widow in the first place. Now, he was in a quandary. What to do?

Troubled by his indecision, he contemplated praying for guidance. Then he remembered he and the Lord weren't exactly on speaking terms.

"Reese." Callie gently touched his arm, a silent show of

solidarity in the barely there gesture. "I would very much like to help you find a wife."

He studied her unwavering gaze and saw that the flicker of resolve was still there. Apparently, Callie had her own agenda in agreeing to the widow's scheme.

What could she possibly hope to gain by agreeing to help him? "You are aware this will put us in each other's company frequently."

"You object to my companion's company?"

"Of course not, that wasn't the point I was trying to make." And didn't that say it all? He, a trained attorney, a man used to applying words to great advantage, couldn't put together a decent argument.

"Reese." Callie gently squeezed his arm to regain his attention. "We are friends, are we not?"

He nodded. "We are."

"Wouldn't you also agree that friends help friends?"

He ran a hand along his jaw. "I would."

"I don't mind if this puts us in close proximity." Her bow-shaped lips curved upward. "I enjoy your company."

"I enjoy yours, too." A little too much. And that was the problem. Reese actually liked Callie. He especially liked this new Callie, the one who dressed in rich, bold colors that made her skin glow and her eyes sparkle.

Her transformation awed him. Her beauty stole his breath.

"If you will give me a chance—" she pulled her hand away from his arm "—I believe I can be of great assistance in your search."

Hadn't he already arrived at that same conclusion? "That is not the point."

"What *is* the point?"

He couldn't remember.

"I need a day or two to think this through," he said,

grasping for any reason to make his exit before he said or did something he couldn't take back.

"By all means." Politeness itself, the widow stepped aside to let him pass. "In the meantime, Callie will draw up a list of suitable young women who meet your requirements."

Another list. As a man who lived his life by them, he was growing to dislike them immensely.

He cast a final glance in Callie's direction.

Smiling serenely, she twined her fingers together in front of her. The slight tremble in her clasped hands told its own story. Callie wasn't as confident as she appeared.

Good. He liked knowing he wasn't alone in his discomfort.

"I will be in touch in the next few days." He nodded to the widow. "I will see myself out."

"Oh, no, that simply won't do." Mrs. Singletary nudged her companion toward him. "Callie will escort you to the door."

After only a slight hesitation, Callie shifted to a spot beside him. "I'd like nothing better."

Beatrix Singletary watched the two young people exit the room. Both so erect in their posture, their shoulders rigid, their spines straight and unbending as their minds.

Her beloved companion. Her trusted attorney. Two wounded souls, refusing to live life to the fullest, tortured by secrets they kept hidden deep within themselves. It was really quite sad.

Neither would admit to needing the other.

Oh, but they did. They needed one another greatly, and would be far better together than apart.

Beatrix looked forward to watching them fall in love. She knew the exact dress that would look best on Callie at their wedding.

Satisfied she'd set them on the proper path, Beatrix knew better than to become complacent. Any number of complications could arise to foil her plan. Thus, she followed behind at a reasonable distance, her steps as silent as her cat's.

Stealth was hardly a necessity tonight.

Determined to show the world they were in control, neither Mr. Bennett nor Callie would look over their shoulders to see if she followed.

They kept a respectable distance from each other, looking neither right nor left *nor* at one another.

Beatrix narrowed her eyes in frustration.

Such discomfort in Mr. Bennett's strides, such awkwardness in the way Callie held her shoulders. Such a battle the two were going to put up to reach their happy ending.

Ah, but Beatrix Singletary refused to be disheartened, nor did she have any intention of giving up.

The good Lord had put Callie in her home for a reason. And that reason was walking stiffly beside the young woman, his chin in perfect parallel alignment with the floor.

When two people were meant to be together, as her dear companion and stern attorney were, they eventually found their way. Especially with a little nudge or two from an older, wiser matchmaker.

After seeing Reese out, Callie returned to her room instead of rejoining Mrs. Singletary in the parlor. Her nerves were too raw, her thoughts in too much turmoil to match wits with the clever woman.

Besides, Callie wanted to be alone while she read her sister's letter. Settling in an overstuffed chair, she carefully placed the pages on her lap. A mere half hour ago, she'd been eagerly anticipating this moment. She'd desperately wanted to read what her sister had to say.

So why wasn't she unfolding the pages?

Why was she hesitating?

Fear, she realized. She was afraid of what she would discover.

Sighing over her cowardice, she turned her head and looked out the window beside her. The Rocky Mountains stood guard, their mighty peaks clearly outlined in the deep purple sky. The rain had moved on. Now, pale moonlight cut shadows across the land while tree branches scratched eerily at the glass windowpanes.

Callie sighed again, pressed her lips tightly together and ignored the letter a moment longer. Something far more troubling weighed on her mind.

Why had she agreed to help Reese find his future bride?

Then again, how could she have not agreed? Mrs. Singletary would have taken over the task if she'd refused. And unlike Callie, the widow wouldn't stop presenting eligible women until Reese was happily settled.

Callie groaned. She didn't object to him getting married, as long as he married Fanny. Anyone else would be intolerable. But how was she to create a list of suitable woman who weren't actually suitable?

What a disaster.

The quickest, most expedient route to fixing this mess was to convince Fanny to return home immediately.

No easy task.

Not if Jonathon Hawkins was to be believed.

Did Fanny have any regret over leaving Reese behind? And if she did, would she put on a brave face, fearing she couldn't come home now that she'd made her initial, *hasty* decision to leave town?

There was one sure way to find out what was in her sister's head. Read the letter Mr. Hawkins had personally delivered.

Callie looked down at the folded paper in her lap.

What if her sister didn't regret leaving town?

What if she did? What if she wanted Reese back?

For a dangerous moment, Callie wished—oh, how she wished—that Fanny was through with Reese once and for all.

Then Callie could… She could…

Find him someone else to marry.

The thought brought on such despair she nearly choked on her own breath.

No more stalling.

She unfolded Fanny's letter with fumbling fingers. She couldn't help but remember Jonathon Hawkins's expression right before he'd pressed the papers into her hand. He'd looked quite confident he was doing Callie a favor by giving her this missive from her sister.

Until tonight, she'd only thought of him as that odious man who'd given Fanny a reason to leave town. But as he'd stared into her eyes, she'd seen a man with nothing but good intentions.

Perhaps she'd misjudged him.

Callie coiled her fingers around the unread letter in her lap. The stiff feel of the paper reminded her that the answers to her dilemma could be right here, beneath her hand.

She lifted the letter until the moonlight illuminated the entire page. The beautiful looping scrawl definitely belonged to Fanny, but appeared much neater than usual, as if she'd taken great care with each word.

A sob worked its way up Callie's throat. How she missed her sister. Taking a deep breath, she smoothed out the pages and began reading….

My Dearest Sister,

I scarcely know where to begin. If you are reading this letter, I can assume Mr. Hawkins has kept his promise and has delivered this to you personally. I am so sorry I haven't answered any of your letters until now. I ask for your forgiveness. It seems a poor substitute to do so in writing, rather than speaking to you in person.

In answer to the question in your last letter, no, I do not regret leaving town. Nor do I regret breaking my engagement with Reese. I should have never agreed to marry him, at least not until I knew more about myself. Though not his fault, Reese proposed to an image I had created, not the woman I am, deep down, and that is solely my fault.

I have happily played a role all my life. The pretty, frivolous young woman. The adored sister. The treasured fiancée. But who is the woman beneath the various masks I wear?

I don't know. However, I am determined to find out. Until I do, I have no business marrying any man.

Please do not hold my departure against Mr. Hawkins. Had he not offered me this job, I would have found another way to leave town.

I close this letter with a single request. When next you see Reese, will you tell him I am doing well and wish him nothing but happiness for the future?

I love you, dearest Callie.

Yours most faithfully,

Fanny

Callie read the letter again and tossed it on the nightstand, only to pick it up and read it one more time. And then another.

Heart pounding, throat burning, she tried to remain detached, but she couldn't. Fanny didn't regret leaving town, but her reasoning for breaking her engagement with Reese was something Callie had never considered. Her sister had been hiding behind a mask, of sorts. No different than Callie herself.

While Callie had buried her true nature behind dull

clothing and severe hairstyles, Fanny had been doing much the same with her fashionable dresses and sparkling personality. The difference, it seemed, was that Callie had always known who she was beneath the facade.

Apparently, Fanny did not.

Callie read her sister's letter once again.

Nowhere did Fanny mention she didn't still love Reese.

The battle wasn't over, then. Fanny could one day change her mind and want Reese back. Despite his assurance otherwise, how did he know he didn't want the same until he was actually faced with the choice?

Cold, hard resentment surged. For a treacherous moment, Callie allowed the dark sensation to fill her. After the pain Fanny had caused, she didn't deserve Reese.

Callie shoved the traitorous thought aside. It wasn't her place to judge her sister so harshly. The Lord's glorious, redemptive love called for mercy and forgiveness.

Besides, she'd agreed to help Reese find a wife, with the express purpose of keeping him from moving on until Fanny could make one final bid to win his heart. Her course was set.

Callie moved to her desk, dipped her pen in the inkwell and began the letter that would hopefully bring Fanny home.

She worked into the wee hours of the night, revising her words until she had them exactly as she wanted them.

The next morning, with very little sleep behind her, she woke groggy and out of sorts. Born on a ranch, she'd never been able to sleep past dawn. She rose with the sun and dressed for the day in her olive-green muslin gown. Thankfully, Mrs. Singletary hadn't raided her wardrobe completely.

Glancing down at herself, Callie admitted the color was drab, the fit unnecessarily large, and for the first time in years, she felt uncomfortable in her own clothes.

She missed wearing the bold colors the widow insisted she don, the ones that brought out the color in her skin.

This sense of dissatisfaction was the widow's doing, as was the wave of rebellion that urged Callie to dress in clothes that highlighted her assets.

Ah, but today was her day off. She planned to spend most of it in the kitchen at Charity House, the orphanage Marc and Laney Dupree had created for children of prostitutes. Boys and girls no other institution would take were welcomed into a loving, safe home and given a solid Christian upbringing, thereby breaking the cycle of sin in their lives.

Callie loved spending her free time with the orphans, many of whom weren't strictly orphans but rather children with mothers who worked in the local brothels. Though indirectly, Callie had a personal connection to Charity House. All three of her older brothers had married women either raised in the orphanage or formerly employed there. Megan, Annabeth and Molly were kind, God-loving women.

Her brothers had chosen well.

Exiting her room, she nearly toppled into Mrs. Singletary. "Oh."

Hands on hips, the widow lowered her gaze over Callie's dress. "You are determined to defy my superior sense of style."

Callie wasn't in the mood to defend her clothing choices this morning. She gave a tight, and slightly embarrassed, sigh. "It's my day off. What does it matter how I dress?"

Mrs. Singletary released her own aggravated puff of air. "You are proving most difficult, Callie Anne Mitchell."

"That is not my intent." With exaggerated dignity, she lifted her chin. "I'm helping out Laney Dupree in the Charity House kitchen today. We're teaching a few interested girls how to bake pies. It's a messy business and I don't mind getting wayward ingredients on this particular gown."

"That explanation is perfectly—" Mrs. Singletary shook her head in amused annoyance "—reasonable."

Callie swallowed a triumphant smile. "I know."

"I had hoped to discuss Mr. Bennett's requirements for a wife with you at some point today. Perhaps together we can make some sense out of his list," Mrs. Singletary continued. "I find his preferences are really rather—"

"Uninspired?" Callie suggested.

"Completely." The widow gave a little shake of her head. "Why, any number of women in town could fit his requirements."

Callie nodded in agreement. If she thought this would end the discussion, she was wrong.

Mrs. Singletary seemed determined to say her piece. "Although the bulk of the task will fall on your shoulders I believe my input will increase your success. Especially as you design your initial list of suitable candidates for him to review."

"You have suggestions?"

"A few."

Callie remained silent for several seconds. If she refused the widow's input would Mrs. Singletary make a *few suggestions* to Reese on her own?

Perhaps. Perhaps not. Callie didn't dare take that risk. "We could discuss this when I return from my afternoon at Charity House."

"That will be fine." The widow started down the hall then quickly turned back around. "I am determined to see Mr. Bennett happily settled before Christmas."

"As am I." Finally, something they agreed upon, and probably the last for many days to come.

Chapter Nine

As he did most Saturday mornings, Reese exited the ridiculously large house he shared with his father and turned in the direction of Charity House. At this early hour the sun hung low, a big, fat orange ball against the blue, blue sky.

The sweet, lilting music of birds singing from their tree branches accompanied him on his short journey to the orphanage, a leisurely stroll that amounted to the equivalent of two city blocks in town.

Alone on the streets, Reese's mind wandered over several pressing concerns, eventually landing on last night's conversation with Mrs. Singletary and her companion. He'd meant what he said when Callie had pressed for a reason behind his bride search. He wanted children. As many as it would take to fill the house and turn the rambling old mansion into a home.

Growing up, Reese had secretly craved a large family. He would have settled for just one sibling, either a brother or a sister. Unfortunately, a week after his seventh birthday, his mother had succumbed to a fever and then died a week later.

His father had never remarried.

Looking back with the benefit of age, Reese wondered if he'd married young with the idea of filling his nursery as quickly as possible. Even at eighteen, he'd been ready to start a family. Miranda hadn't been quite so eager. The one time he'd brought up the subject, she'd laughed the idea away, claiming it was far too early in their marriage to talk about children.

Dark memories threatened to drag him into the past where only hopelessness and sorrow resided. He refused to surrender on this beautiful Saturday morning. The story of his life with Miranda, and the crippling grief he experienced after her death, belonged to his younger self. The man he was now had his entire future ahead of him.

Endless possibilities abounded.

The rewards of marrying again far outweighed the risks. Of course, he still needed to find a suitable woman to marry. A tiny, little, insignificant detail he'd put in Callie Mitchell's care.

He stopped at the street corner and inhaled slowly.

Had he made the right decision? Handing over such an important task to the sister of his former fiancée instead of relying on Mrs. Singletary's guidance?

The widow's arguments for the switch had certainly been sound. Though he didn't fully understand why Callie had agreed to help him find a bride, she *had* agreed. The deed was done.

The course set.

Instead of second-guessing his own actions—or Callie's—Reese crossed the street and focused on the moment, the here and now, prepared to enjoy his day at Charity House.

He passed through a sunbeam warming the cobblestones at his feet. The temperature was perfect for playing outside. Perhaps he would talk some of the children into an impromptu game of baseball, a favorite of the orphans.

One block later, he arrived at the orphanage. Charity House was an uncommonly grand structure, even for this posh neighborhood. Puffy white clouds moved rapidly through the sky above the sloping roof of angles and interesting turrets, the Colorado blue a perfect backdrop for the three-story structure.

With its stylish modern design and perfectly manicured lawns, Charity House looked nothing like an orphanage. Fitting, since many of the children weren't true orphans. Laney and Marc Dupree had created a safe, loving home for the abandoned boys and girls whose mothers often chose their unholy professions over their own offspring.

Did the children realize they lived in one of the most exclusive neighborhoods in Denver? That the gas lamps sitting atop poles at every street corner were of the highest quality? That the other mansions marching shoulder to shoulder in elegant formation along the lane housed some of the wealthiest families in the West?

What did it matter, as long as they were happy and safe?

Pleased he could play his part, small as it might be, Reese unlatched the wrought-iron gate and strode up the front walk.

Marc Dupree exited the house. Dark-haired and clean-shaven, the owner of Charity House wore a gold brocade vest and matching tie, the kind a banker or even Reese himself would wear for a day at the office.

Laney Dupree joined her husband a moment later. Petite and fine-boned, she was as beautiful as her home. She wore a simple pale blue dress with a high lace collar today. Her mahogany-colored hair hung loose, framing her stunning face with long wavy curls.

The couple clasped hands and approached Reese as a single unit. A gnawing ache twisted in his stomach. Reese and Miranda had never had that close, unspoken connection. He'd loved his wife desperately, with the unbridled passion of youth, but now, he wondered.

Would they have settled into a mature marriage, one full of contentment, comfort and peace? Or would they have continued living on the edge, all but laughing at danger and taking unnecessary risks with their lives?

He would never know.

The couple separated and Laney pushed slightly ahead of her husband, her smile radiant and full of welcome. "Good morning, Reese."

"Laney. Marc." He nodded to both individually, then dug into his coat pocket and produced the bank draft he'd brought with him. "For Charity House."

Laney reached out before her husband could and took the money. She looked down at the amount. "Oh, Reese, this is especially generous."

"It's from my father and me."

"Still…" She trailed off, her gaze full of silent gratitude.

"You do good work here, Laney, *important* work, work for the Lord." Reese didn't always understand God's ways, but he didn't deny that the Lord's hand was on Charity House. "I wish I could contribute more."

"You do plenty, not only with your money, but with your time." She folded the bank draft and handed it to her husband. "Thank you, Reese. And, please, pass on my gratitude to your father, as well."

"I will." Feeling slightly uncomfortable, he turned to Marc. "It's a beautiful day. What do you say we put together an impromptu baseball game?"

The other man's smile came quickly and easily. "Great minds think alike. I already sent most of the children outside. They're in the backyard picking teams as we speak."

On cue, Reese heard laughter floating on the light breeze.

"Come on." Marc gestured for Reese to follow him and Laney up the porch steps. "We'll take a shortcut through the house."

They entered through the main parlor. Everywhere Reese looked he saw order and charm, comfort and beauty.

He found the attention to detail admirable. But it was the smells of home that tugged at his heart.

The tangy aroma of soot from the fireplace mingled with lemon wax from the floors and furniture. That sweet, homey bouquet, as well as the scent of baking pies, transported him back to his childhood, when his mother was still alive.

An unexpected bout of longing captured him, longing for a home and a family of his own, for a comfortable, settled life with a good woman by his side. The sensation came fast and hard, digging deep, slowing his steps. For a painful moment, the loneliness in his soul spilled into his heart.

His gut roiled.

Then he heard a familiar female voice, followed by a soft, throaty laugh.

The storm brewing in him calmed.

His senses unnaturally heightened, Reese became aware of additional chattering and giggles from young, girlish voices. *The sound of family.* He breathed in slowly, the scent of apples and cinnamon filling his nose.

The smell of home.

A sense of inevitability pushed him forward. When he stepped into the Charity House kitchen, his gaze sought and found Callie. He had one coherent thought—*her.*

She's the one.

He shoved the disturbing notion aside before it could take root.

The moment Reese's gaze locked with hers, Callie's lungs forgot how to breathe. The ability to communicate failed her, as well, though she couldn't think why. She knew Reese spent time at Charity House, she'd seen him here before.

Yet, somehow, his presence today felt different. New and special.

Life-altering.

There was so much emotion in his eyes, eyes still locked with hers. She recognized that haunted look, the hint of vulnerability in his stance.

How she wanted to go to him, to comfort and to soothe, as one kindred soul to another.

She didn't have that right.

Regardless of their budding friendship, they were barely more than acquaintances. And as of last night, Callie was tasked with the job of finding him the perfect woman to marry. A woman who would have the sole honor of loving him into eternity, who would provide him with the children he wanted and create a home for them all.

The massive kitchen suddenly felt too small, too hot. Callie shoved a strand of hair off her face with the back of her hand.

Reese shifted to his left, splintering the tense moment, and their disturbing connection.

A moment later, Marc Dupree moved into view. Laney pushed past both men and moved to stand next to Callie. The other woman's presence gave her the strength to battle the rest of her control back into place.

She forced a smile. "Hello, Reese."

"Hello, Callie."

She could think of nothing more so say.

Reese wasn't exactly verbose himself. In the fractured silence that hung between them, he studied the chaos she and the half-dozen girls surrounding her had managed to create since she'd arrived.

"We are making pies," she said unnecessarily and perhaps a little defensively, as well. She'd always been a messy cook.

Until now, she hadn't realized just how messy.

"I enjoy pie." Reese sniffed the air. "Especially apple pie."

One of the girls giggled into her hand.

Reese winked at her, whereby her giggles turned into a fit of giddy laughter. This seemed to open the floodgates and the rest of the girls moved in around him, chattering over one another in an effort to gain his attention.

He was clearly a favorite among the assembled group. Callie understood why. With his wide smile and casual manner, he responded in a way that surely made each girl feel as though she were the most important person in the room.

Watching him now, in this setting, with the animated girls surrounding him, he was so easy to like.

He'd be just as easy to love.

Callie jerked back from the thought.

"All right, girls, that's enough." Laney nudged and pushed until she was in the center of the mayhem. "Let's give poor Mr. Bennett room to breathe, shall we?"

"We're heading outside to supervise a baseball game," Marc announced, dropping a glance over each girl. "Any of you want to join us?"

After sharing a brief glance with the others, the oldest spoke up for the rest. "We're making pies for supper tonight and are only halfway to our goal."

Callie smiled at the girl. At barely thirteen, Laurette Dupree was Marc and Laney's only natural child and already a beauty. With her mother's thick mahogany-colored hair and her father's steel-blue eyes, she was bound to break the hearts of many unsuspecting men one day.

"Since I'm also a fan of apple pie, we'll leave you to your work." Marc gestured for Reese to follow him out the back door.

The two men fell into step with one another.

Halfway through the kitchen, Reese stopped, turned back around and moved in beside Callie. He stood so close she could smell his spicy masculine scent over the baking pies.

Lowering his voice for her ears only, he voiced an odd request. "Don't leave until we have a chance to talk."

Though his words could be construed as a command, the tone he used was soft and engaging and made her stomach pitch.

"If that's what you want," she practically croaked. "I'll be sure to find you before I head back to Mrs. Singletary's."

"Splendid." He stepped back, smiled ruefully, then continued on his way.

Unable to take her eyes off his broad shoulders, she followed his progress as he retraced his steps. Confused and a little shaky, a sigh worked its way up her throat. The man made her feel things, things she'd never felt before, not even when she'd thought herself in love with Simon.

The moment he exited the house, several girlish sighs followed in his wake. Clearly, he had female admirers in this house.

Unable to censure herself a moment longer, her sigh joined the others. A mistake. She could practically feel Laney's gaze slide over her.

Callie kept her expression blank, tried to appear nonchalant. But she was hit with a wall of nerves. Had she just given herself away?

Far too perceptive for her own good, Laney leaned in close to Callie's ear. "*That* was certainly interesting."

Aware six pairs of eyes had swung in her direction, Callie busied herself with pouring another cup of flour into a large mixing bowl. "Don't read too much in to what you think you saw," she warned Laney, as well as herself. "Reese and I have agreed to become friends."

"Is that so?"

"Yes." She didn't expand, but rather attempted to change the subject. "How many pies are we short after that last batch?"

Laney eyed her for a long moment. "We need six more,

seven if we want to bring one over to Pastor Beau and his family."

"Seven it is." Callie dug her fingers into the dough, giving her friend a meaningful stare before rolling her gaze over their wide-eyed, attentive audience. "Let's get started, shall we?"

Laney relented with a brief nod.

The next hour was spent mixing dough, rolling out pie shells and cutting apples into small wedges. The girls giggled and laughed their way through the process.

Not until the last pie was baking, and her helpers were cleaning up at the sink, did Laney pull Callie aside.

"You like him," she said without preamble, keeping her voice low. "Don't pretend you don't know who I mean."

Callie gave a weighty sigh. "Of course I like him. I like all my friends."

"Oh, really." Laney parked her hands on her hips. "So, you and Reese—"

"There is no *me and Reese*."

"Not from where I was standing. In fact—" Laney's lips curved upward "—you two looked very comfortable with one another."

"Reese and I are friends, Laney, nothing more."

"So you already said." Laney let out a soft chuckle. "And before you reiterate your point yet again, no man looks at a woman he considers a mere friend the way I saw Reese looking at you."

Callie swallowed, took a hard inhale. There was no excuse for feeling so dangerously moved by this observation. "You are reading far too much into this."

"Am I?"

"Have you forgotten?" Determined to keep this conversation between the two of them, she spoke the words in a hushed whisper. "He was once engaged to my sister."

"He's no longer engaged to Fanny."

"Not by choice."

That, Callie realized, was a critical detail she must always remember herself. The broken engagement between Reese and Fanny had not been Reese's idea. If he'd had his way, he'd be married to Fanny right now.

Depressing thought.

"Callie." Laney took both her hands. "Talk to me. Tell me what's so wrong with the possibility of you and Reese becoming more than—"

A spontaneous cheer burst through the opened window.

"Mother," Laurette called from the sink. "Is it all right if we went outside and watched the game?"

"By all means." Still holding Callie's hands, Laney smiled at her daughter. "Miss Callie and I will watch the pies."

As each girl hurried out the back door, Callie tried to think of a reason to abandon the kitchen, as well. None came to mind. She nearly despaired, but then rescue came in a tentative, barely there tug on her skirt.

"Miss Callie?"

"Yes, Gabriella?"

"I don't want to go outside." Big, sorrowful brown eyes met hers. "I want to stay here with you."

Moved by the request, Callie crouched down to make herself less intimidating. Somewhere between four and five years old, Gabriella Velasquez and her twin brother, Daniel, had only been at Charity House for a few weeks. According to Laney, their mother had recently died of consumption in a Cripple Creek brothel.

Callie smiled down at the sweet, precious child. She tried not to choose favorites. She tried to give of herself equally to all the children. But something about this reserved little girl, and her equally shy brother, had slipped beneath her guard.

Perhaps it was their unusual silence. Or the way they flinched when anyone, even other children, came near them.

"Oh, Gabriella, of course you can stay inside with me." She picked up the girl and set her on the counter. Callie adored this sweet child with the coal-black hair; sad, dark eyes and overly timid nature. "Want to help me count the pies?"

"I don't know how to count."

Callie brushed the child's hair away from her face, resisting the temptation to press a kiss to her forehead. "No time like the present to learn."

And so began Gabriella's first arithmetic lesson. *One plus one equals two. Two plus two equals four.* Basic, simple math equations every child should know. It was a shame Callie and Reese didn't add up that smoothly.

Chapter Ten

From his position facing home plate, Reese looked up at the darkening sky. Sometime in the past twenty minutes the weather had turned. Black ominous clouds boiled overhead, while a stiff wind carried the earthy scent of approaching rain.

Marc, in his self-appointed role as umpire, trotted out to where Reese stood on the makeshift pitcher's mound, which was nothing more than an empty flour bag. "What do you think? Should we call it?"

Distant thunder punctuated the question.

Reese looked back up at the sky, the children's safety foremost in his mind. "No lightning yet, and the first drops of rain haven't hit. I say we play on a little while longer."

"Agreed." Marc hustled back to his spot behind the catcher and made a circling motion with his hand. "Batter up."

A small, thin boy of about five years old approached the plate with slow, tentative steps. His wide, terrified gaze darted around the backyard, eventually landing on Reese. Taking pity on the apprehensive child, he moved forward several steps closer. Until today, Daniel Velasquez had kept himself separate from the other children, choosing to remain on the sidelines as an isolated spectator.

His willing participation this morning was monumental. And deeply moving.

And Reese wasn't the only one who recognized the significance of the moment.

Daniel's entire team cheered him on, urging him to "swing for the back fence." Even kids on the opposing team shouted out words of encouragement.

Marc ruffled the boy's hair. "Remember how to hold the bat?"

Daniel nodded.

"Let's play ball." Marc settled in behind the catcher.

Bottom lip caught between his teeth, Daniel slung the wooden bat over his right shoulder then blinked up at Reese with eyes that had grown bigger and rounder.

Such courage in so tiny a package, Reese thought. Determined to honor this momentous occasion, he lobbed a slow, easy pitch over home plate.

Daniel swung with all his might. And missed.

Clearly dejected, his shoulders slumped forward and his eyes filled with tears.

"Ball one!" Marc called, then patted the boy on the back. "Try again, and remember to keep your eye on the ball."

Daniel's bottom lip quivered, but he heroically firmed it as he slung the bat over his shoulder a second time.

Reese tossed the next pitch a little lower and a bit slower. Daniel swung again. The very tip of the bat connected with the ball, sending it to a spot near Reese's feet. Not a magnificent hit, but a solid enough whack to qualify.

Cheers erupted from both teams.

"Head to first base!" Marc nudged the boy in the proper direction.

Reese made a grand show of fumbling the ball into his glove. He waited until Daniel had a solid head start before tossing the ball high over the head of the first baseman, who was too busy cheering on the little boy to notice.

Daniel's foot hit the pad and he headed for second base.

Wanting to give the boy a fighting chance, Reese hustled over and picked up the rolling ball before anyone else thought to do so.

With shouts of encouragement from the other children urging him on, Daniel flew over second base and continued on to third.

This time, Reese threw the ball short.

The little boy rounded for home, his mouth set in a determined line, his little legs pumping hard. His foot touched home plate seconds before Reese half-heartedly winged the ball into the catcher's glove.

Marc made a wide sweep of his arms. "Safe."

"You hit a home run." Caught up in the moment, Reese ran over, swooped Daniel into his arms and spun him around and around in the air.

The boy giggled and kicked his legs wildly. "I did it. I did it. I did it."

"Yeah, you did. It was a great hit, too." Heart overflowing with something akin to parental pride, Reese set the boy back on the ground and ruffled his hair.

His teammates immediately surrounded him.

Daniel soaked up the attention with a big happy smile.

Allowing his own smile free rein, Reese watched the celebration from a few feet away. He caught a movement out of the corner of his eye and swiveled his head toward the back porch. Callie stood behind the railing, watching Daniel with her heart in her eyes.

Ridiculously pleased that she understood the magnitude of Daniel's moment of triumph, Reese set out in her direction. Only as he drew close did he notice the little girl peering out from behind Callie's skirt. Reese recognized the child as Daniel's twin sister, Gabriella.

For reasons he couldn't understand, his heart lurched at the sight woman and child made, the very image of mother and daughter. His footsteps faltered. Where had that thought come from?

His pulse quickened, beating harder, faster than before, rushing thick and uneven through his veins.

Now that Callie no longer wore an apron covered in flour and pie dough, he was able to catalog her clothing in detail. Her dress was a drab, dull green, the color not particularly flattering. And yet, she radiated.

He couldn't seem to catch a decent breath.

Gabriella tugged on her skirt and whispered something Callie had to bend down to hear. She nodded and then scooted the little girl in the direction of the porch steps.

Hesitant at first, Gabriella descended at a snail's pace. Callie's face was calm as she watched the child's progress, but she clutched at the porch rail with a tight grip. The flicker of worry in her eyes told its own tale, as did the tightening of her lips, and the sigh that leaked out of her. A protective mother-hen leery over letting her chick branch out on its own.

"Gabriella." Bouncing from one foot to the other, Daniel called out to his sister. "Gabriella. Did you see me? Did you see me hit the ball?"

The little girl jumped off the last step, a smile splitting across her face. "You did really good, Daniel."

He beamed. "You have to try it next time."

"Okay." She paused. "Maybe." Another pause, then she sped over to her brother and joined in the merriment. One of the older girls tugged her close.

Charmed by the scene, and not wanting to miss a second of the festivities, Reese conquered the porch steps two at a time then took Gabriella's place beside Callie. He did a double take. Something had happened to her eyes, they'd turned greener, larger. Prettier. He could lose himself in their depths if he didn't take care.

"Hi," he said, pleased his voice sounded relatively normal.

"Oh, Reese." Callie reached up and brushed at his shoulder as if removing a speck of dust. The gesture was casually intimate and felt exactly right for the moment. "That was very kind of you, what you did for Daniel, ensuring he made it around all the bases."

Her words of praise made him feel strong, courageous, keen on conquering the world and slaying dragons with his bare hands.

Shrugging away the fanciful thought, he rolled back on his heels, came back down again. "It's what any man would have done in my position."

"No, Reese." She brushed at his other shoulder. "Not every man has it in him to be kind to children."

She sounded certain, and a little sad, as if she'd come across her share of bad characters.

Had someone hurt her?

A protective instinct shuddered through him and one thought rose above the others. *I want to fight this woman's battles.*

"You are a good man, Reese Bennett Junior."

Instant pleasure surged at the words that seemed to flow so easily off her lips. "Thank you, Callie."

Her eyes went soft with emotion. "You're welcome."

An odd sensation filled his chest, part confusion, part longing. He moved closer, a mere inch, no more.

The wind kicked up. The world paused, and then…

The swollen rain clouds unleashed their watery assault.

Chaos exploded in the backyard. Squeals and shrieks and giggles filled the air. Running feet. More laughter.

"Everybody inside," Marc shouted over the commotion.

One by one the children scrambled onto the porch. They crowded around Reese and Callie, laughing and tossing water in every direction. At the bottom of the steps, Marc hoisted Gabriella into his arms and set her down near Callie.

When Daniel stood in the rain, blinking up after his sister, looking forlorn and forgotten, Reese retrieved the boy in the same way Marc had rescued his sister.

Back on the porch, he had to shuffle his way through a maze of flaying arms and kicking legs to find a clear spot to set the boy down safely.

Marc took charge, Reese and Callie helping wherever they could. The three of them made quick work of gathering equipment in one pile, wet, muddy shoes in another, before herding the motley group of laughing, soaking wet children inside the house.

Retreating to her timid ways, Gabriella clung to Daniel, huddling close to him, her eyes wide and full of fear.

Callie approached the twins, crouched down to eye level. She spoke in a gentle voice, so soft Reese couldn't make out her words. Daniel nodded enthusiastically, pulling on his sister's arm. A blink of the eye later, the boy had his sister following behind the other children. The little girl didn't look especially overjoyed, and kept glancing back over her shoulder at Callie. But with her brother's encouragement, she obeyed.

Progress.

When the back door banged shut behind the twins, Reese realized he and Callie were alone on the porch. Just the two of them.

Fat raindrops pelted the ground. Thick clouds covered the sky. The muted gray light did nothing to conceal Callie's beauty, or hide the shades of caramel, gold and deep yellow in her hair.

And her eyes, those amazing, grass-green eyes, they stole his breath. *She* stole his breath.

Callie Mitchell was a beautiful woman. Reese realized with a sudden jolt that her appeal had nothing to do with her clothing, or how she chose to wear her hair, and everything to do with the woman herself. She was kind to frightened children, and he couldn't stop staring at her.

Nor could he deny the truth any longer. He was attracted to Callie Mitchell, captivated by a woman most considered unremarkable. Fools, all of them.

Reese knew he should feel awkward in her company, certainly alarmed at the direction of his thoughts. Instead, the sensation moving through him soothed his spirit. Calmed his soul. Urged him to let down his guard and relax, as if he'd finally come home after a long, endless journey.

Now, he was uncomfortable.

He took several steps back, away from Callie, and searched his mind for something innocuous to say. "Finished making pies?"

"Oh, yes." The smile she gave him sent his mind reeling. "All ten of them."

"Ten?"

"Apple pie is a favorite among the children."

He felt his smile return. "Kids with exceptional taste, I knew I liked them for a reason."

She laughed. "Apparently, the joy of apple pie knows no bounds."

"Or age limit," he said, laughing with her. He noticed a smudge on her cheek. Compelled, he reached up and brushed his fingertips across the spot.

Her eyes narrowed.

"Flour," he said, showing her the pads of his fingers.

"Oh." She let out a sweet, nervous laugh. "My secret is revealed. I'm a messy cook."

Affection enveloped him. Why had he never noticed just how striking and dramatic her features were? How had he missed the almond shape of her eyes, or how vivid and intense they were beneath finely arched brows?

Something deep and life-altering was gathering inside his heart. Reese wanted to pull Callie into his arms and kiss her.

He clasped his hands behind his back and cleared his

throat. "Are you heading to Mrs. Singletary's anytime soon?"

"I am, once I say goodbye to the children."

"May I escort you home?"

"Yes, I…" A thousand questions leaped into her eyes. She voiced none of them. "Thank you, Reese, I would like that very much."

Thoughts scrambled around one another in Callie's mind, circling each another like a hawk swooping in for prey. She longed for so much, unable to define exactly what she wanted, yet knowing the man strolling beside her was at the heart of the sensation.

Despite her misgivings over the wisdom of allowing Reese to walk her home, her agreement had made perfect sense at the time. He lived in the same neighborhood as Mrs. Singletary, and would only have to alter his own route home by a mere block.

Callie lifted her gaze to the sky.

The rain had let up, but the air was still damp, the wind still raw. Much like her nerves.

The grind of wagon wheels sounded in the distance, along with the boom of a motor carriage firing into life. A baby wailed. A dog barked. "Do you hear that?"

Reese cut a glance in her direction. "Hear what?"

"The sounds of the neighborhood alive with activity." She swept her hand in a wide arc. "Listen."

He slowed his pace and did what she suggested. He listened.

"It's soothing, isn't it?" She smiled up at him. "Knowing the world moves on around us no matter what's happening in our own lives?"

He stopped walking and turned to face her. "Callie Mitchell, you have the heart of a poet."

"Oh, I…" She thought of her love of the Psalms, especially the ones penned by King David. She enjoyed Shake-speare's sonnets, too, some of Byron's work, as well as Emily Dickenson's. "I suppose I do."

"You continually surprise me."

"Is that a good thing?"

"Exceptionally good." His eyes filled with quiet affection as he reached out and brought her hand to his lips.

The gesture was so unexpected, so sweet and gentle, her stomach dipped. She sighed, wanting this afternoon with Reese to last forever. Lovely conversation, lovely company, she couldn't ask for more. *Wouldn't* ask for more than this one perfect moment with a man she admired above all others.

Complicated emotions blazed to the surface. Forgotten hopes and dreams beckoned, and Callie forgot to wear her hard-earned, outward control.

Something had to be terribly wrong, because she and Reese were easy with one another. Comfortable.

Connected.

Still holding her hand, he guided her off the main path. Callie looked around, saw that they'd entered a small public park.

He led her toward a large leafy tree with several low-hanging branches. Their feet left indentions in the wet, muddy grass. Reese's were large and clearly defined, hers smaller, less pronounced, as if she was floating across the ground.

He let go of her hand, reached up and plucked a stem free from its branch. His gaze turned dark and turbulent as he fiddled with a green leaf, and then another.

Something was troubling him. "Reese? What's wrong?"

"It's Daniel and Gabriella." He wound the edge of the stem around his finger. "Although Daniel took a big step today, as did his sister, they're both uncommonly quiet and withdrawn."

Callie laid a hand on his arm, looked into his eyes. "They've only been at Charity House a few short weeks," she reminded him. "It's not unusual for new arrivals to hold themselves apart from the other children for months, sometimes longer."

"I know." The lines of worry around his eyes seemed to cut deeper. "But it seems unfair that they lost their mother so young and never even knew their father. I can only imagine what their lives were like before they came to Charity House."

"At least they're safe now, living in a loving home where they will be given the advantage of a Christian upbringing, renewed hope and unconditional love."

"I know. *I know.* But, Callie, they're too young to fear the world as they do." He tossed the branch to the ground with singular force. "The secret wounds they carry, it's unimaginable."

The intensity of his words highlighted his concern, a concern she shared. "That's not to say they won't one day find healing. Laney and Marc will take good care of them."

Reese nodded, but the tension in his shoulders didn't release. If anything, his shoulders bunched tighter. As she stared into his eyes, Callie saw the man beneath the stern exterior—a man of great feeling, with a hatred for injustice and the capacity to love deeply.

"I know what you say is true, Callie. Still, it's a pity the twins can't have a family of their own."

"They do have a family, at Charity House. Untraditional, to be sure, but one full of faith, hope and love."

He nodded. "It'll have to be enough."

His obvious concern for two precious children was endearing, and really sweet. Was it any wonder Callie found this man so attractive?

Sighing, she balled her hand into a fist and stared down

at it. She wasn't supposed to find Reese attractive. She was supposed to find him a wife.

She'd nearly allowed herself to forget her duty, a duty she deeply regretted now. She'd only agreed to Mrs. Singletary's scheme in order to stall the process, at least until Fanny came home. Inserting herself into the equation was not part of the plan.

And yet, here she stood, hoping for something that could never be. Her assigned job was to ensure Reese stay unattached through the foreseeable future. An idea began to formulate in her mind. As the sister of five brothers, she had a clear understanding of what men found attractive in women. And, more importantly, what they found impossible to bear.

"Reese?"

"Yes, Callie?"

Oh, my. *Oh, my, oh, my, oh, my.* She really liked the way her name sounded on his lips.

He is not for you.

"It's time we discuss your bride hunt."

Chapter Eleven

At Callie's abrupt change of topic, Reese felt his mouth tighten around the edges. A sardonic laugh rustled in his throat. For the span of three heartbeats he could do nothing but stare at her in muted astonishment.

The woman wanted to discuss his search for a bride? Here? Now? When his mind was back at Charity House, focused on two small children who were…

Far better off than they'd been three weeks ago. Given their new, happier circumstances, he supposed there wasn't much more to say on the matter.

That didn't mean he wanted to talk about his *bride hunt,* as Callie called it. The term didn't sit well with him, made his search seem calculating, perhaps even callous. His brows pulled together in a frown.

Was his approach cold and self-serving? Or was his approach part of a wise, forward-thinking plan?

He shook his head to clear his thoughts, but found he couldn't focus. Not with Callie's pretty green eyes sweeping over his face. "Now is not a good time for this particular conversation."

"I daresay there's no good time for this particular conversation."

She couldn't know how much he agreed with her on this. "No. I suppose not."

Thunder rumbled overhead, a dismal warning that the

storm wasn't over. The wind kicked up again, matching his dark mood and bringing an unseasonable chill to the air.

Callie clutched her arms around her, and attempted to hide a slight shiver behind a roll of her shoulders. Reese caught the movement. "Are you cold?"

"A little."

Honesty, even in the small, seemingly unimportant matters, it was one of the things he liked most about this woman. He wasn't supposed to like her. She was only a friend.

You are allowed to like your friends, he reminded himself.

Not this much.

When she shivered again, he realized he'd been staring. He quickly shrugged out of his coat and settled it around her shoulders. "Better?"

She nodded. "Yes, thank you."

"Let's get you home."

She opened her mouth, probably to say something along the lines of, *but we aren't finished with our conversation yet.* He raised a hand to forestall her. "We will continue our discussion in one of Mrs. Singletary's parlor rooms, where we'll be considerably more comfortable than out here in the elements."

Callie's lips twitched, as if she had something more to say. Another protest, no doubt. Again, he gave her no chance to voice her thoughts aloud. "I have found," he said, "that I think far more clearly when I am warm and dry."

A heavy sigh escaped her. "I do, as well."

"Then, we're in agreement. Off to Mrs. Singletary's we shall go." He tucked Callie's gloved hand in the bend at his elbow and guided her in the proper direction.

Her long-legged strides easily kept pace with his. Though he knew many men preferred small petite women, Reese rather liked a woman with some height and substance to her.

He'd have to remember to let Callie know of his preference.

For now, he concentrated on getting her home before the rain let loose.

Upon entering the widow's house, Winston materialized on the threshold. Reese and Callie had barely entered the foyer when the fastidious butler clucked his tongue in disapproval at the mud they'd tracked in on their shoes.

After a brief smile at Callie—which she returned with a wide one of her own—the man turned his full attention onto Reese. "Mr. Bennett." Displeasure sounded in his voice. "Mrs. Singletary is not at home. Nor was she expecting you today."

"I'm not here to see the widow." He removed his coat from Callie's shoulders and handed it to the other man. "My business is with Miss Mitchell."

"Ah." A disapproving sniff. "I see."

Reese suspected the man did, indeed, see the situation clearly. Perhaps even clearer than he himself did.

"We'll be in the blue parlor," he announced.

Another sniff. "Very good, sir."

Before the butler could say more, Reese took Callie's arm and escorted her up the winding staircase, down the twisting corridors and into the blue parlor. With each step, he shored up his fortitude, knowing the next half hour would require patience.

Extreme patience.

The only saving grace to this highly awkward situation was the realization that Reese could better control his bride search with Callie in charge. Unlike Mrs. Singletary, the younger woman would listen to him, respect his wishes and, thereby, address his needs above her own agenda.

He refused to entertain thoughts to the contrary.

Lips pressed into a flat line, he steered her toward a

chair angled in such a way as to catch the heat wafting from the fireplace.

"I see someone anticipated us." He nodded to the crackling fire.

"This is one of Mrs. Singletary's favorite rooms." Callie smoothed out her skirt and then glanced up at him. "She insists a fire be prepared in the hearth, regardless of the time of year or the weather."

Caught in that beautiful sea-green gaze, Reese found no ready response, other than to say, "Ah."

He folded his large frame in the chair situated next to hers. "I believe you wanted to discuss my search for a bride."

"Indeed, yes." She released a slight smile that highlighted a glint in her eyes, a glint that hinted at an impish, playful spirit beneath the carefully bland exterior.

Reese couldn't think of a worse thing to notice. Why did this woman call to a part of him he'd thought long buried?

Why her? Why now?

He cleared his throat. "Where would you like to begin?"

Face scrunched in a delicate frown, she tapped her chin with a fingertip. "I suppose we should start by reviewing your list of requirements for your future bride."

The censure in her voice was unmistakable. It was the same tone she'd used the previous evening when she'd read his list aloud. "We have already done that, just last night."

"Yes, but as I mentioned then, I believe your qualifications are too vague and unclear, it's as if you threw them together in a matter of minutes."

He steeled his jaw. "I assure you, I spent considerable time drawing up my list."

"Oh, really?" She gave him a look that reminded him of an unbending, ruthless schoolmarm. "Just how much effort did you put into the task?"

"I don't see how that signifies in our discussion."

"Then you won't mind telling me." There was that schoolmarm look again, matched with a tone that would make any young boy cringe.

Fortunately for Reese he was no longer a young boy. "I took a full thirty minutes. However—"

"Thirty minutes? On each item?"

"No." Absurd. "I spent thirty minutes drawing up the entire list."

She gaped at him. "That is all the thought you put into something as important as your future bride?"

"Yes, that is all. *However,*" he repeated, determined to state his case before she interrupted him again, "I have thought on the matter for years."

She went back to tapping her chin, seemingly lost in thought. "Can I assume, then, that you are able to recite all seven items on the list?"

"Of course."

"Excellent." Now the schoolmarm showed up in her posture, rigid and unyielding. "Proceed."

"You are *quizzing* me?"

Her response was a lift of a single eyebrow. "You said you wanted my help. I cannot help you if you refuse to co-operate with the process."

A surprised laugh escaped him. The woman was relentless. A formidable adversary as any he'd encountered in the courtroom.

Did she know he liked nothing better than matching his wits with a worthy opponent?

"Very well." He shut his eyes a moment, controlled a familiar wave of anticipation. "She must be well-educated and articulate, which will also make her an excellent hostess. She should love children as much as I do, and want several of her own, at least five."

Her eyes full of appreciation, Callie nodded. The first sign of approval since they'd sat down.

Reese found himself emboldened by her silent endorsement and continued with more fervor. "She must come from a good family and value strong family ties. As you know, my father is very important to me. She must get along with him, and he with her."

Once again, Callie blessed him with a nod of approval.

His pulse roared in his veins. In his heart, Reese knew he was on the verge of something real, something emotional and exciting.

There was no reason he couldn't enjoy the process of finding himself a wife. With Callie at the helm, he might even have moments of great fun.

As soon as the thought materialized, Reese instantly changed his mind. He did not want to incite questions from Callie, or go into detail as to his reasoning behind the remaining items on his list. Or rather, *one* of the remaining items on his list. The most important one. The one that was not up for discussion or would ever be subject to compromise.

But if he wanted to find a suitable woman to marry, he must press on. He drew in a tight breath. *Press on, Reese. Press on.* "She must be conventional, steady and predictable. I will not, under any circumstances, consider a known risk taker or—"

"Wait. Just wait a minute." Callie stopped him with a hand in the air. "Why are you dead set against a risk taker?"

"That is my business." He turned his head away, shut his eyes a moment, and fought for control. "Accept my wishes on this, or we're done."

Callie didn't know what she heard in Reese's voice. Not anger, precisely, but a hint of underlying pain.

She wanted to reach to him, to offer him comfort and

soothe away that haunted look in his eyes. It was the same sensation she'd experienced when he'd arrived at Charity House today.

She still didn't have the right to push past his guard.

Oh, but the urge to go to him persisted. Warning bells were going off in her head by the dozen, even as she reached her hand out and closed it over his.

"Reese, I'm not asking you to explain." She spoke in her softest voice, the timbre barely above a whisper. "I'm sure most men, given a choice, would wish for their wives to act in a manner that would keep them out of harm's way."

"Then you understand."

Far better than she cared to admit. Oh, how she knew what came from taking risks.

"I do," she said, quickly amending her response and adding, "I suppose so."

Although she knew the dangers of taking risks in her own life, she didn't understand why Reese wanted a steady, predictable woman in his.

What terrible tragedy had he endured? Had he watched his mother die in an accident? Someone else?

As the questions rattled around in her brain, Callie realized how little she knew about this man, nearly nothing about his past. Why was that? Why did she know so little about him when he'd once been betrothed to her own sister?

Perhaps Fanny hadn't been the only one who'd kept herself hidden from her intended. Perhaps Reese had done so, as well.

Something to think about. "You haven't mentioned two items from your list. Do you remember what they are?"

She didn't need him to voice them again. Except, she did. She had a point to make.

A very large point.

Leaning back in his chair, Reese stretched out his legs and turned his head back to hers. His gaze had gone completely blank, free of all emotion. "She must have a good moral compass."

That one still perplexed Callie. "Do you mean to say, she should be a godly, Christian woman with an unshakable faith?"

He didn't answer her question, but instead said, "And finally, she should be a witty conversationalist."

"Because...?"

"I should think it obvious." He crossed one ankle over the other, rested his elbows on the arms of the chair and began tapping out a rhythmic staccato with his fingertips. "If I am to spend the rest of my life with a woman, I must be able to tolerate her company."

Callie blinked at him in astonishment. "Let me get this straight. You believe that if a woman is a good conversationalist, then her company will be pleasing, as well?"

He inclined his head. "Stands to reason."

Could the man truly be that obtuse? Didn't he know there was more to a happy marriage than witty banter?

Apparently not.

Perhaps she should attack the subject from a different angle. "I noticed you left out love as a requirement, both last night and again today."

"Love is not a necessary component to a successful union."

"You would be happy trapped in a loveless marriage?"

"I didn't say I wanted a loveless marriage."

Confounding, baffling man. "But, Reese, you just said—"

He cut her off midsentence. "I expect to like and admire the woman I marry."

Oh, really. "You did not put that on the list."

He waved his hand in dismissal. "It's understood."

Oh, really.

Callie remembered Mrs. Singletary's initial response

when she'd read through Reese's list. She'd muttered something about him being her toughest case to date. Ah, but he wasn't the widow's problem anymore.

He was Callie's.

She studied his handsome face. Dear, misguided, stubborn, *stubborn* man.

He shifted in his seat, scowled. "Callie, why are you looking at me like that?"

"How am I looking at you?"

"As if you fancied the notion of tossing me over a cliff."

She bit back a laugh. "You do realize that would be physically impossible."

His scowled deepened. "I meant it as a metaphor."

She hummed her response from deep in her throat. "Uh-huh."

"Callie, I mean it. I don't like that look in your eyes. It's disconcerting and bodes of—"

"Shh." She held up a finger. "I am trying to think."

His response was a hum so similar to hers she nearly laughed. Wagging her finger at him, she mentally shuffled through the names of various women she knew in town, women who met every one of his requirements, uninspired as they were.

She came up with four names with very little effort. Lovely girls, all of them, at least on the surface, until one spent more than a few moments in their company. Another point of contention Callie had with his list. Reese had failed to include a single personality trait for the woman with whom he planned to spend the rest of his life.

So be it. She would present her initial batch of women. It was nothing less than he deserved.

Feeling a bit remorseful—but only a very little bit— she leaned forward and captured his gaze. "For your prospective bride, what say you to Miss Catherine Jameson?"

"Catherine Jameson? You cannot be serious."

Not in the least, but she persisted, anyway. "She meets every requirement on your list."

"She also laughs like a hyena."

True. But Callie couldn't resist this chance to drive home her point. "I assume you have heard a hyena laugh?"

He shot her a warning glare. "At least once a year, whenever I visit the zoo."

"How wonderful that you have cause to visit the zoo that often."

He did not respond to this, but instead shot her another warning glare.

Callie simply smiled. "What about Grace Mallory? She's very pretty."

Beautiful, actually. And again, fit every one of his requirements.

"No," he said through tight lips.

"No?"

"Her mother is trying."

"You won't be marrying her mother," Callie pointed out oh-so-helpfully, which earned her a third warning glare, this one especially fierce.

She presented her next option. "That brings us to Penelope Ferguson."

"No."

"What's wrong with Penelope?" As if Callie didn't know. The girl had been beyond intrusive at Mrs. Singletary's dinner party last night.

She expected Reese to remind her of this important little detail, but he went with a vastly different argument. "Her name begins with *P*."

Callie bit back a laugh. "You would reject the girl merely because you don't like the first letter of her name?"

"It's unimaginative on her parents' part, giving each of their daughters a name that starts with the same letter as the mother. It's impossible to keep any of them straight."

"Oh, honestly, Reese." Callie pursed her lips. "You must realize that once you are married to Penelope you would at least be able to tell her apart from the others."

"No Ferguson girl. I am firm on this." He wound his hand in the air. "Who else did you have in mind?"

She thought for a moment. "Natalie Blankenship."

Reese held silent a full five seconds. Callie could see his mind working up a reason to reject Natalie along with the others.

"Natalie is charming," Callie added, a little miserably, because the girl was actually suitable. "She's lighthearted and smart and comes up with insights into human nature that are almost always correct."

More silence.

"She's pretty, too." Callie sighed. "Raven hair, blue eyes, exquisite skin."

Reese dragged a hand over his face. "Natalie is too…" His gaze filled with a triumphant gleam. "Short. My neck would not be able to withstand a lifetime of looking so far down just to meet her eyes."

"Now you're just being difficult. She's exactly the same height as Fanny."

"And we both know how that turned out."

Callie gaped at the man.

He held her stare, unflinching, then drew his feet back under him and leaned toward her. "Any other prospects you wish to run by me? Perhaps—" he leaned in closer still "—a woman I will actually consider?"

Well, well. Wasn't he clever? He'd been on to her game all along. She made a face at him. "I was merely trying to clarify my argument about your list of requirements, which as you must realize by now are too vague."

He sat back. "You have made your point."

Nevertheless, she wasn't through. "You must be more specific, Reese, or we will be at this for ages."

"Understood."

"Then you will revise your list at once?"

"I will."

Her pulse quickened at his ready agreement. She'd just bought herself some time. But how much? Enough to contact Fanny and convince her to return home? "And you won't rush the process," she ventured. "But you will truly think through each of your requirements?"

"Yes."

It was her turn to lean into his space. "When can I expect your changes?"

"Soon."

"Could you be more specific?" She must know exactly how much time she had to lure Fanny home.

"Monday," he said through a tight jaw. "I will deliver my revised list to you on Monday."

"Too soon," she muttered, threads of panic weaving through her control. "You must treat this process seriously."

"I *am* treating it seriously."

"Of course you are." She gave him a pitying look. "If you're hoping to end up with a bride whose name begins with the letter *P*."

A reluctant laugh escaped him. "You, Callie Mitchell—" he pointed his finger at her "—are a ruthless opponent."

"Thank you."

"I did not mean that as a compliment."

She sighed. "I know."

His well-cut lips curved. "I will present my new list to you only after a full week of consideration."

Better. So much better. "Deal."

He held out a hand. "Shall we shake on it?"

Why not? She pressed her palm to his and her heart took an extra hard thump. Her mind reeled.

From this moment on, Callie knew her life would never be the same. She'd won today's battle against Reese, but feared she'd already lost the war...for her heart.

Chapter Twelve

Reese kept busy the following week. He had a calendar full of appointments and court dates. Each client meeting required complete focus, the court appearances extensive preparation. In addition, there were contracts to review and business transactions to negotiate.

Even with the vast amount of work demanding his attention, Reese's mind kept returning to the other, more personal task before him, a task he'd put off all week, though he couldn't fathom why. Eight days after his conversation with Callie and the dreaded bride list—as he was coming to think of it—*still* needed rewriting.

Shoving away from the desk in his private study, he swiveled around and gazed out over the back lawn. The early morning sunlight glistened off the dew-covered grass. With the snowcapped mountains in the distance, the manicured lawn was picture perfect, as if painted by a master artist.

Reese rolled his shoulders. The idyllic scene was too perfect, too untouched. Where were the signs of everyday activity? Of life itself?

If he squinted, he could almost see his future children racing across the lawn, their rousing game of tag turning up the grass and leaving divots. Two of the girls would be taking turns on the swing he would one day hang from a high tree branch. Meanwhile, Reese would be tossing a ball around with one of his older sons, his wife looking on, smiling and laughing, their youngest perched on her hip.

He rubbed a hand over his face, blew out a hiss and rolled his shoulders again. Had he waited too long to make such a dream come true? Had time run out?

No children would fill this rambling old house with laughter if he didn't find a woman to marry soon, which would never happen if he didn't get on with the business of drawing up his new list of requirements.

In her cheeky, impertinent way, Callie had pointed out the flaws in his original approach. He had, indeed, been too vague.

She'd won that battle fairly, extracting his promise to dedicate a full week to his new list. A week that had come to an end yesterday afternoon.

He'd delayed long enough.

Lips pressed in a grim line, he swiveled back around and pulled out a blank sheet of paper. He would approach the new list as he would any other assignment, with ruthless efficiency and rigid attention to detail.

He stared at the blank page a full five minutes.

What did he want in a wife?

He thought he knew. Now…he wondered. Perhaps he should start with personality. She should be kind and fiercely loyal. Excellent. He wrote those down.

What else?

He shut his eyes, sorting through possibilities. She should have a soft, feminine manner and know how to talk to frightened children, using the same amount of gentleness as Callie had with Gabriella Velasquez.

Reese opened his eyes and wrote down *soft, feminine manner* then added *patient, gentle and nurturing.*

She should smile often. Yet another image of Callie materialized. Reese liked all her smiles, the sweet ones, the teasing ones, but he especially liked the one she'd given him on the back porch of Charity House. His future wife should also know how to build him up, rather than tear him down. When Callie had praised him for his efforts on Daniel's behalf, Reese had been ready to conquer the world.

He wrote down *pretty smile* and *full of encouraging words*.

A familiar knock on the doorjamb had him turning the paper over, facedown.

His father stepped into the room. "You're up and at it early this morning."

Rising to his feet, Reese glanced at the clock on the mantelpiece, noted the time. Half past eight. "No earlier than usual."

"It's Sunday, son."

Because he wanted to avoid a lengthy dissertation on the importance of honoring the Sabbath—the same argument his father presented every Sunday morning—Reese kept his face blank. "I know what day it is."

"Then why are you already hard at it?" His father's gaze flicked across Reese's desk, narrowed over the stack of contracts he'd brought home with him Friday evening. "The Lord set aside this day for rest."

"I took most of yesterday off. I am sufficiently refreshed."

"You know that's not what I meant."

Reese opened his mouth to speak, then stopped. His father was a brilliant attorney, best known for his litigation skills. Further discussion on the matter would only turn into an argument, which would eventually end in a stalemate.

"You work too hard, son."

Feigning boredom, Reese leaned back against his desk, folded his arms across his chest. "No harder than you did at my age, or the subsequent twenty-five years following."

"My point, precisely." Remorse shifted in the other man's eyes. "I don't want you ending up like me."

"It would be an honor to follow in your footsteps." Reese

uncrossed his arms. "You took what grandfather started and built Bennett, Bennett and Brand into a prestigious law firm with a reputation for honesty and integrity."

"That may be true." Eyes full of unspoken regrets slid past Reese, brushed over the stacks of papers on his desk, then shot back. "But there's no pleasure in a lifetime of hard work if all you have to show for your efforts are a large sum of money in the bank and a stellar reputation."

Hearing the underlying message beneath the words, Reese realized his father was lonely. Why had he not noticed that before?

Would he welcome grandchildren in this house? Would that be enough to fill the void in his life? Surely, it couldn't hurt. "You will be happy to know I plan to marry by the end of the year."

His father stilled. "You are courting a woman, someone in particular?"

"Not yet, but I will be in the foreseeable future."

"Do I know her?"

Reese wasn't sure how to answer that question. Both he and his father could very well already know the woman Reese would eventually marry. Or they may not. Best to skirt the question altogether.

He could, however, offer a bit more information to assuage the older man's curiosity. "I have enlisted Mrs. Singletary's assistance in my search for a suitable bride, at least originally, however—"

"You what?" His father stared at him, mouth gaping open. "Have you gone mad, allowing Beatrix Singletary that much control over your life?"

"She isn't in control of anything." Reese clenched his jaw so tight he felt a muscle jerk. "In fact, she has handed over the task to her companion."

His father looked at him for a long moment, his face

perfectly stunned. "Callie Mitchell is helping you find a bride?"

Reese bristled at the shock in his father's voice, ready to defend himself—and Callie—until he noted the hint of delight in his father's gaze and the twinge of some other emotion that bordered on...satisfaction?

"Why Callie is, she's—" his father gave a small, amused laugh "—the perfect choice."

Perfect? Reese begged to differ. Bossy, pushy, entirely too feisty? Absolutely. "I trust she'll steer me in the proper direction."

"No doubt, no doubt." The echo of a smile filled his father's voice and, for once, he let the matter drop without giving his opinion in agonizing detail.

"I had better be going, or risk arriving late to church." He pulled out his pocket watch, made a grand show of checking the time, then glanced back at Reese. "Will you come with me?"

"Can't." Reese pulled a stack of papers forward, feigning a need to get back to work. "I have several contracts to review before tomorrow morning."

"Attending church is expected of a man in your position."

Reese set down the paper, very slowly, very deliberately.

Getting married was expected. Attending church was expected. He was sorely tempted to behave in a manner that was decidedly unexpected.

He stifled the urge, as he always did. "You know why I don't attend church anymore."

"I do. And I understand your reticence." He gave Reese's shoulder a sympathetic squeeze. "What Reverend Walton said to you at Miranda's funeral was unforgivable."

Reese held silent, irritation burning hot. He shrugged out from under his father's grip and prowled the length of the room with clipped, angry strides.

Reverend Jeremiah Walton had started out as expected, giving Reese familiar platitudes and pat words of condolence. Miranda was with the Lord, safe in Jesus's arms, living in a better place where there was no more pain or sorrow.

Reese had heard it all before, had even prayed there was truth in the rhetoric. But when the man pulled Reese aside at Miranda's funeral and suggested she'd brought on her own death with her reckless behavior, Reese had walked out of the church. Either that, or punch the pompous, self-righteous man in the mouth.

Though he knew Jeremiah Walton was only one preacher, and had left town years ago, Reese had avoided church ever since.

"You'd like Beauregard O'Toole's sermons. They're inspiring without being overly preachy."

Perhaps he *would* get something out of returning to church, especially if he attended Beau's church. He liked the man, respected him, enjoyed debating complicated theological matters with him. In truth, Reese had been feeling empty lately. Perhaps he could use some Godly inspiration and sound, Biblical direction.

Was today the day?

Needing a moment to think, Reese stalked over to his desk and put his hand on the closest stack of papers. On top was the agreement between Mrs. Singletary and Jonathon Hawkins. His associate Garrett Mitchell had drawn up the initial contract and had done a stellar job. The verbiage put the widow and young entrepreneur in a legally binding partnership that benefited both equally.

With Mrs. Singletary's financial backing, Hawkins would soon expand his hotel empire into major cities beyond Denver, Chicago and St. Louis.

"Son? Did you hear what I said?"

Reese had nearly forgotten his father was in the room. "I'll attend church with you soon."

"You say that every Sunday."

He dismissed the perfectly compelling argument with a flick of his wrist. "Perhaps I mean it this time."

His father persisted. "Mrs. Singletary and her pretty companion will be there."

Reese didn't want to see Callie this morning. She would no doubt ask him about the dreaded bride list.

"I'll attend Beau's church with you in the next few weeks," he said again, more firmly. "It is a promise."

His father went to the door and spoke without looking back. "I'm going to hold you to that."

"I'd be disappointed if you didn't."

Chuckling, his father left the room. Reese moved around his desk and turned over the new list he'd begun for Callie.

He'd made a good start, but was it still too vague?

Perhaps.

Rationally, he knew finding a woman to marry wasn't going to be as simple as creating a string of qualifications and then plugging in the most suitable candidate. But he had to start somewhere.

He fished out his original list from a drawer, read through it, his gaze returning several times to the line about children.

He wrote his desire for children on his new list. No use pretending he didn't crave a large brood of happy, healthy offspring. His children would never have to wonder whether their father loved them or not, something Gabriella and Daniel Velasquez had never experienced.

The twins touched Reese in ways he couldn't explain, urging him to do something about their situation, even knowing there was little he could do. They were in good hands.

Callie understood his sense of helplessness. He'd seen

it in her eyes, those bright, deep green catlike eyes. There were times when she seemed open and available, transparently vulnerable yet full of inner strength and grit.

She was also full of mischief, as evidenced by her sassy opinions over his bride list. Opinions that rang a bit too true. He couldn't afford another mistake. One failed engagement was bad enough.

Two, unacceptable.

Callie claimed she needed specifics? Well, Reese would give her specifics.

He picked up a fresh sheet of paper and went to work.

Bright and early Monday morning, Callie stared in disbelief at her closet, her incredibly *bare* closet. No more oversized, ill-fitting dresses, no more ugly frocks or aprons or bonnets or coats or wraps, nothing but the two gowns Mrs. Singletary had loaned her.

The widow had followed through with her threat. She'd gathered up all of Callie's dresses and taken them away, presumably to donate to charity.

Callie felt violated.

Why, *why* must Mrs. Singletary insist on making her into a new creation? Why was it so important that Callie stand out from the crowd?

There was no reason for people to notice her, no need to garner unnecessary attention.

Her past mistake with Simon had taught her a hard lesson. It was best to remain quiet and small, easily ignored. The Bible supported her position on this in several places. *Clothe yourselves in righteousness.* As well as the command from the Apostle Peter, *Do not let your adornment be merely outward, rather let it be the hidden person of the heart.*

Sage words to live by.

She blinked at her closet, reached out, let her hand drop.

This was terrible, another blow, as shocking as the one Fanny had dealt Callie by not responding to her most recent letter requesting she return home at once.

How long was Callie going to be able to stall Reese's bride search? More to the point, what was she supposed to wear today?

Had she not stayed up so late compiling her list of suitably unsuitable women for Reese, she would have taken the time to lay out her clothes before she'd gone to bed. Had she been her usual, efficient self she would have made this shocking discovery the previous evening.

She moved aside the borrowed dresses—they were not hers, regardless of what Mrs. Singletary said—thinking perhaps the widow had missed one of Callie's more suitable gowns.

She came away empty.

With profound reluctance, she stepped back and shut the closet door.

Resentment filled her. She was the widow's companion, not her current *project*. Not some doll to be dressed up and paraded out into the world.

"Meddlesome, interfering, intrusive woman."

"Who would that be, dear?"

Callie whirled around. Mrs. Singletary stood in the doorway, brows lifted, eyes twinkling with good humor.

More than a little miffed at her employer, Callie couldn't find it in her to feel embarrassed over her softly muttered words, words meant for her ears only. As her own mother always said, eavesdroppers never heard anything good about themselves.

Still…

Callie shouldn't have spoken so plainly. The widow meant no harm, even if her tactics were a bit heavy-handed. "What have you done with my clothes?" she asked, proud that her voice came out calm and mildly curious.

"We discussed this, Callie." The widow moved deeper into the room. "I have sent the bulk of your wardrobe to the Home for Destitute Widows and Orphans. Though, I must say, I felt a little guilty doing so."

"As well you should," Callie muttered.

The widow lifted a delicate shoulder. "Your clothing was beyond ugly, ghastly really. Those poor women deserve better."

Outrage had Callie sputtering. "That, why that is just—"

"True?"

"Mean."

"And yet, also true."

With no ready comeback, Callie paced through her room. Back and forth, back and forth. She ended up at her closet again, threw open the door and scowled at the two gowns hanging there. "What am I supposed to wear today?" She touched the crimson grown. "This one is too fancy and the blue is too…"

Fetching, she nearly said. Thankfully, she refrained. Too telling and, depending on her tone, could be misconstrued as ungrateful.

Though she didn't appreciate the widow's tactics, she knew Mrs. Singletary had acted out of kindness rather than ill will.

Nevertheless, Callie would have to visit a local dress shop as soon as possible, or perhaps Neusteters department store. She could not do so in her nightgown. She would have to wear the blue dress, after all.

"Not to worry, Callie." Mrs. Singletary drew alongside her and linked arms. "I have made an appointment with my personal seamstress. She will be here tomorrow morning at nine o'clock sharp."

"I am quite capable of shopping on my own."

Mrs. Singletary laughed in delight. "We both know my fashion judgment is far superior to yours."

At the widow's teasing tone, Callie felt her own laugh work up through the layers of frustration and anxiety. She pressed her lips tightly together.

"In the meantime, I have found several other dresses in my wardrobe that will suit you."

"But of course."

"What did you say, dear?" The widow asked the question while motioning someone into the room from the hallway.

"It was not important, Mrs. Singletary."

The widow hummed in response, even as she guided one of her maids into the room.

Callie didn't recognize the petite black-haired girl. No more than seventeen, maybe eighteen, she held two dresses draped over her arms, one in a rich emerald-green and another made in the most beautiful shade of lavender Callie had ever seen.

She eyed both creations, her gaze hovering over the lighter of the two. "I thought you said no pale colors."

"Lavender is the exception." The widow led Callie to her dressing table, pressed her gently into the chair. "Julia, could you please come here."

The maid carefully set the two dresses on the bed and did as Mrs. Singletary requested.

"Callie, this is my newest maid, Julia."

The two women greeted one another with a smile.

"Julia comes highly recommended by Polly Ferguson and is considered a wonder with hair."

Knowing where this was headed, dreading it all the same, Callie held silent. What could she say, anyway? *My hairstyle is perfectly acceptable, Mrs. Singletary.*

The widow was a force to be reckoned with in this mood. Runaway freight trains could learn a thing or two from her.

"I trust my friend's opinion, of course," Mrs. Singletary said to Julia. "But, alas, before I allow you to work your talents on my hair, I wish to test your skills on my companion."

"Yes, ma'am, perfectly understandable." Julia turned her attention to Callie. Picking up a small clump of hair, she studied the curling blond locks with squinted eyes. "You have beautiful hair, miss, the color is extraordinary."

"Thank you."

"You are in good hands, Callie dear. I shall be off." The widow beamed at her before heading to the doorway. "I have much to do before my attorney arrives."

Callie didn't bother sighing at the way her heart lifted at this pronouncement. She was actually growing used to the sensation.

Mrs. Singletary paused at the doorway then turned back around and moved toward the bed.

In silence, she considered the newest two dresses, bouncing her gaze between Callie and the bed. At last, she picked up the lavender dress. "You will wear this one today. And this one—" she fingered the green gown "—when we attend the theater this evening."

"Yes, Mrs. Singletary."

"One last request." The widow captured Callie's gaze in the mirror. "I would find it most helpful if you would sit in on my meeting with Mr. Bennett today. I will expect you in one hour and twenty minutes."

A week ago, Callie would have thought Mrs. Singletary's request strange and disconcerting. Not today.

A week ago, Callie would have worried that Mrs. Singletary had an agenda in asking her to join her business meeting with Reese.

Not. Today.

Because, today, Callie accepted the truth about her employer. Beatrix Singletary was shrewd and cunning.

And she always, *always* got her way.

Chapter Thirteen

Whenever Reese met with Mrs. Singletary at her home, he kept the conversation brief and to the point. Today was no exception. With a complete lack of fanfare, he laid out the particulars of Jonathon Hawkins's requests. "The hotelier wants three changes to the initial contract Garrett Mitchell designed."

Concern shifted in the widow's gaze. "Do not tell me Mr. Hawkins is having second thoughts."

"Not in the least. I don't believe you will find the stipulations troublesome."

This seemed to satisfy the widow's misgiving. "Carry on."

"The first is minor, a simple case of rewording." He pointed out the newly worded passage with his index finger. "The second is a bit more complicated. It states if either of you decides to sell your share of the properties, you will give the other first rights to the purchase."

The widow considered the changes in silence, her eyes tracking over the page.

At last, she nodded her head. "I see no problem with either provision."

"Agreed." He flipped to the next page. "The third change is no more complicated than the other two, but could prove a problem if you aren't in agreement with Mr. Hawkins on the matter. He wants—"

The widow held up a finger as if she had something to say, then brought it back down. "Go on."

"Mr. Hawkins is insisting the hotels retain the Dupree name and asserts this point is nonnegotiable." Since Beatrix Singletary did not take ultimatums well, Reese continued before she could speak. "As you already know, the original Hotel Dupree was owned by Marc Dupree before he married Laney and joined forces with her at Charity House."

"Ah, yes, hence the hotel's name." The widow's brow furrowed. "That still doesn't explain why Mr. Hawkins insists on keeping the name."

"He was one of the first residents of Charity House."

The widow blinked at him in surprise. "I knew he had a personal connection with the Duprees, but..." Mrs. Singletary stopped to draw a breath. "I had not realized it was so direct."

"He believes his success in business is in large part due to Marc and Laney's influence in his life, especially Marc's. Maintaining the Dupree name on all current and future properties is his way of honoring their legacy."

The widow turned her head to the side, giving Reese her profile as she mulled over this last piece of information. "And if I refuse to maintain the Dupree name?"

Reese inhaled slowly. "The deal will fall apart and Mr. Hawkins will withdraw from further discussions."

She turned back to face him. "Maintaining the Dupree name is that important for him?"

"Yes."

"Very well." She picked up the quill beside her hand, dipped it into the ink pot and then flipped to the last page of the contract.

Reese couldn't refrain from asking, "You are not put off by Mr. Hawkins's refusal to negotiate on this point?"

"Indeed not—I admire the man's sense of loyalty." With a flourish, she signed her name on all three copies, set down the pen and then leaned back in her chair. "I believe I will very much enjoy working with him on this project."

"I will deliver the signed contracts to him this afternoon."

At the same moment he reached for the pages, a knock came from the other side of the door.

Mrs. Singletary flashed him one of her cagey grins. "The young woman has exquisite timing."

Reese's stomach lurched. He wasn't sure what the widow meant by the comment, but he had no doubt who the young woman was with exquisite timing.

In anticipation of Callie's entrance, Reese rose to his feet. He straightened the contracts into one neat pile then flipped open the lid of his briefcase.

Feeling a strange tightness in his chest, he shoved the contracts beneath the revised bride list.

Soft footsteps stopped a few feet behind him. "Hello, Reese."

He looked over his shoulder. Felt his gut roll again as he turned around fully. The sight of Callie in a perfectly cut, fashionable, light purple dress ratcheted his heartbeat to an alarming pace. She'd done something different to her hair again. This newest style highlighted her long neck and arresting features.

The impact was like a punch to his heart. "Good afternoon, Callie." He wasn't surprised by the rustiness of his own voice. The woman made him uneasy, now more than ever. "You look quite lovely today."

"Thank you." She produced a slightly nervous smile.

Reese swallowed, hard.

He shouldn't be this attuned to the woman. She was Mrs. Singletary's companion, tasked with the duty of finding him a bride. She was only in his life to assist him in sorting through potential candidates. She would eventually fade into the background while Reese wooed another woman.

The thought didn't sit well.

Callie was not a porcelain doll on some shelf, to be dragged out when needed, then flung aside when she'd done her duty.

She deserved better.

As though reading his mind, she stared at him intently, almost defiantly, her green, green eyes running across his face, as if her entire focus was on him. No one but him.

He felt a spark of something long hidden away, a desire to toss away lists and ledgers, to once again discover the joy of a spontaneous act.

Dangerous, dangerous thinking. Riddled with disaster.

Reese was no longer a boy of eighteen. He and Callie had only just become friends. He must ignore this surge of affection and focus on his goal. To find a wife who would make him a decent companion and a proper hostess, a woman who would help him fill his nursery.

Mrs. Singletary shoved her way between them.

Reese balked at the intrusion. In a show of silent solidarity, he moved to stand beside Callie.

The widow smiled fondly at them both. "How is the bride hunt coming along?"

Oh, she was a sly one, broaching the subject with the calmness of one announcing it looked like rain coming on the horizon. One day, Reese would like to see Beatrix Singletary on the wrong end of a matchmaking plot.

Callie stepped forward. "We have hit a slight snag in Reese's bride search, but not an insurmountable one." She smiled over at him. "I have charged Reese with the task of revising his original list of requirements. We will proceed once he's finished."

"Which, you will be pleased to discover, I am." He dug inside his briefcase, pulled out the slip of paper on top. "I present to you—" he thrust out his hand "—my new list."

Callie's mouth formed a perfect O, but no words came forth. Nor did she reach for the paper.

Why not? She'd told him to draw up a new list and take his time doing so. He'd followed her directive, coming up with the most exacting specifics with the most precise language possible.

He pressed the paper into her palm.

She lowered her gaze. Almost instantly, her head shot back up. For a moment her mask of exquisite, maddening control fell away and emotion shone through.

There. There in her eyes, he saw astonishment and alarm and, most baffling of all, hurt.

Somehow Reese had managed to hurt her. That hadn't been his intent. He might have been a bit too precise with a few of the items, for levity's sake only. He'd thought Callie would see the intended humor.

He touched her arm, wanting her to understand.

She shifted out of his reach. His hand dropped away.

Uncomfortable silence hung between them.

"I see you two have much to discuss." Mrs. Singletary inserted herself into the conversational void, her voice a mix of flatness and droll irony. "I'll leave you to it."

Reese held himself motionless as the widow exited the room. Only after she shut the door did he shift his stance. He'd never been restless or edgy. Until Callie.

She turned to him, her gaze unreadable.

It was then that he realized she wasn't telling him he'd been too vague this time around. Nor was she pointing her finger at him in outrage, or scowling at him like a schoolmarm—pity, that—or telling him he'd still gotten it all wrong.

Reese had a brief insight that if he would only let down his guard, and open his heart, even a little, this woman would light up his world as no one ever had before.

He cleared his throat, as he seemed to do far too often

when he was alone in Callie's company. "Is there something wrong with my list?"

"No." She shook her head. "Or rather, yes. I mean, no."

"Which is it? Yes or no?"

"Oh, Reese, your new list. It's so very…specific."

Annoyance burst into life. "Which is what you said you wanted. You told me my requirements were too vague. You insisted I should be more specific."

A sigh leaked past her lips. "I see you took my words to heart."

"Of course I did. You were right, Callie, I hadn't spent the proper amount of time or thought on the first go-round. Any number of women could have fit my original requirements, including highly unsuitable women. So I—"

"Reese." She held up her hand to stop him from continuing. "I'm afraid you might have been a bit too specific this time around."

He scowled. "Which item are you referencing?"

Lowering her head, she studied the page. "You have listed you desire a woman with brown hair."

"What's wrong with brown hair?" Miranda's had been a wild flaming red. Fanny's, pale blond. It made sense for him to avoid both colors.

"Do you realize how many shades of brown hair there are?"

He eyed her warily. "Is that a trick question?"

"There are scores. Golden brown. Reddish brown. Dark brown. Black brown."

Why was she harping on hair color? "Any shade of brown will do."

Something flashed in her eyes, something that looked like hurt. A protective instinct took hold of him, followed by a desire to make her smile. Before he could stop himself, he took her hand, brought it to his lips. "Attend the theater with me tonight."

"I…" She cocked her head *"What?"*

"Callie Mitchell." He pulled her closer, pressed her palm to his heart. "Would you do me the honor of being my guest?"

She drew her hand free, tucked it against her waist. "I am already attending the theater with Mrs. Singletary."

"Then you two must sit with me and my father in our box. I insist," he added when it looked as though she might protest. "If the play is boring, we will discuss my bride list further."

It was the last thing he wanted to do but, at the moment, seemed the absolute right thing to say.

"I'll let Mrs. Singletary know of your invitation." She lifted her chin. "The final decision will be up to her."

"Fair enough." He would make sure the widow accepted. Callie *must* sit beside him tonight.

The desire to have her close, sitting in the seat next to him, shouldn't fill him with such anticipation. But it did.

Reese refused to analyze his motivation.

So he wanted to provide Callie with an evening that brought her joy and happiness? They were friends, after all. It made sense that he would want to please her. To restore her pretty smile. A night at the theater seemed the perfect place to start.

What could possibly go wrong?

All this talk of marriage was beginning to depress Callie. She needed a distraction, if only for an afternoon. With Mrs. Singletary taking tea with a friend, that left her several hours to fill before she had to dress for the theater.

Any activity would do, as long as it took her mind off of Reese's latest list of requirements. Brown hair, indeed, what was the man thinking?

Twirling a lock of her pale blond hair, Callie tried not to think about his other requirements. Most of which she would never hope to meet. She could not speak at least two other languages besides English, only Spanish, and not very well. She could not play a musical instrument.

She could not sing in tune.

Really, Reese had been alarmingly specific this time around.

Telling herself she was merely curious, Callie picked up his list and read it again, from top to bottom, more slowly this time. Other than wanting children, there was only one other requirement she met. Her name did not begin with the letter *P*.

She rolled her eyes to the ceiling, a bubble of laughter escaping through her pursed lips. The man was impossible. Really quite funny. And oh-so-endearing.

She looked back at the list, sighed miserably.

No scandal in her past.

The fatal blow. A gut punch, as her brothers would say.

Technically, Callie hadn't actually ignited a scandal when she'd run off with Simon. But her behavior had been shameful. At the very least, her judgment would forever be suspect. *Bad company corrupts good character.*

What would Reese think if he found out what she'd done?

Tears pricked at the back of her eyes. She wrapped her arms around her middle and tried not to cry.

Shoring up her emotions, she retrieved her Bible from the nightstand. She searched around in the Psalms for some verse, any verse, to make her feel less dismal. Nothing. She landed on *1 Peter.* She read for a while, mostly skimming the passages until she was in the fourth chapter. Everyone had a talent, so the Apostle claimed, gifted to them by God.

Perhaps tapping into her talent might help with her sour mood.

Lowering to her hands and knees, she fumbled around beneath her bed, found the box of paints, brushes and round canvases she'd tucked away. She sat back on her heels and ran her palms over the rectangular wooden box.

Back at school, Callie had loved art classes. It wasn't until she'd taken a course in miniature portraiture that she'd discovered her true talent. One she pursued for her own enjoyment.

She took out a blank, three-inch oval canvas and positioned it on the small writing desk near the window. Natural light was always best for the intricate detail work required for small portraits.

Once her paints were mixed and sitting in colorful piles on the palate, she began.

Time evaporated.

Confusion and hurt disappeared, leaving only the creative process. She'd nearly forgotten the joy of putting an image on canvas, of making a picture out of nothing but an idea, the closest she would ever come to understanding the beauty and order of the world God had created with His hands.

Hours later, when the sky had faded to a dull purple and the light in her room took on a gray cast, Callie sat back and studied her handiwork.

A bride and groom stared back at her. The bride wore white, in the same style as the crimson gown Mrs. Singletary had loaned her. Callie looked closer at the image. Without realizing it, she'd painted her own face on the bride.

The groom wore a black formal suit with tails, a crisp white shirt and bow tie beneath. His hair was nearly as black as the suit, his eyes one shade lighter and his face…

She leaned in closer still, gasped.

The groom's face belonged to Reese.

Callie had painted a wedding portrait of them together.

A sound of dismay whistled in her throat. To dream of more than friendship with him was one thing, but to put that secret hope on canvas? Insufferable.

As she cupped the tiny canvas in her palm, she admitted the truth at last. Her heart yearned for Reese.

Which meant her heart was headed for disappointment.

Even if, by some strange twist of events, he turned his attention onto her, Callie could never win him for herself. He belonged to Fanny. And even if he didn't, her past mistake would always be with her, looming as a dark reminder of her true nature.

"Miss?" Julia popped into the room, holding several magazines against her. "Where are you?"

"Over here," she called out.

"Why are you sitting in the dark?"

"Time got away from me." She swiped at her eyes. "I hadn't realized dusk was upon us."

Julia walked through the room, turning on lamps and wall sconces as she progressed. "Mrs. Singletary sent me to style your hair for this evening's event."

As if waiting for her cue, the widow herself sauntered into the room. "Let's try something more festive for our evening at the theater." She took one of the magazines from the maid. "Something like, say—" she flipped through the pages "—this one here."

Julia leaned over the magazine. "That would look rather nice on your companion, but what about this one instead?" She flipped the page and placed her finger on another image.

While the two consulted over Callie's hairstyle, ignoring her completely, she took the opportunity to slip the portrait she'd painted in the back of a drawer of her writing desk. She then stored her paints under her chair as stealthily as possible.

Thankfully, neither woman paid her any attention.

"I hear the Gibson Girl is all the rage out East," Julia remarked, turning the page once more. "It looks like this."

"Oh, my, yes. That would suit Callie quite well, quite

well indeed." Mrs. Singletary's voice filled with satisfaction. "It is decided. Carry on, Julia. You have one hour to transform my companion into a Gibson Girl."

Having issued her command, the widow swept out of the room.

Much to Callie's relief, Julia performed her duties in silence. She wasn't in the mood for conversation.

When she was fully dressed, Callie turned in a tight circle and faced the mirror. She hardly recognized herself. Sighing in pleasure, she stroked her hand down the silk damask in a stunning emerald green. The color was exquisite and added a golden tone to her skin.

The dress itself had a rounded neckline bordered by a thin row of lace and pale green flowers. She'd never worn anything so lovely, had never seen her hair look both disheveled and elegant at the same time.

The maid looked at her expectantly. "What do you think?"

"You are very talented, Julia."

The girl grinned. "It's as if the hairstyle were created just for you."

Callie touched her hair, most of which was piled high on her head in a loose topknot with a waterfall of curls caressing her cheeks. *Soft* and *romantic* were the words that came to mind.

A wave of pure happiness crashed over her. Why not embrace her transformation, if only for tonight? Why not revel in being an attractive woman?

She studied her image in the mirror a moment longer. She looked young, beautiful and innocent. For that one instant, she felt as if she was all three.

Chapter Fourteen

Reese thought he'd conquered the dangerous leanings of his youth. For fourteen years, he'd consciously avoided situations that might lead to messy, emotional entanglements.

Yet here he stood, raging inside, battling against his very self, merely because Callie Mitchell had entered the theater's atrium. Every effort to hold off the rush of feeling sweeping through him proved useless.

He hardly recognized himself.

The way his heart dipped in his chest did not belong to the man he'd become, a man renowned for his restraint, who adhered to a rigid set of rules and personal standards.

Dressed in a deep green dress that highlighted her blond hair and trim figure, Callie called to the part of Reese he'd locked tightly away. She sparkled like a precious jewel, her entire being lit from the inside out.

He was not the only man who noticed.

A jolt of possessiveness shuddered through him, making him uncomfortably aware that he loathed the idea of sharing Callie with anyone tonight.

When their eyes met over the crowd, Reese felt another catch in his throat. He took the moment in, like a dream, then shook himself free.

"Ah, Mr. Bennett, there you are." Mrs. Singletary shouldered through the crush of theater patrons, Callie following beside her. "Please tell me you have not been awaiting our arrival down here in the crowded atrium."

"I have, indeed." His voice was that of a man doomed to a fate he could no longer prevent. "I wanted to make certain you found your way to my box without incident."

"How very gentlemanly of you."

He inclined his head.

Callie shifted closer to him, presumably to be heard over the din. Whatever reason, Reese's collar felt too tight.

"Has your father joined you this evening?"

Reese enjoyed the way her winged brows knit delicately together as she asked the question, the way she looked him straight in the eye.

"He is already upstairs. Come. Allow me to escort you the rest of the way." He offered his arm to Callie, waited until she threaded her gloved hand through the crook of his elbow before turning to Mrs. Singletary and going through the process a second time.

Keeping both women near, he focused on conquering the stairs at a sedate but steady pace. By the time they reached the final landing the crowd had thinned to a mere smattering of theatergoers seeking out their reserved seating.

Reese released the women. "Ladies." He moved the curtain aside. "After you."

Inside their box, his father immediately took over the pleasantries. Reese hung back.

Propping a shoulder against the wall, he watched Callie laugh at something his father said. She looked comfortable. Relaxed and happy.

Reese was no longer a fanciful man, yet the sight of her unfettered joy gave him immense pleasure.

The more time he spent in Callie's company the more he grew to appreciate her understated beauty and unique personality. Beneath the starch was a kind, pure heart and an intelligent mind.

She took his breath away.

The sensation had little to do with the change in her outer appearance. Something profound was happening to the woman, an overcoming of her innate shyness that brought her inner beauty to the surface.

What must it have been like, he wondered, to live in the shadow of a sister like Fanny?

Reese studied Callie's lovely face. She looked a lot like Fanny. And yet, not at all.

Callie was far more beautiful.

Reese couldn't believe it had taken him this long to notice.

Smiling, she turned her head toward him. Their gazes merged and Reese was caught once again inside a pair of beautiful sea-green eyes.

His pulse thundered in his ears.

Still smiling, Callie broke away from his father and Mrs. Singletary.

The thunder turned into a roar.

Out of the corner of his eye, Reese saw his father take Mrs. Singletary's arm and guide her to the seats in front of the railing in their box. Their bent heads and hushed voices indicated they were in a deep conversation.

Neither looked back at Reese and Callie. They might as well be alone.

He fought back a bout of uncharacteristic nerves.

"Reese?" Callie's hand came to rest on his forearm. "Are you unwell?"

How like her, he thought, to react with genuine concern.

"I am perfectly well." How like him, to immediately deny anything less than faultless control.

"You are sure?" Callie persisted. "You seem different tonight, not quite yourself."

How right she was.

"Busy day at work. My head is full of—" *you,* he nearly

blurted out, catching himself just in time "—complicated legal matters."

She squeezed his arm, the small gesture one of quiet understanding and affection. "You work too hard."

"I suppose, sometimes I do." The admission did not come easily, but even in this small matter Reese didn't want to mislead this woman.

Her mouth gentled and her eyes warmed and he thought his head might explode from the wonder of her.

"Are you a fan of comedies?" he blurted out.

Two perfectly winged eyebrows arched upward. "Changing the subject?"

Absolutely.

Reaching to one of the plush velvet chairs behind his father and Mrs. Singletary, Reese picked up a playbill. "I was referring to tonight's performance. Shakespeare's *As You Like It.*" He read the title aloud, then slid his gaze across the lead actor's photograph. "A Simon Westgrove is playing the role of Orlando."

"What?" Callie yanked the two-page brochure away from Reese, ran her gaze wildly over the cover. "It can't be. It's just not possible."

Her stunned reaction was completely unexpected, as was the way her face had paled to a dingy gray.

"Callie." He took her arm and steered her to the back of the box, away from his father and Mrs. Singletary to afford a degree of privacy. "What is it? What's wrong?"

"It's. Oh, Reese, I..." She glanced up at him, her eyes glassy and unseeing, as if she was lost in another time, another life. "I do not like this play. Or—" she choked out a bitter laugh "—this particular actor."

Although the play wasn't especially a favorite of Reese's, either—the plot relied too heavily on deception—he sensed the lead actor was the real cause of Callie's sudden anguish.

"You have seen Simon Westgrove perform this play before?"

She nodded, her eyes miserable.

"When I was attending school in Boston I frequented the theater often. I…" She broke off, blinked several times, took a slow, deep breath and then squared her shoulders.

Another slow breath, a jerk of her chin, and then the rigid, controlled Callie Mitchell slid into place.

Gone were the soft eyes and warm smile, replaced with a cold, rigidly blank stare.

Reese suspected he knew why. "Do you know Simon Westgrove, personally?"

"Yes." She didn't expand, but the shadows lurking in her eyes spoke volumes. The famous actor had done something to hurt Callie.

Reese wanted to whisk her out of the theater, to someplace safe, somewhere that would restore her sweet smile and the kind, approachable woman who hugged frightened children.

"Do you want me to tell Mrs. Singletary you are ill?"

Her spine stiffened. "Don't be absurd."

The lights flickered, indicating the start of the play. They silently took their seats in the chairs directly behind Mrs. Singletary and Reese's father. He leaned close to Callie. "I will escort you home and—"

"That won't be necessary." She spoke without looking at him. "I am perfectly happy to remain in my seat for the entire performance."

Happy? No, she wasn't.

Wishing to soothe away her pain, he reached for her hand. He acted on impulse and entirely without an agenda other than to offer Callie his silent support.

She barely acknowledged him, except to close her fingers tightly around his.

Musical notes filled the theater. A hush came over the audience.

The curtain began its ascent.

Callie shut her eyes briefly, drew in several deep breaths, and then several more. Reese knew the technique well, employed it often himself. She was gathering her composure, and having phenomenal success.

She barely flinched when Simon Westgrove entered the stage and recited his opening line.

She was so in control, so brave, Reese wanted to pull her close. He leaned over her instead and said, "You are safe with me."

He wasn't sure where those words came from, but he sensed they were the ones she most needed to hear right now.

She held perfectly still for one beat, two. Then, slowly, very, very slowly, she turned her gaze to meet his.

The impact of her misery was like a punch to his gut. "Callie—"

"Thank you, Reese." She pressed a fingertip to his lips. "You cannot know how much your presence means to me."

Tears pooled in her eyes. Blinking rapidly, she ruthlessly held them in check.

Compelled, he lowered his head, brought her hand to his lips then straightened. Though he didn't look at her again, he kept their fingers entwined.

She did not attempt to pull away.

Only when the curtain descended over the stage for intermission did she unclench her fingers from around his.

Staring straight ahead, she did not applaud the performance. She did not move a muscle.

Reese ached for her.

"Well, I say." Mrs. Singletary stood and turned to smile at them. "That Simon Westgrove is everything the rumors contend. Marvelously talented, indeed."

Though her reaction was nearly impossible to detect, Reese felt Callie stiffen beside him.

The widow's eyes narrowed. "Are you not enjoying yourself, Callie?"

She produced a broad smile. "I am having a grand time." Her voice sounded brittle.

The widow's eyes narrowed even more, but she must have caught Reese's imperceptible shake of his head because she merely patted Callie on the shoulder and said, "I am glad to hear it, dear."

She turned to Reese's father. "Come, my friend, I have a mind to see who else is in attendance tonight."

The older man's lips curved. "The usual suspects, I presume."

"You jaded old man." She slapped playfully at his arm.

"You think me wrong?"

"I dare say, no." She linked her arm through his. "But I refuse to admit defeat until I have checked for myself, which I do not wish to do alone."

Reese's father chuckled. "And so you won't."

They left with no further fuss.

Reese waited an additional three minutes before breaking the heavy silence in the box.

He could go for the direct approach, or attempt to interject some levity into the situation.

"The play was wretched. The worst I've suffered through in years." He waved a hand in dismissal. "Predictable storyline and dreadful acting, especially from the untalented male lead."

His tactic worked. Callie laughed. It was a strained, paltry sound, and lacked all signs of joy, but Reese claimed it a victory.

"Thank you, Reese." Callie swiped at her cheeks. "That was exactly what I needed to hear."

"Want to talk about it?"

She shook her head.

"I'm a good listener."

She craned her neck forward, glanced at the box on their left, then over to the one on their right. "So, I would humbly suggest, are many others here tonight."

Message received. Reese began a lengthy exposition on his reasons for disliking the play.

Simon. Of all the actors, in all the acting companies traveling across America, Simon Westgrove was in Denver, performing the role of Orlando. The same character he'd played the night Callie had first met him.

Her breath snagged on a skittering heartbeat, even as the memory of her folly took hold.

Her inability to see beyond Simon's slick surface, to the man beneath the handsome face, had nearly led her into ruin. She'd fallen for his considerable charm, his charisma, his skill in donning a role and making it his own. There was no denying he was a brilliant actor. On and off the stage.

She'd believed him when he'd said she was beautiful, when he'd called her the most extraordinary woman of his acquaintance. She'd thought him in love with her, had never once questioned his devotion, until she'd run away with him and he'd made it shockingly clear he had no intention of marrying her.

The moment she'd discovered his duplicity she'd immediately left him. She'd returned to her dormitory before dawn, thereby avoiding others finding out about her foolishness. Not even Fanny had been aware of her absence.

Callie had been so naive, so gullible.

She wanted to cry.

And there sat Reese, a man worth a hundred Simons, offering his silent support, not even knowing why she needed it.

If he knew the cause of her despair, would he remain by her side, offering his allegiance?

She didn't dare test him.

Reese drew her to her feet. "You look like you could use a change of scenery."

She didn't argue as he led her to the back of the box. However, when she realized he was directing her out onto the landing and possibly beyond, she pulled him to a stop. "I'm sorry, Reese. I don't think I can bear facing other people right now."

She could hardly bear her own company.

Nodding, he let go of her hand. "Will you tell me what's wrong?"

"I want to." She really, truly did. "But you will think differently of me if I do."

Not that, Lord. Anything but that.

She couldn't stand knowing he might think less of her after she told him what she'd done. Her life had been far easier when Reese hadn't thought of her at all.

"I'd rather discuss anything but me." She took the cowardly approach and deflected the conversation back onto him. "For instance, your most recent bride list."

Something flickered in his eyes, something that looked like annoyance. He shook his head, even as he reached out and drew her against him with heartbreaking tenderness.

As they stood hidden from view, one of his hands cupped the back of her head and urged her to rest it against his shoulder. He said nothing, simply held her in silence. The moment couldn't have been more profound or poignant had he kissed her.

Encircled in Reese's arms like this left her dizzy with emotion. Nothing had ever felt more right, or so wonderful.

"I think you should strike hair color off your list." She whispered the words into the lapels of his suit, trying desperately not to cling to him.

"Any particular reason why I should?"

Because I don't have brown hair.

Tears burned behind her eyes, but she held them back. "You must remain open-minded to all possibilities, or risk missing out on the perfect woman to marry."

"Are you suggesting I consider even women with streaks of gray in their hair?"

He was trying to make her laugh. The dear, dear man. She swallowed back a sob. "Especially them."

A sound of amusement rustled in his chest. "I'll take that under advisement."

"Reese?"

"Hmm?"

She pulled back to look into his eyes. "I heard from Fanny last week."

Why had she inserted her sister into this tender moment? Callie knew the answer, of course. Because she couldn't allow herself—or Reese—to forget who stood between them.

Surely he would set her away from him now.

He did not.

He did, however, loosen his hold. "I'm glad, Callie." He swept his gaze over her face. "I know how important your relationship with your sister is to you."

But just how important was *his* relationship with Fanny?

"Jonathon Hawkins personally delivered her letter to me the other night at Mrs. Singletary's dinner party."

Reese's eyes never left her face. "Did she write something that upset you?"

Her answer came immediately. "Yes." She shook her head. "I mean, no. Not really."

Clasping his hands behind his back, he took a step away from her. The distance between them was no more than a few feet. It felt like a gaping, impossibly large chasm that could never be breached.

Callie sighed. How appropriate they were having this conversation at the theater. "Fanny claims she broke your engagement because she was merely playing a role with you and couldn't be sure who she really was beneath the facade."

"That's what she told me, as well, when we spoke last."

Why didn't he appear more upset? Why did he seem detached, indifferent even?

"Don't you want to know what she else said?"

"No, Callie, I'm not curious in the least." He held her gaze with unwavering resolve. "I'm quite comfortable with the way Fanny and I left things between us."

"You seem sincere."

He held her gaze for several more heartbeats, some silent message in his eyes. "I am, very."

Okay. "About your bride hunt…"

He took a deep breath. "What about it?"

She looked over her shoulder, assured herself the adjoining theater boxes were completely empty before continuing. "I have come up with several names I wish to run by you."

His expression cooled. "Perhaps we should sit down for this."

"If you wish."

They returned to the plush velvet seats they'd left only moments before. As Callie settled into her own chair and waited for Reese to follow suit, she looked out across the auditorium to the box she'd occupied with Mrs. Singletary a few weeks ago.

So much had changed since then.

What had started out as infatuation for a man she only knew as her sister's ex-fiancé was building into something more, something stronger and lasting. Callie was beginning to understand Reese on a whole new level.

He was more than a brilliant attorney, more than a man of unquestionable integrity. He was kind and loyal, a man who worked too hard but found time to play baseball with orphans.

He deserved happiness. If not with Fanny, then with the woman of his own choosing.

Callie would no longer hinder the process. She would find him the perfect bride. Fanny had made her decision. She'd had her chance and had thrown it away. Callie was through protecting her interests where Reese was concerned.

"I think you should consider Violet Danbury." The twenty-year-old met all of his requirements, on *both* his lists.

"No."

"She is perfectly suitable," Callie argued.

"She is named after a flower." He spoke as though that was reason enough to cross her off his list.

Callie blinked at him, confused. "Does that mean you won't consider Lily Manchester, either?"

"No flower names. They're ridiculous."

He was actually rejecting two perfectly suitably women because they were named after flowers? After also refusing to consider women who names began with *P?*

Why was he being so difficult?

Callie's breath backed up in her throat.

Was it possible that Reese was intentionally sabotaging the process? He winked at her. *Oh, my.*

She stared into those smiling eyes, eyes full of silent affection directed at her. Hope spread to the darkest corners of her soul. Would he, possibly, maybe, consider Callie a suitable candidate?

Oh, please, Lord. Please.

As soon as she lifted up the silent prayer she caught sight of Simon's photograph on the playbill. Reality slammed into her. Callie was many things. Suitable she was not.

Chapter Fifteen

Callie endured the following morning of dress fittings with a philosophical mind-set. Four times, she stretched out her arms and held perfectly still while Mrs. Singletary's personal seamstress draped and pinned fabric over her.

But, really, what did it matter if Callie wore fashionable gowns or tattered rags? Who would ever care if her hairstyle was copied out of current magazines or pulled tightly against her head in a severe bun?

Her future was set. Her foolish mistake with Simon would forever cast a shadow over the rest of her life. She slumped forward.

"Stand up straight, miss." The dressmaker, a small woman with a beak nose and rust-colored hair, scolded her in a thick Irish brogue. "Or we will be at this all day."

It was a sufficiently terrifying threat. They'd been *at this* for what felt like hours already.

Callie dutifully stiffened her spine and stared straight ahead, feeling more like a doll than ever before. Dressed up, paraded out at parties, manipulated in every direction, then randomly discarded.

Mutiny swelled at the apropos metaphor for her life. She was worthy of more, so much more. She'd made a mistake. One. Mistake. She wasn't alone in that, the Bible even taught that *all fall short of the glory of God.*

Her past did not have to define her future. She was a child of God, forgiven and loved.

She'd been betrayed by a fast-talking, charming actor trained in playing a role and deceiving others. She could either spend the rest of her life feeling shame over her lapse in good judgment, or accept the Lord's mercy.

The past was the past. The future, hers for the taking.

Why couldn't she reach for what she wanted? For *whom* she wanted?

An image of chocolate-brown eyes, broad shoulders and attractive, sculpted features came to mind. Her heart gave several hard, thick beats. Reese. *Oh, Reese.*

A wistful sigh escaped her lips.

"Did you say something, dear?"

"No, ma'am." Callie caught Mrs. Singletary's gaze in the mirror. "Just deep in thought."

"Ah. I completely understand." The widow picked up her cat and cuddled the animal close. "More times than not, I have found an evening at the theater often calls for reflection the following morning."

Refusing to give anything away, Callie schooled her features into a bland expression. "Very insightful."

"Yes, yes. Now, let me see where we are." Stroking Lady Macbeth's head, the widow circled around Callie. "Excellent work, Mrs. O'Leary. That particular shade of blue suits my companion quite well."

"I thought it might." The dressmaker tucked a piece of fabric at Callie's waist, pinned it into place and then stepped back to study her handiwork. "Perfect."

The widow agreed. "When can we expect the finished garments?"

"This one will be ready by the end of the week, the others within two more."

Nodding in satisfaction, the widow captured Callie's gaze in the mirror once again. "You have been very patient today. When we are through here, I will treat you to lunch at the Hotel Dupree."

Callie would rather stay at home and rest. Her muscles ached from holding them in stiff, awkward poses. But she'd never been a patron at the restaurant where she'd once worked. It would be nice to see the other side. "I'd very much enjoy accompanying you, Mrs. Singletary."

"Excellent."

An hour later, dressed in another of Mrs. Singletary's castoffs, this one a gold sateen with blue-and-green trim, Callie followed her employer to a table in the Hotel Dupree dining room. Settling in her seat, she took in the elegant decor, ran her fingers over the fine china and silver place settings.

She'd barely set her napkin in her lap when Jonathon Hawkins joined them at the table. He greeted Mrs. Singletary first, then turned his smile onto Callie. "Miss Mitchell, it's a pleasure to see you again."

"And you, as well." To her surprise, Callie meant every word. She'd half expected to feel animosity toward the man. But the anger simply wasn't there anymore. Mr. Hawkins had merely offered Fanny a job in another city, and only *after* she'd broken off her engagement.

"I have taken it upon myself to order for the three of us," he said, dividing his attention between Callie and Mrs. Singletary. "My chef makes a memorable sea bass, as I'm sure Miss Mitchell can attest."

"Indeed, he does."

"Well, then, I bow to your expert opinions," Mrs. Singletary said. "We shall indulge in the sea bass today."

After a few more pleasantries, the widow and Mr. Hawkins proceeded to discuss the new decor of the restaurant, which segued into other changes he had in mind for the hotel.

Apparently, Callie had been invited to a business luncheon, where she understood only a third of the terms. When the conversation turned to types of lumber best suited for crown molding, she decided to take a short break.

"If you will both excuse me." She set her napkin on the table. "I'd like to freshen up before our meal is served."

"That'll be fine, dear." Mrs. Singletary waved her off with a distracted sweep of her hand.

In no particular hurry, Callie made her way through the restaurant and into the lobby. The hotel was teeming with activity. Groups of people lounged on the luxurious leather furniture. Some of the guests were reading books, others newspapers, while still others partook in animated conversations.

Everyone looked happy, satisfied and completely at their leisure. The Hotel Dupree had become a destination in and of itself. She was proud to have once played a small part in its success.

Recognizing the employee behind the registration desk, Callie decided to say a quick hello. She hadn't seen Rose since taking the position as Mrs. Singletary's companion. It would be lovely to catch up with the other woman.

Callie's steps faltered when she realized she wasn't the only person heading in the same direction. A few steps ahead of her was someone else, a man. Her throat turned dry as dust. She recognized that bold swagger, that arrogant tilt of the head.

The sight of *him,* the dark figure from her past, sent her into an air-gasping fluster. She swallowed hard against the biting pressure rising in her stomach, cinching around her heart.

Simon was here.

In the Hotel Dupree.

What were the odds? *What were the odds?*

Callie swayed, her balance momentarily thrown off. She stumbled backward, then quickly righted herself. She had to get away before he noticed her, before he could hurt her again.

The force of her panic frightened her.

Spinning on her heel, she retraced her steps. Shame and fear made her movements clumsy, awkward. *I have to get away.*

"Callie? Callie! Come back."

She ignored the call, keeping her head down as she hurried back the way she came, praying no one noticed the urgency in her steps.

"Callie." A hand clasped her arm and whirled her around.

Infuriated, she yanked free of the offensive grip. Her stomach roiled. Her eyes stung. She tried to move, but she was hit with a spasm of immobility, her feet frozen in place. All she could do was stare at the man who'd once been the sole player in her dreams, now the lead actor in her nightmares.

His face was more handsome than she remembered, his demeanor more polished and slick. Oh, but his eyes were the same steel-blue. How had she not seen how cold and detached they were?

How had she missed the depravity in his gaze?

"We meet again, my beautiful, beautiful girl. Or as I like to think of you—" his lips curved into a sly, knowing grin "—the one who got away."

The intimacy of his words made her feel tainted. Was it any wonder she'd spent the past four years avoiding masculine attention? Her eyes stung with the threat of tears. She swallowed them back. "Excuse me, Simon. My employer will be wondering where I am."

"Wait." His hand returned to her arm.

She shrugged away from him.

He tucked his hands into his pockets. For a moment, the brilliant actor slipped away and all that remained was a spoiled man who always got his way, by any means possible.

"I have never forgotten you, Callie." He said her name in a low voice as he moved in close, far too close. "I have always regretted losing you."

She couldn't fathom why he would say such a thing. What could he possibly hope to gain? Surely he couldn't think she would fall for his lies a second time? "I don't believe you, Simon, not after the way you callously deceived me."

His shoulder lifted in a leisurely shrug. "We had a misunderstanding."

"A misunderstanding?" She nearly spat the word. "Is that how you remember it?"

Another lift of his shoulder. "Had you not bolted out of the hotel so quickly I would have explained my position in greater detail."

"You explained yourself quite well." To her utter humiliation, a tear leaked out of the corner of her eye.

His hand came to her face, wiped at her cheek.

She slapped him away.

He gave a dramatic sigh, but didn't reach for her again.

"You have become even more beautiful in the years since we last met." Like a hungry cat seeking easy prey, his eyes roamed over her face. "I made a grave mistake letting you go."

"I left *you,* the very moment I discovered your wicked agenda."

And that, Callie realized, was what she'd nearly forgotten through the years since leaving school.

She hadn't given in to Simon that night. She hadn't fallen completely for his lies. She'd walked away on her own steam, with her virtue still intact.

"My sweet, sweet Callie." Simon's smile didn't quite meet his eyes this time. "Still so pure, so untouched, so wholly innocent. Other than your beautiful, exquisite face, those were the traits that most intrigued me about you."

He moved in closer, reached for her.

She took a large step back.

Undeterred, Simon closed the distance between them once more. *Again,* Callie stepped back.

So involved in their conflict, she didn't notice that a third party had joined their scuffle until an angry masculine voice dropped into the fray.

"Touch her again, Westgrove, and I'll make sure it's the last thing you ever do."

Callie jerked around so hastily she lost her footing. Reese caught her, steadying her at the waist. Once her balance was restored, he let her go, though it took Herculean control not to whisk her up in his arms and carry her out of the hotel lobby.

"Reese." Her thunderstruck gaze met his. "What…what are you doing here?"

"I have a meeting with Jonathon Hawkins."

"Oh." She looked away, but not before he saw the humiliation in her eyes.

He'd never seen Callie wear such an expression before, a combination of shame, regret and fury. Emotions he knew were directed at the man standing behind her.

Reese's gaze focused and hardened on Simon Westgrove.

Had he any doubts as to whether Callie knew the famous actor personally, they'd been dispelled the moment he'd walked into the Hotel Dupree. Even from across the lobby, Callie's obvious panic told its own story, a story Reese knew he wasn't going to like.

Now was not the time for questions, save one. "Are you all right?"

She nodded miserably.

His chest filled with a need to protect, to wipe away that

look of anguish on her face. He drew her close, securing her beside him. Trembling, she leaned into him.

Westgrove arched a brow. "It appears I have been replaced in your affections, Callie, my love."

She stiffened, either at the words or the endearment, Reese couldn't be sure. One thing he did know, Callie wanted nothing to do with the actor, who was grinning with far too much intimacy in his gaze.

"It's time you left, Westgrove. Callie doesn't want you here."

"I say we let the lady speak for herself."

The silence that met those words seemed to last a lifetime.

Then, Callie snapped her shoulders back and straightened her spin. "Mr. Bennett is correct. I don't want you here, Simon. I never want to see you again."

"You heard the lady." Reese took a hard breath. "Off you go."

"How sublime." Westgrove barked out a laugh. "I've landed in a badly scripted play with a couple of two-bit actors on stage with me."

The other man could malign him all he wanted, but Reese wouldn't stand for him disrespecting Callie. He started forward.

"No, Reese." Callie rested her hand on his arm to stop his pursuit. "He's not worth it." Before he could respond she turned her head and glared at the other man. "Go away, Simon."

"Is that your final word on the matter?" His gaze shifted from her to Reese then back to Callie. "I cannot persuade you to run aw—"

"*Go.*"

The man paused. A shadow flickered in his eyes, then was gone. "Right. Your loss, sweeting."

After throwing an audacious leer in Callie's direction,

Westgrove sauntered away. He moved through the lobby with a casual, relaxed stride as if he hadn't a care in life.

Reese drew in several steadying breaths, debating whether to stay with Callie or follow after the actor and have a private...*word* with the man.

Callie's struggle to catch her breath made the decision for him. Reese gently lifted her chin until she looked him directly in the eyes. As she blinked up in silence, he ran his gaze over her face, taking careful inventory.

"What did Westgrove do to you?" Reese was surprised by the rage in his voice.

Callie lowered her head. "I don't think I can tell you."

He could see she would rather keep her secret safely hidden. How well he knew the need to conceal parts of the past, to suffer through the tormenting pain alone.

If he didn't encourage Callie to unburden herself with him, would she turn to someone else? With whom could she confide? None of her brothers were in town. Fanny was gone. The only support in Callie's life was Mrs. Singletary. Her employer.

A frown tugged at Reese's brow as he pondered how alone Callie was in the world right now, with only the widow to champion her.

And him. Callie had him, too. He badly wanted to give her his unwavering support, his unconditional acceptance. The trick would be convincing her to let him.

"Let's sit down, over there." With a jerk of his head, he indicated the far right corner, where two wing-back chairs were surrounded by large potted plants. The makeshift alcove was private, but not indecently so.

When Callie nodded her agreement, Reese took her arm and guided her across the marble floor, their footsteps striking in a shared rhythm like hammers to nails.

She sat primly, her spine perfectly erect. Regardless of her stiff posture, Reese was struck by the graceful way she entwined her fingers together in her lap. There was nothing hard about this woman, nothing coarse or brazen. She personified gentleness and goodness.

He placed his hand over hers. "Tell me what happened with Westgrove."

Lowering her head, she held silent a moment. Then, slowly, she looked back up. Her gaze was full of unspeakable pain. "You'll think differently of me once I do."

She'd said much the same thing once before.

What had Westgrove done to her? "I meant what I said at the theater last evening. You'll get no judgment from me, no condemnation."

"I don't know quite where to start." Her voice was very low, very quiet. The sound called to mind broken trust and betrayed innocence.

Emotion wrapped around him, a bone-deep urgency to protect Callie—always. If Westgrove appeared again, Reese would likely beat the man to a pulp.

For now, he focused on earning Callie's trust. One step at a time. "How did you meet him?"

"I met him in Boston. Fanny and I were in our final year at Miss Lindsey's Select School for Women. I was mad for the theater back then, and went as often as I could." She smiled ruefully, and a little sadly. "A friend of a friend worked at the theater and introduced me to Simon. I was instantly dazzled by his charm and wit. He seemed equally enamored and said all the right things to turn my head. I believed I was special in his eyes."

With slow, deliberate movements Reese sat back in his chair. "You let him court you?"

"I suppose that's what you could call it. He was very persistent, very convincing with his attentions, he…" She broke off, darted her gaze around the lobby.

"Go on," he urged.

There was another moment of hesitation before she continued. Reese didn't interrupt her again, but let her tell the tale of Westgrove's treachery.

With each new piece of evidence pointing to the man's despicable nature, anger stormed inside Reese. He tried not to show it, but the discovery that Callie had been lied to so completely—*used* so dishonestly—filled him with a protective fury unlike he'd ever experienced before.

Over the next part of the story Callie's voice hitched. "When Simon asked me to run away with him, I thought he meant to marry me."

She continued on, explaining in a halting tone all the events of that evening.

Reese's hands balled into fists. "Westgrove should answer for his behavior."

"Oh, Reese, I carry my own share of the blame." She choked on a sob. "The part of me raised by Godly, Christian parents should have known not to agree to run away with him. I should have *known* not to meet him in a hotel."

"You were young, Callie. He preyed on your innocence."

"And I let him." She dropped her gaze and then, as if determined to fight off her embarrassment, boldly lifted her chin. "Once I realized he had no plans to marry me, I immediately left the hotel lobby and returned to my dormitory."

"He didn't follow you?"

"No, and he never tried to contact me again. Ironic, isn't it?" Her glassy-eyed gaze shifted around, landing in no particular spot. "After all these years, I cross paths with him in another hotel lobby?"

"I'm sorry, Callie." It angered him that a woman who deserved only affection and tenderness had been treated with disrespect, with such ugly intent.

Reese had never been prone to violence, but he felt his temper rising with vicious force, urging him to crush the man who'd hurt this beautiful, special woman.

"Now you know my secret." She met his gaze. "And the full extent of my shame."

"You have no reason to be ashamed." Reese carefully took her hands in his. "You were lied to and betrayed. But when the real test came, you resisted temptation. That doesn't make you dishonorable, it makes you incredibly brave."

"You...you think me brave?"

"Callie Mitchell." He brought her hands to his lips, kissed both sets of knuckles. "You are the bravest person I know."

Chapter Sixteen

Several days after her altercation with Simon, Callie's emotions were still in turmoil. In truth, she didn't know quite what she felt about the encounter. Relief, to be sure. She'd faced her past. Though she could have handled Simon on her own, Reese's timely appearance had been a blessing. His kindness afterward had given Callie the confidence to set aside her shame and freely accept God's grace.

Where did that leave her now?

She'd spent so much time looking back, allowing her past to define her present, that she didn't know how to move forward.

Live your life. One day at a time.

Yes. Yes!

Drawing in a long breath, she looked around the overly decorated parlor in Polly Ferguson's home. As usual, Callie had accompanied Mrs. Singletary to her weekly meeting of the Ladies League for Destitute Widows and Orphans. She attempted to focus on the earnest discussion about poverty among single, unattached women in Denver, but she'd lost the gist of the debate.

Though she had her own opinions on the subject, and cared a great deal about the plight of the poor, her efforts to sort through the various positions proved unsuccessful.

Her mind kept wandering back to the Hotel Dupree, to the makeshift alcove out of the main traffic area. Reese had been incredibly gentle with her and so sweetly outraged on her behalf. His defense of her had meant more than he could know.

He'd even called her brave.

Reese really was a wonderful man.

Now, she could not stop dreaming of him, of hoping one day he would see her as more than a friend, perhaps even consider her for his bride. Problem was, if he did propose to her, Callie couldn't accept. Not as long as he insisted on avoiding a love match. She would accept nothing less.

They were at cross purposes, she and Reese, facing an obstacle perhaps even greater than his previous relationship with Fanny.

"Pass the scones, Miss Mitchell."

"Oh." She jerked at the command. "Yes. Of course, Mrs. Ferguson."

After placing one of the buttery pastries on her own plate, she handed the serving tray to the woman sitting on her left.

In her role as hostess, Polly Ferguson presided over today's meeting from a brocade settee on the opposite side of the room. The matriarch was bracketed by two younger copies of herself. Phoebe and Penelope even wore gowns in the same shade of pale pink as their mother.

Philomena Ferguson, the third oldest daughter, was also in attendance. She sat on Callie's right. Barely twenty years old, Philomena was well-spoken, well-educated and, in Callie's estimation, the most likeable of the Ferguson sisters. With her unusual hazel eyes and flawless complexion, she favored her brother Marshall in both looks and temperament.

Callie believed she and Philomena could forge a friendship, given time. If pressed, she would also admit the girl suited most of Reese's requirements for a wife. Her hair was a beautiful golden *brown,* with natural caramel streaks that complemented her pretty eyes. Or course, her name did start with the letter *P*.

"Is the rumor true, Beatrix?" Polly Ferguson eyed Mrs. Singletary with a stare that had a bit of cunning wrapped around the edges. "Is Reese Bennett Junior actively seeking a wife?"

Callie winced. While she'd been lost in thought the conversation had turned in a more gossipy direction.

Had someone overheard her conversation with Reese at the theater last week? No other explanation made sense. She groaned inwardly. She'd been careful to keep her voice low, barely above a whisper. Not careful enough.

Mrs. Singletary—*bless her*—deflected her friend's question with ease. "Now, Polly, wherever did you hear such a tale?"

"It makes sense, doesn't it?" Mrs. Ferguson leaned forward, her narrowed gaze giving her a hawklike appearance. "Mr. Bennett is the most eligible bachelor in town. And now that he's in sole charge of his family's law firm, he must be in search of a wife."

"I have no doubt my attorney will make some young woman a wonderful husband." Mrs. Singletary cast her gaze to the ceiling. "It's certainly something to ponder, at any rate."

Oh, Mrs. Singletary was good. She actually sounded as though this was the first time she'd considered Reese for one of her matchmaking schemes.

Clever ploy.

But her friend wasn't fooled. "Now, Beatrix, I find it hard to believe you aren't personally involved in Mr. Bennett's search. Everyone knows you enjoy making a good match."

The widow chuckled. "Everyone would be right. But, regrettably, I am not in league with Mr. Bennett."

"Is that so? Well, according to my source, he was overheard discussing a list of qualifications he wishes in a bride. If he wasn't speaking with you, Beatrix—" Mrs. Ferguson's gaze turned shrewd "—then who?"

Mrs. Singletary cocked an eyebrow. "It's quite the mystery, isn't it?"

Pretending grave interest in her plate, Callie pinched off a small bite of scone. Oh, but her insides turned over, making knot upon knot upon knot. She'd inadvertently put Reese at the center of Denver's gossip mill.

She must warn him.

"It would be a great coup—a feather in your matchmaking cap, if you will—to make a match for Mr. Bennett, especially if the bride was one of my lovely daughters."

Phoebe and Penelope twittered among themselves, openly plotting how best to gain Reese's attention. But as it so happened, their names started with *P*.

Now that the subject had been broached, a barrage of questions began. Callie almost felt sorry for her employer. Except Mrs. Singletary didn't appear the least bit troubled by the verbal attack. In fact, she looked secretively amused as she fielded the onslaught of questions with her usual aplomb.

At one point, her delighted gaze caught Callie's.

Callie frowned in return. She found none of this amusing. Every woman in the room was now speculating as to which young lady in town Reese would ultimately choose to marry.

He must be informed of this horrible turn of events, before the competition to win his heart began in earnest.

As Callie decided how best to approach the subject with him, Mrs. Singletary skillfully turned the conversation to her annual charity ball next month.

It was a smooth transition, aided by Philomena, who suggested a portion of the funds raised be used to buy winter coats for the destitute widows and orphans in town.

The group was debating which one of their members should head up the decoration committee when Laney Dupree entered the parlor. "Sorry we're late." She shoved her hair off her face. "A busy morning at the orphanage."

"Well, you are here now." Mrs. Singletary patted the empty seat beside her. "Come, sit by me."

Laney hesitated, perhaps because she wasn't alone. A young woman about Callie's age accompanied her. The newcomer was quite beautiful. Her black hair offset her pale white skin and heart-shaped face, while her eyes were an unusual shade of blue, nearly lavender. Callie had only read about such a color in books.

Laney made the introductions. "This is Miss Temperance Evans, our newly appointed headmistress for the Charity House School."

Miss Evans's responding smile was dazzling. "Thank you for including me in your meeting. I look forward to helping your cause however possible."

The cultured British accent fit the beautiful face to perfection, as did the yellow silk organza gown.

"We were just discussing my annual charity ball before you arrived." Mrs. Singletary directed her words at Laney. "You have such an eye for detail, I wonder if we can lure you into heading up the decorations this year."

"I'd love to take on the duty." Laney claimed the seat next to the widow. "I already have several ideas."

"As do I," one of the older women declared.

A shuffling of seats followed.

While the older women deliberated over the benefits of roses versus lilies, and gold accent over silver, Penelope and Phoebe eyed Temperance Evans with suspicion.

Proving herself the more gracious of the Ferguson daughters, Philomena scooted over to make room for Temperance next to her.

Once she took her seat, Callie offered the woman a scone.

"Thank you."

Callie smiled. "Tell me, Miss Evans, what made you decide to settle in Denver?"

"My parents brought me here as a child so I could experience the great American West. I fell in love with the area, especially the mountains. When I learned about the headmistress position at Charity House, I decided to leave London—" she lifted her hands in a show of surrender "—and here I am."

There was more to Temperance's story. Callie heard it in her overformal tone.

So, apparently, did Phoebe Ferguson. "You traveled halfway across the world to run a school for prostitutes' children?"

"I did."

"Why?"

"I have a fondness for children." Miss Evans did not explain herself further.

Penelope took over the interrogation, screwing up her face into a disbelieving scowl. *Not* a becoming expression on the girl. "You seem awfully young to run a school."

"I am twenty-three."

"I would have guessed eighteen."

"That's quite enough." Philomena didn't actually snort, but she came perilously close. "Leave the poor woman alone."

An argument immediately broke out among the three sisters, the two oldest joining forces against the younger. Philomena held her ground throughout the fray. Clearly she harbored a quiet strength and a spine of steel beneath the serene expression she usually wore.

When Phoebe stomped out of the room, and Penelope

followed her in a near identical display, Callie gave in to a sigh.

"Good riddance," Philomena mumbled.

With Miss Evans leading the way, conversation turned to the rigors of sea travel during the rainy season. Philomena warmed to the subject.

Callie listened in silence. Both women made excellent observations and seemed perfectly levelheaded. If she presented their names to Reese as potential candidates in his bride search, would he seriously consider them?

Or would he find a reason to reject them as he had all the others? A prayer flashed through her mind, coming straight from her heart. *Oh, please, Lord, let him find fault with every woman I present.*

Unable to focus on the contract beneath his hand, Reese swiveled in his chair and looked out his office window. People of every shape and size hurried along the sidewalks en route to their respective destinations.

There was a rhythm to their steps. Not so, inside his head. Thoughts buzzed around chaotically, with no apparent destination to drive them in a satisfying direction.

Shutting his eyes, he attempted to clear his mind. But his thoughts kept circling back to Callie. And the trauma Simon Westgrove had put her through.

After discovering the full extent of the actor's treachery, Reese had been tempted to hunt down the man and make him pay for what he'd done to her. Fortunately for Westgrove, the acting troupe had left Denver that very afternoon. Reese had missed the train's departure by a full hour.

At least the man couldn't hurt Callie anymore. Reese hoped she would forever let go of the shame she'd been carrying through the years. Her only mistake had been to fall in love with the wrong man.

Callie's situation was additional proof that love was a

dangerous prospect, especially when deeply felt. For Reese, the emotion had been so strong he'd nearly gone mad when he lost Miranda.

Loving like that couldn't be good. Of course, love came in many forms. It didn't have to hurt, or end in tragedy, or bring about pain.

Perhaps he could even love his wife, as long as he kept the emotion from growing too deep, or becoming too fervent.

If his head ruled his heart, he would find a suitable woman to marry—a woman who would make a good wife, a proper partner in life and a devoted mother to their children.

Was he being overly optimistic?

Ever since holding Callie in his arms, he'd felt something shift inside him, urging him to expect more from his wife than companionship.

Looking back, Reese could admit his feelings for Miranda had been entirely too strong, while his feelings for Fanny had not been enough.

He needed to find a balance.

In that regard, the bride list made practical sense.

Then why did the thought of checking off qualifications until he found the most suitable candidate not seem as wise as it had before?

Blowing out a hiss of frustration, he stood and moved closer to the window. Leaning an arm on the frame, he looked out unseeingly over the city then focused on the mountains beyond.

"I've come to warn you."

By now, he should be used to the way his gut rolled at the sound of Callie's voice. He swallowed once, twice, three times.

Once he had his reaction under control, he glanced over his shoulder.

Callie stood in the doorway of his office, her hands twisting together at her waist, her brows scrunched into a frown.

Something was wrong.

Had Westgrove returned?

Reese hastened toward her. Whatever had happened, he would stand by her. The intense urge to alleviate her worries nearly flattened him.

He'd once thought this woman hid a world of feeling behind her cool facade, but Reese now knew the truth. The world of feeling was inside him, bubbling to the surface whenever he was in the same room with her.

This was not the way things were supposed to be. He wasn't supposed to want to champion this woman, to protect her from all harm, to make her happy above all other pursuits.

Yet he couldn't bear any other man having that honor.

Reaching out, Reese took her hands, lowered his gaze over her. She was wearing the blue dress she'd worn weeks ago. The beginning of her transformation. He noted again how the color highlighted the green in her eyes and made her skin glow.

Everything in him pinpointed to one specific goal. Erase her misery. "Callie, what's upset you?"

"I...I don't know where to start."

"Has Westgrove—"

"No." She shook her head. "It's not Simon. He is good and truly gone from my life."

The relief quickening through Reese's blood nearly brought him to his knees.

"Oh, Reese, I'm afraid something terrible has happened and it's my fault."

Her unease cut him to the core. Still focused on his goal, he pulled her into his office and, despite knowing it was a bad idea, shut the door behind her. They were alone.

Completely.

Alone.

And yet, all he could think was how to soothe away that look of worry in Callie's eyes. He resisted placing a hand on her face, though he desperately wanted to cup her cheek and tell her everything was going to be all right.

He couldn't know that for certain. Not until she told him why she'd come to him. "Tell me what has happened."

"We were overheard."

Someone had been listening to them at the Hotel Dupree? The monumental consequences immediately struck him. Although Callie hadn't actually done anything wrong with Westgrove, she'd agreed to run away with the man, had gone so far as to meet him at his hotel. Her actions, if taken out of context, could prove her ruination. "Who heard us?"

Perhaps it wasn't too late to stop the gossip. If he could address the person directly, explain the situation, perhaps he could prevent the worst of the talk from spreading.

Callie sighed. "I don't know for certain. But Mrs. Ferguson brought up your bride search this morning at the Ladies League for Destitute Widows and Orphans tea." She sighed again. "Penelope and Phoebe are already plotting how best to win your heart."

His bride search? That's what they'd been overheard discussing? So relieved to find *he* was the center of gossip, and not Callie, Reese threw back his head and laughed.

Callie's mouth dropped open. "How can you find this amusing? Women all over town will be throwing themselves at you now."

"I can assure you, I don't find any of this amusing. But the idea of any woman plotting ways to win my heart? It's absurd."

"Love is not absurd."

"No," he agreed, sufficiently sobered. "It's very serious

business. But I meant what I said, Callie, I am not seeking a love match."

Pressing her lips tightly together, she eyed him for a long silent moment. Something flickered in her eyes. Hurt, perhaps? Disappointment? A combination of the two?

"Why are you so resistant to falling in love?" she asked.

"I've already explained my position."

"You are being incredibly single-minded." She punctuated the accusation with a scowl.

He suspected she was attempting to appear fierce. The expression only managed to make her look wholly adorable. Unable to resist, he reached out and placed a hand on her shoulder.

She stared up at him, her gaze searching his. "I told you about Simon. I shared my past with you. Won't you trust me with yours?"

Perhaps it made him a hypocrite but he couldn't, he wouldn't, talk about Miranda with Callie. "No."

"Whatever happened, I'll not pass judgment."

He believed her. Sorely tempted to unburden himself, he opened his mouth but couldn't get the words to form together logically in his mind. "I appreciate your offer, Callie, but still, no."

"Will you at least discuss your bride search with me?"

He gave her a wry smile. "Isn't that what brought on this latest snag we find ourselves in now?"

She sighed. "The floodgates are open, Reese. Every woman in town will soon be vying for your attention."

He chuckled at the dismay in her voice, placed his other hand on your shoulder. "Surely not *every* woman. Let's not forget, I can often be stern and overly rigid."

"Untrue. You are handsome, kind, gentle, especially with children, not to mention upright and full of integrity. Any woman in her right mind would consider herself fortunate to receive a marriage proposal from you."

Her defense of him was charming. "Some would say I dislike chaos."

"You simply appreciate lists."

He chuckled again, the sound rumbling from the depth of his soul. This beautiful, sweet, fiercely loyal woman understood him. "You do know me well."

Compelled, he drew her into his arms.

"Reese." She spoke his name on a whisper. "I don't think this is a good idea."

"No, it's not."

"Nor do I think—"

"Now, see, that's the problem. You think too much. We both do." Maybe, just this once, they needed to stop thinking and indulge in a bad idea...together.

Course set, he pressed his mouth to hers.

Callie stiffened in his arms. Less than a heartbeat later, she leaned into him.

All thought disappeared.

For a second, Reese allowed himself to indulge in the sensation of holding a woman he cared about, whose company he thoroughly enjoyed.

After a moment, he lifted his head and stared into Callie's wide green eyes. Caught inside her beautiful gaze, a condition he was growing to appreciate, he forgot all about lists and timetables and adhering to tight schedules.

He jerked back.

Callie Mitchell was a dangerous woman.

As if coming out of a trance, she drew in a slow, careful breath of air. "I better go, before Mrs. Singletary worries."

She turned.

"Callie, wait. We have to talk about what just hap—"

"Please, Reese. Please don't say another word." She wrenched open the door and all but ran out of his office.

Watching her scurry down the hall, she looked as though she couldn't get away from him fast enough. The realization brought a moment of searing pain. A pain so similar to grief Reese had to reach for the doorjamb to steady himself.

One lone, coherent thought emerged, bringing with it a bright spurt of hope. He'd been searching for a wife in the wrong place and in the wrong way.

Time to start a new list.

Chapter Seventeen

Throughout the next week, whenever Callie found herself alone—a state that occurred far too often for her peace of mind—her thoughts returned to Reese.

Sitting in the hard, straight-back chair facing her writing desk, she pulled out the miniature portrait she'd painted, cupped it in her hands and studied the image in the bright morning light.

She'd painted Reese smiling.

The expression reminded her of the way he'd looked when she'd informed him that word had gotten out about his bride search.

His reaction to the news still mystified Callie. He'd seemed completely unconcerned that women all over town would soon be throwing themselves at him.

Was he that immune to falling in love? That resistant? Did he actually believe his life would be happy without it?

God's second greatest commandment called His children to love one another. Love was important, necessary, a prerequisite for a good, healthy life.

Callie knew Reese had the capacity for deep emotion. She'd seen him with the orphans at Charity House. No man had that much patience without love in his heart.

A terrible thought occurred to her. Had someone broken his heart?

Was Fanny the culprit? He claimed not. But what if Reese was still pining for his former fiancée?

Callie wasn't sure she had the courage to push them together, not anymore, not after all she and Reese had shared in the past month. Besides, her sister refused to come home and make things right with him. Fanny had thrown away her chance with Reese.

But…if he truly loved her sister, how could Callie stand in their way? How could she not do everything in her power to bring them back together? Reese deserved happiness. As did her sister.

Lowering her head, Callie studied the miniature portrait in her hand, ran her fingertip over his face. She paused over his mouth, remembering how in the midst of their talk about love he'd kissed her.

Her finger shook as the memory refused to fade.

He'd been so gentle with her, both at the theater and at the Hotel Dupree. And again when he'd held her in his arms and pressed his lips to hers. He must care for her.

Of course he cares. We are friends.

Friends don't kiss friends, not the way Reese had kissed Callie. His behavior baffled her. He seemed almost calculating in his pursuit of a bride, but Callie knew he wasn't that heartless. He was wonderful, extraordinary.

She thought she might cry.

Why had he pursued Fanny first? Why, all those months ago, hadn't he looked at Callie the way he had in his office the other day?

Would she have accepted his suit at the time?

She didn't know. She truly didn't know. Ever since returning home to Colorado she'd allowed her mistake with Simon to define her.

Had she spurned Reese without even knowing it?

"Callie, are you ready to go?"

Jumping at the question, she quickly tucked the miniature away in her desk and looked up at her employer. "Nearly there. I just have to finish pinning my hat in place."

"Hurry, hurry, dear, we don't want to be late for church."

"I'm coming." Callie secured the final three pins and checked her reflection in the mirror. She was growing used to her transformation, even appreciating the changes Mrs. Singletary had insisted upon. But it was more than just the outer wrappings.

The new Callie no longer hovered around the edges of life. She no longer melted into the shadows. She held her head high, wore dresses tailored specifically for her and styled her hair in the latest fashions of the day.

Smiling at her reflection, she picked up her reticule and turned. "All set, Mrs. Singletary."

She was talking to the widow's back.

Callie scurried after her employer, eventually catching up with her outside the mansion. Since they were only a few blocks away from the church building, and the day was already warm, Mrs. Singletary suggested they walk. Callie agreed. They took the most direct route and thus managed to arrive a full ten minutes before service started.

Now they were no longer walking, Callie looked up at the sky. The sun shone bright, hugging the church building in its golden arms. The pretty steeple pointed straight toward the pristine blue heavens. The mountains in the distance marched in a craggy row, looking like sentinels on duty, safeguarding all who moved in their shadows.

"Lovely," she whispered to no one in particular.

Mrs. Singletary hummed her agreement as she waved at someone she knew.

Callie started up the steps. She conquered only two when she realized her employer hadn't joined her. "Aren't you coming, Mrs. Singletary?"

"Go on ahead, dear. Sit wherever you like. I wish to speak with Laney Dupree before I head inside." She took off toward her quarry.

Callie smiled after her employer.

When she'd first taken the position as the widow's companion, she hadn't expected to attend church with her. She'd assumed her employer would wish for a more formal service than the one they enjoyed at Denver Community Bible Church.

Mrs. Singletary had surprised Callie, stating she'd supported the church loosely connected with Charity House and always would as long as she had breath in her lungs.

Denver Community was led by Reverend Beauregard O'Toole, a member of a famous acting family who'd chosen ministry over the stage. All were welcome in Pastor Beau's church, no matter their current situation or what they'd done in the past.

It was a sentiment Callie had agreed with in theory, but she was only just now coming to understand what it meant to accept God's grace fully. Or, as the good reverend often said, "Who better to appreciate God's unlimited mercy than the lost, misguided and hurting?"

A movement caught Callie's eye. She turned, felt her smile widen. Reese had come to church with his father today. The elder Mr. Bennett was already engaged in an animated conversation with Mrs. Singletary and her friends. Reese stood off to one side.

He did not look happy. Actually, his eyes had taken on a hunted look. Perhaps that was due to the fact that he was being quickly surrounded by a swarm of women, all of whom were openly competing for his attention. They'd sufficiently corralled him.

Other than plow someone over, he was good and truly stuck. A captured audience.

Easy prey.

As a friend, Callie should hurry over and rescue him. She decided to let him suffer a few moments longer. It served him right for laughing at her, when she'd only sought to warn him of this very thing. Now that word was out he was actively seeking a bride, he might as well get used to the female interest.

With slow, even steps, she approached the perimeter of the crowd surrounding him and lifted up on her toes.

"Mr. Bennett," she called over the uproar. "Mrs. Singletary has insisted you and your father sit with her this morning. Stop dawdling, please, and do come along."

Thoroughly trapped, he spread out his hands in a helpless gesture. A silent plea filled his anxious gaze.

"Oh, honestly. Step aside, ladies." Callie shouldered her way through the bulk of the crowd. Angry female objections arose.

Callie ignored them.

Taking hold of Reese's sleeve, she tugged. Hard.

A little stumble on both their parts, more objections, then—finally—she managed to pull him free.

For a moment, his gaze turned inward, as if to contemplate how he'd ended up on the wrong end of his bride search.

Callie resisted the urge to remind him she'd warned him this would happen. Instead, she silently looped her arm through his and attempted to guide him toward the church entrance. He refused to move. For a moment, there was an alarming intensity to the man, his features severe with concentration as he stared into her face.

"I believe I owe you an apology." His voice held a sheepish tone. "You were right."

"Though I never get tired of hearing those three little words, I'm afraid you've lost me." She sent him a smiling glance. "What was I right about?"

"I have become the center of unwanted female attention." He sounded so perplexed and baffled she didn't know whether to laugh or quiet his concerns.

She chose something in between.

"You'll be fine," she said in her most soothing tone, patting his arm with her free hand. "That is, as long as you never leave your house again."

His lips dropped into a frown. "Not funny."

"I thought so."

They entered the church before either could say more. All heads turned in their direction. Or rather, all *female* heads turned in their direction. Although the attention was unnerving, Callie knew most were looking at Reese. Speculating as to why he was with her.

Refusing to be intimidated, she lifted her chin and moved deeper into the building. The pew she usually shared with Mrs. Singletary and Reese's father was still empty. They were probably still chatting outside.

A loud squeal of delight rent the air. "Miss Callie. Mr. Reese. Over here. Hey, we're over here."

Seated in the back row with several of the other Charity House children, Daniel Velasquez bounced up and down while waving his hands frantically in the air. His sister copied his every move.

Dressed in their Sunday best, their hair combed and eyes shining, the twins looked adorable. They also looked set apart, with a large empty space between them and the other children in the pew.

Daniel shouted their names again, this time adding, "Won't you come sit with us?"

Callie would like nothing better, but it wasn't her decision alone. She turned to discuss the matter with Reese, but he was already pulling her toward the children.

There was a moment of jostling and organizing and arguing over who would sit where. In the end, Callie and Reese ended up in the middle of the pew with Gabriella on Callie's lap and Daniel on the other side of Reese.

As if on cue, the first strains of organ music wafted through the air. Everyone stood. Callie attempted to set

Gabriella on her feet, but the girl clung to her, wrapping her arms around her neck in a death grip. Shifting her hold, she settled the child on the church pew.

With her arm around the little girl, Callie had to sing the hymn from memory. Obviously sensing her predicament, Reese held out his hymnal so Callie could see it, too.

She breathed in slowly, restraining a sigh. He smelled so good, clean and fresh, soap mixed with pine. She took another short breath, leaned in closer and began singing the selected hymn in earnest. Her voice melded with Reese's. They sounded good, as if they'd been singing together all their lives.

Despite her efforts to stay focused on the song, her thoughts turned fanciful. She imagined her and Reese together like this every Sunday, with their many children beside them, taking up an entire church pew.

Shocked at the direction of her thoughts, Callie shook away the image.

Out of the corner of her eye, she glanced at Reese, only to discover he was watching her. Something quite nice passed between them, a feeling that instilled utter contentment.

The singing came to an end. There was another round of jostling for position, whereby the children ended up in the same places they'd started.

Reese shared a smile with Callie over their heads. He then nodded to his father and Mrs. Singletary as they passed them on their way to a pew closer to the front of the church.

Pastor Beau took his place behind the pulpit amid more than a few female sighs. It was the same reaction he received every Sunday. Not only was the preacher on fire for the Lord, but he also had the trademark O'Toole tawny hair, classically handsome features and mesmerizing eyes.

As was his custom, he began with a bang. "The scandals

of our lives can become the story of God's redemption. But only if we allow Him full access to our pasts."

Callie nearly gasped. It was as if Pastor Beau was speaking directly to her, giving her permission to release the shame of her past once and for all.

"Today is a new day, meant to be lived under grace."

Heads bobbed in agreement, Callie's among them.

"Ah, but living under grace is not as easy as it sounds." He lowered his voice and nearly everyone in the congregation leaned forward. "We often let our pasts hold us back from living a victorious life. We cling to the memory of our mistakes and wallow in the pain of our broken dreams."

Reese stiffened. Callie slipped a glance in his direction, surprised to find he looked as though he'd been punched in the face.

She reached out and covered his hand. He remained rigid under her touch.

"God is the God of our todays and tomorrows," the preacher continued. "But He's also the God of our yesterdays. He reaches into our pasts, forgives our offenses and settles all claims against our conscience."

Reese shifted in his seat. Cleared his throat. Mumbled something under his breath.

"The Lord's goal is not to condemn us, but to heal us. But God doesn't do any of this without our permission. We must be willing participants in our own redemption. I ask you this…" A pause. "Do you have the courage to put the pain of your past into His hands?"

Reese leaned over and said something in Daniel's ear. The boy nodded, then moved in beside Callie as Reese slipped out of the pew.

The sermon continued, but Callie couldn't concentrate on the rest of the message.

She desperately wanted to go after Reese, but she couldn't up and abandon the children.

What seemed an endless amount of time later, the sermon came to a close. "Let us pray."

Callie bowed her head, lifted up her own silent prayer for Reese, for whatever trouble haunted him enough to exit the church in the middle of the message.

"Lord," Pastor Beau began, "help us forget those things which are behind us, and reach forth unto those things which are before us. Teach us to forgive ourselves as You have already forgiven us. We ask this in our Savior's name, Amen."

After the closing hymn, people began shuffling out of the church. Though Callie wanted to run out of the building and seek out Reese, she stayed with Gabriella and Daniel until one of the older children promised to see the two back to Charity House.

"But we want to stay with you, Miss Callie."

Smiling down at Gabriella, she smoothed a hand over the glossy dark head. "I'll stop by the orphanage later this afternoon. We'll bake cookies."

"Will Mr. Reese be with you?" Daniel asked.

Since she didn't know where he'd gone, Callie hedged. "I'll see what I can do, but no guarantees."

When she was outside and once again alone on the steps, Callie's gaze roamed the immediate area. People lingered, clumped in groups, but she saw no sign of Reese. Driven by a strange urgency, she walked around the side of the building, where the cemetery was located.

Her gaze landed on a tall figure nearly hidden in the shadow of a large ponderosa pine tree. Reese. Head bent, he was staring down at a grave. A second later, he sat on the ground beside the weathered headstone.

The pang in her heart was fueled by sorrow. Sorrow for Reese, for the evident loss he suffered of a loved one.

Callie watched him several minutes longer before setting out in his direction.

* * *

Reese had no idea how long he sat beside Miranda's grave. He figured not long, maybe only ten minutes. The final strains of the closing hymn still quivered on the air. People were only just spilling out onto the church steps. He didn't want anyone seeing him here in the cemetery. No one would, unless they came looking for him.

Callie would come. He'd seen the worry in her eyes as he'd shifted around her in the pew. A part of him wanted her to find him so he could share his burden with her.

Another part wanted her to stay far away.

Of all the days he'd chosen to return to church, he had to come when Beau gave a sermon about forgiveness and letting go of the past. One line had hit Reese especially hard. *God reaches back into our pasts, forgives our offenses and settles all claims against our conscience.*

Could it be that simple? Could it be a matter of releasing the pain of his past to the Lord, asking for healing and then…what? What came next?

Did he boldly reach for a different kind of future than the one he'd been pursuing for fourteen years?

Reese lifted his gaze to heaven, a wordless prayer forming in his mind. He was tired of remembering Miranda's death, instead of celebrating her life. Tired of the lingering grief that hit him when he least expected it. He wanted…

He wanted…

Freedom.

He wanted to set the past firmly behind him. That, he realized, was why he now sat at Miranda's grave. He needed to settle the past, to finally let his wife rest in peace. Not because he wanted to be free of his memories of her, but because he wanted to be free of the broken dreams that kept him from living fully in the present.

Where did he start? What words did he use? His heart felt numb in his chest.

He and Miranda had been so young when they'd married. Her recklessness had fueled his impulsiveness. Fire to fire, flame to flame, they'd burned bright, too bright.

Frowning over the memory of their shared impetuousness, their foolish thoughts that they were immune to misfortunes, he picked up a stone and rolled it around in his fingers. The dirt covering the rock felt hot and dry against his skin, much like his long ago dreams of a happy marriage with the beautiful Miranda Remington.

A shadow blackened the sun overhead. "Reese?"

At the sweet familiar voice, the riot of emotions swirling inside him calmed. Callie had found him, perhaps thinking she'd come to his rescue. And maybe she had.

In that moment, Reese knew he would tell her about Miranda, and he would do so today. But at what cost? Callie would want to know the truth, all of it, and that would require giving her a piece of his soul.

She lowered to a small wrought-iron bench situated between him and the tree, but said nothing.

From his position on the ground, he looked up at her. Her gaze was fastened on Miranda's headstone, sweeping quickly over the etchings. Reese didn't have to follow the direction of her gaze. He knew every word, every line by heart, including the final three. *R.I.P. Miranda Remington Bennett. 1863 to 1881.*

Callie's brows pulled together, as if calculating the dates in her mind. Reese saw the exact moment she made the connection.

Her eyes filled with a hundred unspoken questions. She spoke but one of them aloud. "Miranda was your—" her gaze returned to the headstone "—sister?"

"My wife."

Chapter Eighteen

Despite her shock over Reese's astonishing revelation, Callie did not push him to explain himself further. Not yet. He needed time to gather the words that would best tell his story—a story she doubted few people had heard. Perhaps only his father knew the full tale. And maybe not even him. Maybe Reese carried his terrible loss deep within him, where no one could know the magnitude of his pain.

Oh, Reese.

Wanting to ease his suffering, but not sure if he'd welcome her interference, Callie patted the empty space on the bench beside her. He gave one firm shake of his head, clearly preferring to sit on the ground beside his wife's grave.

Callie's heart took a tumble at the obvious implications. She did not try to coax him away again. However, a few moments later, he joined her on the bench, after all.

Holding silent, he stretched out his long legs and rolled his shoulders, but he didn't look in her direction. She studied his profile. Enveloped in shadows cast by the tree overhead, his face appeared pale and gray.

Callie's heart took another tumble.

Whatever had happened to Reese's wife was clearly a tragic tale. When he continued staring straight ahead, she could stand his silence no longer. "Your wife died, back in—" she cut a glance at the headstone "—1881?"

"That's right." At last, his eyes met hers. "Miranda and I were married September of that same year."

Fourteen years had come and gone since his wedding, more than half of Callie's life. Reese's wife had died the same year they'd married, when Reese had been no more than—Callie calculated the years in her head—eighteen years old. *So young.* It explained much about his current approach to finding a bride.

"I'm sorry, Reese." She reached out and covered his hand with hers. "I'm truly sorry for your loss. There aren't words for what you've suffered."

"None that have been invented, at any rate." His stilted tone hinted at a storm of pent-up emotion held firmly in check.

"Will you tell me about your wife?" As soon as she asked the question, Callie realized she was quite possibly asking him to bare his soul. "Unless, of course, you'd rather not."

"I want to, Callie. I really want to tell you about Miranda." He clutched tightly at her hand. "But I don't think I can do it without your help. Ask me whatever you wish and I'll try to answer honestly."

"All right." The muscles in her stomach quivered as she cast about for her first question. "How...how did you meet?"

His brows pulled together in concentration, as if he was following the memories back through time, all the way to the beginning. "I met her at a party at the Carlisles'. What prompted the occasion doesn't matter. I remember being furious at my father for insisting I attend. Because I had other plans that evening."

He went quiet as he drew his hand free of hers and set it on the arm of the bench. "Plans, I have no doubt, that would have landed me a night or two in jail." He let out a wry chuckle. "It wouldn't have been the first time."

"I shudder to ask."

"Probably for the best." He shifted a bit, released another laugh, this one self-deprecating. "I was an outrageous rebel in my youth. Impulsive, bone-stubborn and determined to find trouble wherever I could."

Callie could hardly imagine the person Reese described. He was such a deliberate man now, upright and straight, full of staggering patience. She couldn't imagine him behaving in a manner that would *land him a night or two in jail*.

"Go on," she said softly when she realized he'd fallen silent again.

His gaze lost somewhere in the past, he blinked at her in confusion.

"You were telling me about the party where you met your wife," she prompted. "Your father insisted you attend, and…"

"Right." He nodded. "The party. The moment I saw Miranda from across the room I fell completely, hopelessly in love. I know that sounds clichéd, but it's the truth. I was smitten from the moment I laid eyes on her."

His own eyes shuttered to slits, his gaze once again somewhere faraway.

After a moment, still glassy-eyed, he continued. "She was laughing when I walked up to her. I was captivated by her beauty." He smiled softly. "She had unruly red hair and startling, pale blue eyes. I asked her to marry me that very night. She said yes. We were wed a week later."

A flood of surprise washed over Callie. "So quickly?"

He smiled again, and Callie felt it deep within her soul, the pull of attraction she felt for him. Pray he didn't see her feelings written on her face.

"I was young, Callie. Impetuous. Miranda was equally spontaneous and untamed. We had one glorious, wild, uninhibited month together." He bent his head. "Then she was gone."

One month? He'd only been married one short month?

So little time for happiness, Callie thought, so few days to be with the one he loved. "How did she die?"

He wiped a hand across his mouth. "Miranda loved horses. They were her greatest passion. She insisted we ride every day, sometimes twice a day, sometimes even more. I happily obliged her. It never occurred to me do anything else."

"Of course not. You loved her and wanted to make her happy."

"I did." He ran his hand over his mouth a second time. "She found great pleasure in challenging me to race at the most unexpected moments. It didn't matter where we were, in the heart of town, near an open field, in the midst of a crowded neighborhood. She died on one of our races."

There was sorrow in his eyes, unmistakable guilt in his voice. "Reese." Callie turned slightly to face him. "I was raised on one of the largest ranches in Colorado. I know horses better than most. Accidents happen, no matter how careful the rider is or how skilled."

"Nevertheless," he continued as if he hadn't really heard what she said, "Miranda's death could have been prevented."

"You don't know that for sure."

"We were racing in a field we'd never ridden across before. Neither of us cared. We never cared. We were both that reckless."

You were both that young, she thought, remembering her own penchant for wild, spontaneous acts.

"Miranda was winning, as usual, laughing at me over her shoulder. But then her horse stumbled and went down hard." He tilted his head to the sky, released a slow breath of air. "After a series of rolls, Miranda ended up under the animal. It happened so fast. By the time I caught up to them, the horse was back on his feet. Miranda lay still on the ground."

"She… You…" Callie's voice broke over the words. "When you found her, was she dead?"

He shook his head. "Not dead, but nearly. She hung on for three days. Three endless days that crawled along at a slow, wretched pace. Yet when I think back to that time, those collective moments seemed to have passed in a single heartbeat."

"Oh, Reese."

"I willed her to live. I prayed unceasingly. I begged God to take me instead of her. To no avail. She breathed her final breath in my arms."

"I'm sorry." The words felt so inadequate.

"For months afterward, I wanted to die, too." He turned his haunted gaze onto Callie. "Maybe a part of me did die. The impulsive boy of my youth was gone for good, replaced by the man you see before you now."

A man who valued lists and structure above spontaneity and recklessness. So telling, Callie thought, so incredibly heartbreaking. Because after fourteen years, Reese still blamed himself for his wife's death.

In that, at least, Callie could ease his mind. "Reese," she began, thinking the best route just might be to lead him to the truth, instead of simply telling him. "Whose idea was it to race across that field?"

"I…I don't remember."

"I think you do," she said softly.

Angry shock leaped into his eyes. "You know nothing about what happened that day. You weren't there."

Knowing how badly he was hurting, Callie was tempted to back down. But no. This was too important. *Lord, give me the courage to continue.*

She took a deep breath and repeated the question. "Reese, whose idea was it?"

"Hers," he hissed. "It was Miranda's idea to race across that empty field."

"And yet—" Callie gentled her voice to a whisper "—you're still blaming yourself for her death."

"Of course I blame myself. I didn't have to agree to her challenge that day." His chest heaved with the vehemence of his response. "I could have discouraged her. I *should* have insisted we turn around."

"Would it have mattered?"

"I—" He broke off, lowered his head. "No."

Callie brought one of his hands to her face, pressed her lips to his open palm. "Maybe it's time you forgave yourself for your wife's death."

He continued staring at her, pressing his lips into a grim line. He looked down at his hand, at the spot she'd kissed, then folded his fingers into a fist.

"Are you still in love with her?" Callie asked.

"A part of me will always love Miranda. I'm who I am because of her." He unclenched his fist, spread his fingers out wide. "But Beau's sermon released something inside me, something that's been coming on for some time, a need to put the past behind me, once and for all."

Callie knew just how easy it would be for Reese to continue holding on to the blame for his wife's death, instead of allowing God to heal his pain. Hadn't she done much the same thing with Simon?

"I left the church and came here to Miranda's grave with the idea of letting her go." He flexed his hand. "It's time I forgave her for dying on me."

"And time," Callie ventured, knowing she was risking his ire, "you stopped blaming yourself for not preventing the accident that took her life."

He nodded. "Yes. It's time I forgave myself, as well."

Did he know what a huge step he'd just taken? Did he realize the ramifications? "You recently called me brave. But you're the one who's brave, Reese. So very, very brave."

He didn't respond.

Cupping his face between her palms, she kissed him firmly on the lips. "Thank you for telling me about Miranda."

She dropped her hands, blinked away the sting of tears and attempted to stand.

"Don't go." He pulled her back down beside him. "I still have something to say, something important."

Callie waited, holding her breath, fearing what was about to come out of his mouth yet knowing he needed to have his say.

"On several occasions you've asked me why I don't want a love match. Now you know the answer."

She did. But she didn't like it.

"I've already loved once in my life. Once was enough. I know how much it costs to give someone my heart, and the terrible price that must be paid when love is lost. I'll not willingly go through that pain again."

Callie lowered her head a moment, her heart beating wildly against her ribs. "I understand." She pushed the words past the lump in the throat. "I'll continue helping you find a suitable bride, but I won't expect you to fall in love with her."

He eyed her for a long, tense moment. "Thank you."

She nodded, feeling helpless and sad and more than a little defeated.

"Come on." Rising, he reached out and pulled her to her feet. "We had better return before my father and Mrs. Singletary get it into their heads to send out a search party for us."

Callie tried to laugh, but the sound came out scratchy and rough. A perfect match to her mood.

Tucking her hand in the crook of his arm, Reese led her out of the cemetery and around the building to the front of the church.

His father and Mrs. Singletary were waiting for them on the front steps.

"Ah, there you two are." Mrs. Singletary dropped a large, satisfied smile over them. "Mr. Bennett and I were discussing where we should partake in our noonday meal. We have decided upon the Hotel Dupree because, as Callie can attest, the chef makes a memorable sea bass."

The elder Mr. Bennett smiled. "I enjoy a good sea bass."

The idea of food made Callie's stomach churn, as did the prospect of sitting through a meal making small talk. She opened her mouth to refuse, thinking she would claim a headache, when she remembered her conversation with the Velasquez children. "That sounds lovely, but I'm afraid I won't be able to join you."

Mrs. Singletary, being Mrs. Singletary, insisted on an explanation. "Why ever not, dear?"

"I promised a couple of the Charity House children I'd bake cookies with them this afternoon."

The widow continued holding Callie's gaze.

The penetrating look caused her to add, "I mustn't disappoint the children."

"No," the widow said in an ironic tone. "We wouldn't want that."

Callie extricated her arm from Reese's only to have him reach out and take her hand. "I believe I'll join Callie at the orphanage."

"You will?" she asked, shooting him a surprised look. "Why?"

"I have a fondness for fresh baked cookies. And—" he divided a long, steady stare between his father and Mrs. Singletary "—a massive dislike of sea bass."

Beatrix watched two of her favorite young people depart on their walk to Charity House. A short walk, indeed, seeing as the orphanage's backyard spilled onto church property.

Oh, but it did her soul good to witness the changes in

their relationship. Not long ago they were quite awkward in one another's company. Now they fell into perfect step, matching each other's stride, as if they'd been strolling together like that all their lives.

She smiled fondly after their retreating backs. At last they were comfortable together. Indeed, they made a far cozier picture than when she'd insisted Callie walk Mr. Bennett to the door after her dinner party. They'd barely looked at one another that night. Now, their heads were tilted close in hushed conversation.

Only after they turned the final corner did she allow her smile to turn smug. "They are falling in love."

She predicted an autumn wedding, the plans already materializing in her mind.

If his masculine snort was anything to go by, apparently the man standing beside her had a differing opinion. "You think you're so clever, Beatrix."

Not prone to feigning false humility, she answered the odious question without hesitation. "I am clever, Reese, dear, as evidenced by my vast and ever-increasing fortune, which, as you may recall—" she lifted her nose in the air "—has greatly benefited your own overflowing coffers."

He started to say something, probably, *I earned most of the money without your help,* but she cut him off.

"Do you object to your son marrying my companion?"

"I think they make a lovely couple. I am quite fond of Miss Mitchell. I hope something comes of it." The corner of his mouth turned down. "That's not the point."

Her brows rose. "But of course that's the point."

He jabbed a finger in the air between them. "You shouldn't meddle in other people's lives."

"Don't be ridiculous. If not me, then who do you suggest should guide otherwise stubborn individuals to their happily-ever-after?"

His lips tightened. "You should leave the future up to the Lord. Stop playing God."

The very idea. It was insulting. "I am but a humble servant of our Lord, directing misguided men and women in the proper direction. I never force a match."

"No?"

"I nudge."

"Beatrix, you cannot continue interfering in other people's lives. One day you will make a false step."

She waved this off with a flick of her wrist. "Don't be silly. I know exactly what I'm doing."

For the barest second he looked appalled that she would dare claim such a thing, then, in a stern tone, he said, "No one is infallible. You will make a mistake. It's only a matter of time. I urge you to cease and desist—"

"Reese Bennett, you may be smart. You may be highly successful in your given field." *You may be entirely too handsome for your own good.* "But you will not tell me what to do."

He stared at her.

"I mean it."

To her great surprise, he laughed.

Finished with their conversation—with the man himself—she turned on her heel and headed down the pathway to her home. Walking, or rather marching, with her head held high, served the very necessary purpose of cooling off her temper.

"Beatrix, darling," the odious man called after her. "Haven't you forgotten something?"

Her feet ground to a halt. Instead of turning around completely, the man didn't deserve that much courtesy, she shot a haughty look over her shoulder. "What would that be, Reese, *darling?*"

"You promised to introduce me to the Hotel Dupree's famous sea bass."

"You still wish to dine with me this afternoon?"

"I would like nothing better." The smile he gave her was quite devastating.

She pressed her lips tightly together in what turned out to be a failed attempt at returning that handsome smile.

"Come, Beatrix." He reached out his hand. "My carriage is ready and waiting to take us across town."

Well, why not? She spun back around and, in silence, head still lifted, took his outstretched hand.

When their fingers connected, then entwined, the smirk he shot her was full of masculine arrogance.

"You should know I am only accompanying you because, once given, I never break a promise." She looked at him with narrowed eyes, daring him to comment.

With nary a word, he helped her into the carriage and settled on the opposite seat. His gaze warmed. "I apologize for upsetting you, Beatrix. It was unconsciously done."

She noted he didn't actually ask for forgiveness for what he said, merely for upsetting her. As apologies went, she supposed it wasn't the worst she'd ever heard. Not the best, but certainly not the worst.

She could continue making him suffer, but no one would ever accuse Beatrix Singletary of carrying a grudge. "Apology accepted."

"So quickly?" He leaned back in his seat and chuckled softly. "You do realize I was prepared to grovel."

Ha, she knew better than that.

"Nevertheless," she began, feeling far more generous than he deserved, "at times such as these, it helps to have a short memory."

He inclined his head. "You are graciousness itself."

"Of course I am."

Having seized the last word, she leaned back in her seat and set out to enjoy a fine meal with equally fine company at a very fine hotel.

Chapter Nineteen

With each step she and Reese took toward Charity House, Callie felt the tension seep out of him. He seemed more relaxed, as if a dark shadow had been lifted from his heart.

How well she knew the feeling, and how happy she was to see the light restored in his eyes. Ignoring the little flutter in her heart, she smiled up into his face.

He smiled back.

They were a single unit in that moment, united by the revelation of their individual secrets to one another. If only Reese wasn't resolved to lead with his head, Callie thought.

If only she could settle for less than love in her own life. Perhaps then they could forge something lasting, something that would keep them together forever.

When they turned the final corner to the orphanage, she pulled him to a stop. "Tell me the real reason you chose to come with me to Charity House instead of dining with your father and Mrs. Singletary."

"I *really* dislike sea bass."

She laughed. "Very funny. But, seriously, Reese, why?"

He shot a glance over her shoulder, smiled secretively. "I've been thinking it's time Beatrix Singletary found herself on the other end of a little matchmaking."

"You're joking."

"Not even a little." Returning his gaze to hers, he lifted an elegant shoulder. "My father seems the perfect choice."

She couldn't think why. "But they disagree on most topics."

"Precisely." He leaned forward, lowered his voice. "Take a moment and think about it, Callie."

Contemplating the notion, she tapped her chin with her fingertip.

"Mrs. Singletary and your father, as a couple? Why that's brilliant." Half appalled, half amused, another bubble of laughter slipped past her lips. "A bit startling, but brilliant."

"I've been known to think fast on my feet." He leaned over and gave her a boyish grin. "A talent that can be quite handy in the most startling, brilliant ways imaginable."

Laughing in perfect harmony, they entered Charity House side by side. But then Reese pulled away, mentioning something about needing to find Marc.

Callie reluctantly let him go.

Feeling slightly abandoned—all right, a lot abandoned— she adopted a more leisurely pace than the long, clipped strides that had taken Reese so quickly away from her.

She'd barely moved into the main parlor when a small hand tugged on her skirt. A surge of affection seized her heart.

"Hello, Gabriella." Callie crouched down to eye level, studied the pretty little girl. "I forgot to tell you this morning, but you look quite lovely in that dress. I particularly love the pink bow tied at your waist."

"Look what I can do." The child executed a perfect twirl.

"Very impressive." Callie hugged the girl's thin shoulders.

Gabriella clung for several seconds, then squirmed free.

"Where's your brother?" she asked, mildly concerned. It wasn't typical to find one Velasquez child without the other nearby.

"He's in the tiger room. He and the other boys are playing with toy soldiers."

"Sounds like…fun?"

"Uh-uh." The little girl scowled adorably. "I'd rather bake cookies with you."

"Already halfway done," said a familiar voice from the doorway.

Smiling, Callie straightened to her full height. Temperance Evans stood silhouetted in a ray of sunlight, looking really quite beautiful as she returned the gesture.

"Don't tell me you cook, too?" Callie asked.

"No, no, no." The headmistress gave a brief shudder. "My mother always used to say that if you can make sense of a recipe, you can make any dish. But I've discovered it's a bit more complicated."

Callie didn't disagree. Even something as basic as deciphering simple measurements could present a challenge to someone unschooled in the various abbreviations.

Miss Evans frowned down at the child holding onto Callie's hand. "You are not to be in the main parlor, Gabriella. It's against house rules."

Though her words were somewhat stern, Miss Evans ran a gentle hand over the child's hair as she added, "You must rejoin the other little girls playing jacks on the back porch."

Gabriella buried her face in Callie's skirt. "I want to stay with you."

Frustration flashed in the headmistress's gaze, followed by a genuine note of sympathy.

Before Miss Evans could decide which emotion to give in to, Callie spoke first. "What do you say, Gabriella?" She pried the little girl away from her skirt. "Want to come with me and see what's happening on the back porch?"

"No." The child stared at the floor. "I want to go find my brother."

Miss Evans sighed.

Callie leaned down and captured the child's gaze with her own. "You don't want to play jacks?"

The child's eyes welled with tears. "I want Daniel."

"Go on, Miss Mitchell. Take the child to her brother."

Less than five minutes later, Callie stood on the edge of the tiger room, named after the massive mural painted on the far wall. The scene depicted a large jungle cat prowling through a detailed world of vines, trees, beautiful waterfalls and all sorts of colorful, exotic animals.

The boys, grouped into two separate teams, were facing off in what looked like a ferocious battle of some sort. They weren't alone, either. Reese and Marc Dupree were on the floor with them, squaring off with one another from opposing sides.

They were so involved in their game, nobody noticed Callie and Gabriella. Callie took the opportunity to watch the skirmish in silence. Or rather, she watched Reese.

Her heart dipped to her toes. Reese. Oh, Reese. This was what he would be like as a father. Sprawled out on the floor, tin soldier in hand, playing as if he were another one of the children, caring little for the dirt and smudges on his clothes.

Daniel, sitting on Reese's left, caught sight of his sister. "Gabriella, come be on my team. We're playing marshals and outlaws."

The little girl rushed over to her brother and plopped down beside him.

After patting her on the head, Reese handed Gabriella a tin soldier. "We're the good guys, *Marshal* Velasquez."

The little girl beamed up at him.

"You have too many people on your side," the boy sitting beside Marc whined.

"Yeah," another one added. "That's not fair to us."

"Callie, come quick." Marc motioned her to take the empty spot next to him. "It's up to you to even out the numbers."

Even out the numbers. That had been nearly the exact

same argument Mrs. Singletary had used when she'd insisted Callie attend her dinner party all those weeks ago.

Much had changed in her life since that night. She was no longer a piteous wallflower content to hide in the shadows. Nor was she satisfied with camouflaging her light behind ugly clothing.

The woman she was today fully embraced the transformation her employer had originally hoisted upon her. Happily willing to accept she was a child of God, worthy of love.

Reese had been instrumental in the change. Was it any wonder she loved him?

She loved him? Why, yes. She did. Callie loved Reese. The realization should have come as a shock, but instead it spread through her like warm honey, sweet and appealing yet also a little sticky.

Callie knew while she might never win Reese's heart, she had to try.

"Move aside, boys." She settled in beside Marc, and then locked her gaze on Reese. "Let the battle begin."

This was the woman Reese had always suspected lurked inside Callie. Beneath the ugly clothing and off-putting facade was a beautiful, fierce warrior princess. A woman who bravely stepped out of the shadows and tackled life head-on.

Mesmerized, Reese watched her take up her position as one of the *outlaws.* Appropriate, given that this woman could easily steal his heart if he didn't take care.

There were far worse fates a man could suffer.

Why, Reese wondered, had he avoided her all these years? Why had he kept his distance for so long?

He knew, of course.

Deep down, he'd sensed her fighting spirit, her passionate loyalty for the people she loved. That hidden ferocity had alarmed him. He'd been too hobbled by guilt over Miranda's death to recognize the beauty of Callie Mitchell. By thinking he needed to maintain control at every turn, he'd steered clear of this charming, daring, magnificent woman.

In an ironic twist, it was Callie who'd helped him let go of Miranda and allow his wife to finally rest in peace.

Toy soldier in hand, a husky growl came out of her throat, followed by a delighted giggle. Reese couldn't take his eyes off her.

He made a mental note to add *not afraid to get dirty* and *willing to play with toy soldiers* to his latest bride list.

Even dressed in her Sunday best, Callie battled as valiantly as any of the boys in the room. But, alas, her efforts—and those of her team—weren't enough. The good guys won.

Daniel and Gabriella jumped up and down, cheering with the rest of their teammates.

As Reese watched the siblings' uninhibited celebration, joy and relief filled him. He couldn't be more pleased by their transformation.

Wondering if she'd noticed the change in the children, as well, he glanced over at Callie. A mistake. He'd let his guard drop a second too long. In the next instant, he was tackled playfully by his teammates. Fingers and elbows jabbed at him. He took a foot in the gut, one in his chest, and all he could think to do was...

Laugh.

It felt good to laugh. Freeing.

Not only was Miranda finally at peace but so, too, was he.

Hovering from a spot overhead, Callie peered down at him with one of her prettiest smiles. "Want help up?"

He rolled out from under the tangle of arms and legs, then stretched out his hand. "Please."

The moment their palms pressed together he felt it, the

sensation of coming home, of finding his place in the world, of letting go the fight.

Strangely lightheaded, he let Callie pull him to his feet. Staring into her eyes, his throat began to burn with unexpected emotion. He swallowed. "You are a fierce opponent, Miss Mitchell."

"Something you should keep in mind, Mr. Bennett."

"I like a good challenge."

"Then considered yourself warned. One day, victory will be mine."

"Watch yourself, Reese." Smiling, Marc clasped him on the shoulder. "The Mitchells give no ground. They take no prisoners. It's a marvel we lost the game."

Eyes narrowed, Callie pointed a finger at Reese. "We'll get you next time."

He started to say something along the lines of *you're welcome to try,* when he caught a movement in the doorway. The new schoolmistress stood beside Laney Dupree, watching the shenanigans from a safe distance.

Both women were smiling, but only Laney carried the smile into her eyes.

In fact, Temperance Evans looked excessively stiff. Her gaze was distant, as well. Standing intentionally apart from the action, she reminded Reese of Callie.

Or rather, the old Callie. The new Callie was the most approachable woman he knew. He was growing quite fond of the changes in her.

"I see we missed out on all the fun," Laney said with a hint of remorse in her tone.

Miss Evans looked more than a little relieved.

Carrying two of the younger boys upside down in either hand, Marc sauntered over to his wife and kissed her square on the mouth with a loud smacking sound.

"Oh, stop." She playfully pushed at his chest. "You're embarrassing yourself."

That earned her a dry chuckle from her husband.

Grinning, Marc set the boys on their feet. At the same moment, Laney announced, "Milk and cookies are waiting in the kitchen."

Cheers erupted, followed by a mass exodus toward the door.

Marc halted the stampede with a piercing whistle. "Everyone, freeze."

Silence dropped over the room like a cannonball falling from the sky.

"You know the rules."

"No running inside the house," half the children said, while the other half grumbled under their breath.

Shoving away from her spot at the door, Miss Evans took charge.

"Follow me, children." She turned on her heel, then glanced back over her shoulder. "Remember, we walk in an orderly fashion, single file, no pushing or shoving."

She didn't raise her voice, or speak overly harsh, yet every child obeyed her directives, lining up one by one, single file, tallest to shortest, Gabriella near the rear behind her brother.

Marveling, Reese stepped aside to let the children pass.

Once the last little boy trooped into the hallway, Marc let out another, softer whistle. "I bow to your expertise," he said to his wife. "Miss Evans was a perfect hire."

"I do so love being right."

He gave her another loud peck on the cheek. "I know that, my love."

Everyone laughed.

"You know, Laney—" Marc wiggled his eyebrows "—playing Marshals and Outlaws is hard work. I could use a cookie myself. What about you, Reese?"

Reese adopted the same hopeful tone as the other man. "I wouldn't say no."

Marc leaned around him. "Callie? What about you?"

"I also enjoy cookies."

"Then follow me." Laney motioned them into the hall-way. "Quickly, now, before they're all gone."

As if in silent agreement, Reese and Callie took up a position side by side and fell in step behind the Duprees. Only as they wound their way to the stairwell did Reese realize Callie had grown unnaturally quiet. The fight hadn't exactly left her, but she seemed less...bold. Not quite as feisty.

He glanced over at her, noticed her face held a thoughtful expression. A lot was going on in that complicated mind.

Wondering if he was the cause of this alteration in her mood, he waited until they hit the first-floor landing then tugged her off to one side.

Marc halted, as well, a question in his eyes.

"I need to speak with Callie before we join you in the kitchen."

Brows traveling toward his hairline, Marc's gaze turned suspicious.

Reese rolled his shoulders in annoyance. "We'll stay out in the open. Where you can see us."

This time, Marc looked to Callie for confirmation.

"I have no objection," she said.

"Out in the open." Marc pointed at Reese. "Move too far away from my line of vision, and I'll come looking for you."

"Understood." As soon as Marc rounded the corner, Reese took Callie's shoulders and turned her to face him. "All right, out with it."

Her eyes widened. "Out with what?"

"What's on your mind? And don't say 'nothing,' I see the inner wheels spinning."

She pressed her lips tightly together and said nothing.

"Come on, Callie. You're thinking so loud my ears hurt."

Sighing, she lifted a delicate shoulder. "I'd rather not speak of it here."

He touched her arm. "You can tell me anything."

She drew her bottom lip between the teeth, glanced at a spot behind him. Shaking her head, she pulled him into the shadows and lowered her voice to a mere whisper. "It's Miss Evans."

"The schoolmistress?" He jerked in surprise. "What about her?

Callie went silent on him again, but her eyes held a troubled light. That couldn't be good.

"What's wrong with Miss Evans?"

"Nothing. Not a single thing. If you must know." Callie looked left, then right, then left again. "I like her."

So she'd found a new friend. That was nice. But why was she telling him? Why the stealth and whispered conversation?

As if reading his mind, Callie gave him a meaningful stare. "She's perfect."

"Please." He made a sound deep in his throat. "No one is perfect."

Another sigh, this one full of female frustration. "She's perfectly suitable. For you. You must realize she fits all your requirements for a..." She mouthed the word *bride*.

For several heartbeats, Reese stood in stunned silence. She was foisting Miss Evans on him? *Now?* After all that had happened between them? When his head was so full of Callie he couldn't think straight?

"Say something," she whispered.

He couldn't think what to say, so he went for levity. "Uh...*something?*"

Lips pursed, she shook her head at him. "She fits every one of your requirements and a few you haven't listed."

Did this woman not realize how miserable she sounded? Did she not realize how heartening it was for him to discover Callie didn't want him pursuing Miss Evans? "I don't like her."

"What's wrong with her?"

She's not you.

He nearly blurted out the truth in his heart, but decided now wasn't the time. Not with them skulking in shadows as if they had something to hide.

"Her smile rarely meets her eyes," he said. "Doesn't bode well for easy, lighthearted conversations."

"Oh, honestly." Callie threw her hands in the air. "Are you trying to be difficult?"

Actually, he was. But, again, now wasn't the time for that particular conversation. He had a new bride list to finalize, with an entirely different set of requirements, ones Callie would surely approve of this time around. Seeing as she was his inspiration.

He looked over his shoulder again, back into the kitchen. Miss Evans was handing a cookie to one of the smaller children. The smile she gave the little girl was warm and friendly and completely rendered his earlier argument moot.

Callie followed the direction of his gaze and sighed heavily. "She's very beautiful and appears to have a great affinity for children."

She was so adorably upset by this admission he couldn't help but tease her a little. "I may have responded in haste. Perhaps I'll allow her further consideration, after all."

"Did you know she can't cook?"

Amused at Callie's sudden switch in position, Reese pretended to consider this new piece of information. "Not at all?"

"She can't even follow a simple recipe."

Reese stifled a laugh. "She's a smart woman. I'm confident she can learn."

Lowering her head, Callie sighed a third time. Or was it the fourth? He'd lost count. "If you really like her," she began, "I suppose I could teach her the basics."

"You'd do that for me?"

She nodded, looking profoundly unhappy. He didn't think he could adore this woman any more than he did right now.

"That's very generous of you, Callie." And very, very educational.

She was jealous of Miss Evans. Simply because she thought the woman would make him a suitable bride.

A plan began formulating in his mind. It would take time to implement and would require much preparation on his end.

Reese was a patient man, highly skilled at carrying out a properly prepared plan.

Beginning tomorrow, he would start over with his bride hunt. He would pursue just one woman from this point forward. The *only* woman he wanted, the most suitable woman for him.

The trick would be to convince Callie that *he* was equally suitable for *her*.

Chapter Twenty

Over the following weeks, Callie noticed a discernible change in Reese. He seemed more attentive, making a point to seek her out at parties or the theater or whenever their paths crossed. If he had a meeting with Mrs. Singletary, he lingered over mindless discussions with Callie about the weather, both before and after his appointment.

At Charity House he found ways to include her in whatever game he'd chosen to play with the children.

He always behaved above reproach, treating her as though she was a woman worthy of his respect. Other than that one time in his office, he didn't attempt to kiss her again. No, he treated her with generosity and tenderness, as if she was precious in his sight. As a result, Callie was getting to know Reese on a whole new, deeper level.

She was also falling more in love with him by the day. Not the man she'd wistfully watched from afar, but the man she knew him to be now. A man who worked hard, cared deeply for his family and friends, and who adored all children.

What he didn't do was discuss his bride hunt with Callie. No matter how many times she broached the subject, no matter what tactic she employed to get him talking, he managed to dodge the conversation altogether.

Only two causes made sense. Either he'd turned to Mrs. Singletary for help once again. Or he'd made up his mind and had chosen a woman to become his bride. The latter seemed unlikely. With all the attention he'd been paying Callie, how would he have time to pursue any woman? How could he—

A gasp flew past her lips. She quickly pressed a hand to her mouth. But… Oh. Oh. Reese was pursing…*her?*

"Oh, my!"

Situated behind the desk in her private study, Mrs. Singletary looked up from the guest list she held in her hand. "Did you say something, Callie?"

"No, I…I just…" She couldn't form thoughts in her mind. Her heart beat wildly in her ears, stealing what little concentration she had left. "I…thought of something I forgot to do for tonight's ball."

The widow placed the list on the desk in front of her. "What is that, dear?"

Think, Callie. Think. "I…haven't picked out my hairstyle yet."

"That's leaving it a bit late. The ball will be starting in a few hours."

Callie stood, looked frantically around, pivoted toward the exit. "I need to consult the magazines Julia left in my room."

Without waiting for the widow's response, she hurried out of the office and strode quickly through the winding corridors. She desperately needed the sanctuary of her own room, where she could sort through the chaotic thoughts running around in her head. Reese had chosen her.

He'd chosen *her* for his bride.

But…why hadn't he made his decision known to her? *He's had weeks.*

What could he hope to gain by not informing her of his intentions?

So focused on puzzling out his strange behavior, she nearly tripped over the cat trotting beside her. Fluffy tail pointed straight up in the air, Lady Macbeth barely swerved out of the way.

Callie smiled down at the skittering cat. "Seeking escape, are you?"

The spooked animal darted in front of her feet once again. Prepared for the move, she redirected her steps, skirting disaster by less than a foot.

Lady Macbeth rushed ahead of her, pausing at her bedroom door. The moment she twisted the doorknob, the cat shoved inside and dashed under the bed.

Callie didn't blame her for wanting to get away from the household commotion. For three days straight, Mrs. Singletary's home had turned into a hive of activity in preparation for her annual charity ball.

Vast quantities of people came and went throughout the day, bringing with them large amounts of food, an assortment of desserts, flower arrangements and who knew what else.

Rugs had been rolled up and tucked away in the attic. The floor in the main ballroom had been waxed and polished, twice. Buffet tables had been set up in several rooms on both the main and second levels of the house.

Aside from the outside help, Laney Dupree had also put Mrs. Singletary's staff to work on the decorations, including Callie. Her fingers were numb from polishing scores of silver candlesticks, dishes and serving trays.

As the widow's companion, Callie would be expected to act as one of the hostesses this evening. Until then, she would enjoy a bit of solitude. She quickly shut her bedroom door and clicked the lock in place.

"It's safe to come out now."

Lady Macbeth peered out from under the bed, gave Callie a narrow-eyed glare then dashed back into her hiding place.

"Can't say I blame you, you're out of harm's way under there, might as well stay put."

That way Callie wouldn't have to worry about tripping over the skittish animal as she took to pacing. Her heart overflowing with emotion, she tracked around the perimeter of the room.

Reese was actually courting her. How had she not made the connection? The gentleness, the sweet, affectionate attentiveness, all spoke of a man wooing the woman he preferred above all others.

She wanted to be his bride, so very much, but only if he loved her. She didn't want him to propose because he deemed her suitable according to some list he'd drawn up as he would a legal brief.

She wanted his heart, all of it, and would settle for nothing less. Unfortunately, he'd given the bulk of it away already, when he was more boy than man. *I've already loved once in my life. Once was enough.*

Oh, Reese.

Callie spun in a tight circle, retraced her steps, maneuvering around the furniture when necessary. She knew Reese cared for her, but that wasn't the same as love.

The fact that Callie refused to settle for second best in his heart was really his own fault. He'd taught her to accept her worth as a cherished child of God.

"Typical man. He's ruined everything. *Everything.*"

Marching over to her writing table, she yanked open the drawer and pulled out the portrait she'd painted of her and Reese. She'd titled the picture Bride and Groom.

Wishful thinking. If Reese proposed and she refused him, would he marry someone else? The thought was a black stain upon her heart.

"Callie? Are you in there?" A rapid knocking sounded at the door. "Do let me in, dear. I'm worried about you."

Sighing, she carefully set the painting on her desk. She

should have known Mrs. Singletary would follow her after that hasty departure. The widow was nothing if not perceptive.

"Coming," she called.

The moment she opened the door, Mrs. Singletary grabbed her by the shoulders and stared into her face. After several seconds of intense scrutiny, she released a slow exhale. "You're all right."

"Of course I'm all right."

"You left so abruptly I wasn't entirely sure." She looked over Callie's shoulder. "May I come in?"

"Yes." Callie stepped back and let her pass.

After a brief glance around the room, Mrs. Singletary chose to perch herself on the edge of Callie's bed. "Won't you tell me what's upset you?"

Surprisingly close to tears, she sank down beside her employer and drew in a steadying breath. "It's hopeless."

"Nothing is ever hopeless." The widow draped her arm around her shoulders. "With God all things are possible."

Then why did her situation feel so completely *impossible?*

"I'm in love with Reese." She was astonished at how easy the admission came.

"I know." Mrs. Singletary removed her arm from around Callie's shoulders and took her hands. "Love is a marvelous thing. A treasured gift from God. Something to be celebrated."

Not when it was one-sided. Giving in to her sorrow, she buried her face in her hands and let the tears come at last.

"Oh, dear. Those aren't tears of joy."

Callie had never cried in front of her employer, but now that she'd begun she couldn't seem to stop the flow. "I'm in love with Reese, but he's not in love with me."

"Well, that's just silly. Of course he loves you. I dare say he's besotted."

The woman sounded so confident that Callie experienced a small flutter of hope. "Why… How…?" She dropped her hands and gaped at her employer. "How do you know?"

"It's quite simple, dear. I've watched him watching you. He does it all the time, especially when he thinks no one is paying attention." The widow leaned in close. "I *always* pay attention."

Something tugged at Callie's heart, something new and wonderful. Something that felt like anticipation. "He—" she swiped at her cheeks "—watches me?"

"Indeed, yes. He can't keep his eyes off you. At the theater he watches you instead of the play. Moreover, you're the first person he seeks out at any gathering and the last he speaks to before he departs."

If half of what the widow claimed was true, Reese could very well ask her to marry him soon. It was a gloriously wonderful thought and so horribly terrible.

She knew he cared for her, perhaps even deeply. But that wasn't the same as loving her. "He was married once before. Did you know that, Mrs. Singletary?"

Her words were met with several beats of silence. "You jest."

"Fourteen years ago."

"How did I not know about this?"

"The marriage lasted only a month before his wife died in a riding accident. He was only eighteen at the time, and…" Callie blinked rapidly to stave off another onslaught of tears. She'd cried enough. "His wife was the love of his life."

They both fell silent, staring at one another. Callie saw the widow processing this new piece of information, saw that keen mind of hers evaluating what it all meant. "You are sure about this?"

"He told me himself." *I've already loved once in my life-time. Once was enough.*

"Well, hmm. That certainly explains a lot." The widow rose, then began to pace through the room, following nearly the same route Callie had taken.

Eyes burning with unshed tears, she tracked the woman's progress until she could stand the suspense no longer. "Do you now understand why the situation is hopeless?"

Mrs. Singletary held up a hand. "Hush, dear. I need a moment."

Callie gave her two. Then said, "But, Mrs. Singletary, you have always claimed that we each have only one true soul mate."

"I know what I said. But perhaps it's time I reevaluated my opinion on the matter." She halted at the writing desk, picked up the miniature portrait Callie had made of her and Reese. "Did you paint this, dear?"

"Yes."

"It's quite lovely." She set the portrait back on the desk and returned to sit beside Callie. "Despite his previous marriage, I still believe Mr. Bennett is in love with you."

Callie squeeze her eyes tightly shut, trying desperately to hold back the burst of hope spreading through her. "I want to believe you."

"It seems you have an important decision ahead of you."

Callie opened her eyes. "I…do?"

The widow rose, peered out into the hallway, then came back to stand over her. "You can either let your fears determine your future and thus live the rest of your life alone. Or you can take a leap of faith and seize a lifetime of happiness with the man you love. The choice is yours."

"But even if Reese does love me—"

"Oh, he does."

"How can I trust it's enough? How will I know if *I'm*

enough? What if Reese..." She broke off, unable to finish the rest her thought.

No, she must continue. She must speak aloud her greatest fear. "Mrs. Singletary, what if Reese grows to resent me?"

"For what, dear?"

"For being alive?" She swallowed. "For not being Miranda."

"There are no guarantees in life, or in love. That's where faith comes in. You must allow the Lord to direct your path. In the meantime, let's get you dressed." Mrs. Singletary stuck her head back in the hallway. "Julia. Hurry, hurry, our time is running short."

The maid popped into the room, breathing harder than usual, as though she'd run the entire length of the long corridor.

"My companion must look her very best this evening." Mrs. Singletary took the maid's hand and dragged her toward Callie. "She should wear her hair up, I think, with perhaps a few tendrils hanging loose around her face."

"Whatever you think best, Mrs. Singletary."

"Then up it shall be." She headed toward the door, paused. "Think about what I said, Callie. The only way you will lose this battle is if you refuse to fight."

With those sage words, the widow swept out of the room.

Reese entered Mrs. Singletary's home behind an unfamiliar couple. It seemed all of Denver had been invited to the widow's annual charity ball.

Handing his hat and gloves to one of the hired butlers, he entered the crowded foyer and looked around. Women were dressed in formal gowns made of colorful silks or satins. They wore elbow-length white gloves and fancy adornments in their hair. Jewels glittered around their necks.

In contrast, the gentlemen wore formal black tailcoats and trousers with white vests and matching white bow ties.

Looking for one woman in particular, Reese scanned all the female faces but didn't find the one he wanted most to see.

Shouldering his way through the bulk of humanity lingering in the open foyer, he continued searching for the only woman he wanted to see tonight. The crowded drawing room on his right was filled to capacity with clusters of people chatting among themselves.

No Callie.

Although, he had to admit, there were an uncommon number of attractive young women in attendance tonight. He felt the bulk of their gazes following him as he moved on to the next room. The overabundance of female interest in him had failed to die down in the weeks since news had gotten out of his bride search.

It seemed everyone wanted to know who he would marry.

He planned to end the speculation tonight.

He had his final list tucked inside an interior pocket of his jacket. After weeks of writing and rewriting, agonizing over what to put in and what to take out, he was ready to present his requirements to Callie.

He needed to find her first.

Music floated through the house. Tables draped in gold-and-silver satin lined nearly every room. Trays of fruit and cheeses were surrounded by piles of smoked fish, roasted fowl and thinly sliced cuts of beef. Several tables were dedicated to desserts.

At last, he caught sight of Callie in the grand ballroom. She was dressed in a gossamer gown that was neither blue nor green but a mesmerizing combination of the two. The bodice was form-fitting, trimmed with lace, while the skirt draped in flowing waves of fabric past her slippered feet. Her hair was piled on top of her head with a loose waterfall of curls hanging around her face.

As he'd seen her do countless times in the past, she watched the dance floor from a discreet distance. The sight made his gut twist. She should be taking a turn around the ballroom with the other couples, with him as her partner.

Easy enough to rectify.

She must have sensed his gaze on her because she turned her head and smiled at him. She was different tonight, bolder, more sure of herself. As inevitable as the day giving way to night, his heart picked up speed. His blood raced through his veins.

His throat seized over an unsteady breath.

He set out in her direction.

She set out in his.

They met halfway and he took her hand. "You are a vision tonight."

Though she boldly held his stare, the slight tremble in her fingers spoke of her nervousness. "Thank you, Reese. You're looking quite handsome yourself."

"I look like every other man in the room."

She smiled again, an expression of infinite caring and affection. "Perhaps in what you are wearing, that is true. But you stand out above all others, in looks and character."

He'd asked himself many times over the past few weeks, why this woman was the one he wanted to marry. *Why her?*

Now, as he stood entrapped in her gaze, he wondered why he'd ever doubted his decision to pursue her.

"Shall we dance?"

She bit her lip. Even without that telltale sign, he could sense her hesitation. He silently willed her to say yes.

Her answer came in a brief nod. He drew her into his arms and spun her out onto the dance floor.

Gazes locked, they danced in silence for most of the song. It came to an end all too soon and they stepped apart.

Reese wasn't through holding her. "Dance one more with me."

"I have been tasked with refilling the dessert tables whenever they fall low. I cannot neglect my duties." She sighed. "Nor can I monopolize you all evening."

The strains of the next waltz filled the air. "Once more," he insisted.

"People may misunderstand your intentions."

"My intentions are wholly honorable." Sweeping her into his arms, he gave her no more chance to argue. "Besides, you owe me a respite."

Her eyebrows arched at haughty angle. Ah, there she was. *His* Callie.

"Countless women have been showing up at my law firm all week with the sole purpose of insisting I dance with them at the ball this evening."

Letting out a delighted laugh, she shook her head. Then, as if concerned he might actually be telling the truth, her eyes rounded. "Surely not."

"I might have exaggerated the number." His tone came out more amused than he'd felt at the time. "It wasn't *countless* women, just two."

Eyes narrowed, head titled, she considered this a moment. "Let me guess, their names begin with the letter *P*."

"Right on the first try." He spun her in a circle.

She matched him step for step. "I forbid you to dance with either Phoebe or Penelope Ferguson tonight."

He drew back in laughing surprise. "You forbid me?"

"Don't think you can defy me on this, either." The mock scowl she gave him was as endearing as the rest of her. "I will make a scene if you do."

"I wouldn't dare risk a scene."

They danced the next twelve notes in companionable silence.

"I've made up a new bride list," he said.

Her feet stumbled to a halt and she blinked up at him in horrified silence.

It was hardly the response he'd expected.

At last, she found her voice. "You did what?"

"I have designed a new list. I brought it with me." He took her arm and guided her off the dance floor. "I thought we might review it together later, perhaps when the ball is winding down."

"You have revised your list," she repeated.

"You'll be pleased to discover that I put much thought into this last and final one. It's very detailed. I'm hoping you'll approve of the changes."

She glanced at him without smiling. "So you are still seeking a bride?"

"Not precisely." He was attempting to tell her he'd picked out his bride—*her*—but he was making a hash of it. "I've already made my decision. You see, Callie, I—"

A small commotion at the front of the ballroom cut off the rest of his words. Reese swiveled his head and, for a perilous moment, his mind went blank.

He'd expected this evening to be memorable. Had hoped and planned for it to be so.

But he hadn't foreseen this shocking twist.

After months of being gone, after innumerable unanswered letters from her sister, Fanny Mitchell had chosen tonight to make her return to Denver.

As she took the dance floor with her partner, Reese clasped Callie's hand and watched his ex-fiancée waltz back into their lives.

Chapter Twenty-One

Fanny looked spectacular, Callie thought glumly. She was poised and sophisticated beyond her twenty-two years, and even more beautiful than when she'd left town. The blue silk gown she wore complemented her delicate beauty, while the artfully arranged mass of blond curls set off her exquisite face and startling amber eyes.

As if she didn't know—or perhaps didn't care—that she was the center of attention, she twirled around the dance floor in Jonathon Hawkins's arms. A triumphant return, timed for utmost effect.

But to what end?

If Fanny had come to the ball in an effort to halt any remaining gossip over her broken engagement, she'd failed. The ballroom buzzed with whispers and speculation. Gazes swung between Fanny and Reese.

Callie thought she might be sick.

Not wishing to add substance to the rumors already circulating through the ballroom, she discreetly tugged her hand free of Reese's.

He continued staring straight ahead. "Did you know she was coming tonight?"

"No. Did you?"

Reese shook his head.

They fell silent again, both of them watching Fanny, as were most of the other party guests.

Callie stared blankly at the spinning couple, her thoughts in turmoil. Why had her sister chosen tonight to make her long-awaited return? Why had she not let Callie know she was coming home?

Was Reese happy to see Fanny? His stiff posture hinted that he was more taken aback than pleased. Callie couldn't drum up the courage to look at him to find out one way or the other.

The whispering intensified around them, turning into open speculation. She thought she heard her name linked with Reese's, followed by an unfounded conjecture that she'd played a role in her sister's broken engagement.

Now gazes were turning to study her and Reese, making a connection that wasn't there. Or hadn't been there until recently.

The music played on and Fanny continued whirling around the dance floor with Mr. Hawkins.

Callie's stomach churned in perfect rhythm with their steps. She wanted to be glad her sister was home, truly she did, but did Fanny not realize that her sudden appearance would generate talk, much of it ugly? Did she not hear the whispers following her across the dance floor?

"Why did she have to come back tonight?"

Reese shook his head, obviously as baffled by Fanny's behavior as Callie. "Your sister has interesting timing."

Indeed.

If Fanny had arrived even hours before the ball had begun, Callie would have been better prepared for the whispers. She would have found a way to temper the gossip… somehow. She loved her sister—she did. Hadn't she sent innumerable letters begging Fanny to come home?

Now that her sister was here, Callie wished she would have stayed away.

Guilt washed through her at the thought, turning her heart bleak. Where was the joy over seeing Fanny again?

Her sister was her best friend, the woman who knew her better than any other. Yet, Callie still wanted her gone.

This time, a spark of resentment followed the thought, leaving an unattractive blight on her soul. This insight into her character was not a pretty one.

"I must greet her properly," she said, mostly to herself, but Reese responded, anyway.

"As should I." He shook his head in resignation. "She's given us little choice."

They shared a bleak smile.

"Come." He took her hand and set it on his arm. "The waltz is drawing to a close. We'll catch up with her as soon as she steps off the dance floor."

More than a few curious glances followed their progress across the room.

They approached Fanny and Mr. Hawkins on the very edge of the parquet floor. Neither seemed to notice their arrival. They were each looking steadily into one another's eyes, a silent message flowing between them. With a shaky smile, Fanny lowered her head.

Mr. Hawkins cleared his throat. "Thank you for the dance, Miss Mitchell."

Fanny continued staring at her toes. "It is I who should thank you, Mr. Hawkins. I'm afraid I didn't sufficiently think through my actions. Had you not asked me to dance I don't know what I would have done. You saved me from certain humiliation."

"I'm glad I could help." He started to say more, but caught sight of Callie and Reese. "Ah, Miss Mitchell. Mr. Bennett." He divided a look between them. "Always a pleasure to see you both."

Callie greeted him with her a short nod and then turned her attention to her sister. "Welcome home, Fanny."

"Callie." Fanny's head lifted and a look of unfiltered

relief filled her gaze. "I'd hoped you would be here this evening."

As she stared into her sister's eyes, Callie recognized the discomfiture there, the worry that her return would not be received well. Whatever lingering anger she'd been holding toward Fanny suddenly disappeared. All that was left was love. Love for her sister. Love for her best friend. Fanny had made her share of mistakes recently. Then again, so had Callie.

Judge not, lest you be judged.

"Oh, Fanny." Callie pulled her younger sister into a warm, tight embrace. "I've missed you so."

"I've missed you, too, Cal. So very much."

They clung to one another for several seconds, neither caring that they were making a spectacle of themselves with their joyful reunion. Or that the whispers and chatter had increased.

Fanny stepped back first.

Her gaze dropped over Callie, traveling from head to toe. "Why, Callie, you're beautiful. And your dress..." A smile curved her lips. "It's absolutely stunning and so perfect for your coloring."

A few months ago, the compliment would have alarmed Callie. She would have retreated behind her cool mask, concerned she'd attracted unnecessary attention. Now, she accepted her sister's admiration with a gracious smile and a genuine thank-you.

"My, how you've changed, Cal." Fanny clasped her hands delightedly. "Is this newfound confidence due to Mrs. Singletary's influence?"

"And Reese's." Callie answered without hesitation, not quite realizing what she'd revealed until the words had passed her lips.

Reese. He stood silently beside her, his shoulders not

quite touching hers. Tall, strong and vigilant, ever watchful, she found strength in his presence.

She dared a glance in his direction, but he wasn't looking at her. He was looking at Fanny, his expression unreadable.

Fanny turned to face him directly.

A hush fell over the surrounding crowd, spreading through the ballroom like yeast through leavened bread. It was as if the entire room was poised in anticipation, eager to witness firsthand this unexpected reunion between the estranged couple.

"Hello, Fanny." Reese gave her a brief nod, his smile slipping only a fraction. Callie doubted anyone noticed but her. "Welcome home."

"Thank you, Reese." Fanny looked momentarily disconcerted, then returned his smile with a bright one of her own. "It's wonderful to be back in Denver."

"Is your return permanent?" Callie asked, hoping to alleviate the tension falling over their awkward little group.

"I haven't yet decided." Something flickered in Fanny's gaze as she glanced at Mr. Hawkins. "The terms of my employment aren't quite settled."

Mr. Hawkins frowned, the gesture one of genuine masculine puzzlement. "Miss Mitchell, I am more than willing to meet your requests."

Fanny lifted her eyebrows. "*All* of them?"

After a slight pause, he nodded.

"Wonderful." Her eyes lit with triumph. "Nevertheless, I wish to think it over before I give you my answer."

Her response earned her a frown. "I understand. However, you should know…" His face took on an unbending expression. "I will not wait indefinitely for your answer. You have a week to make your decision."

Fanny gasped. "But, Mr. Hawkins, I—"

"One week. Not a day more."

After a quick word of farewell to Reese and Callie and a brief nod in Fanny's direction, he was gone.

Additional tension descended in his wake. Expectant silence hung heavy on the air. Not quite understanding what she'd just witnessed, Callie shared a confused glance with Reese.

He lifted a shoulder, then, ever the gentleman, stepped into the void. "Fanny, would you care to dance?"

Eyes still on Mr. Hawkins, hands clenched at her sides, Fanny drew in a sharp breath. "Thank you, Reese, I believe I would. Very much."

As he guided her sister onto the dance floor, Callie was filled with admiration for Reese. The sensation was followed immediately by gloom. Though Reese had merely been smoothing over an awkward moment, Fanny was once again in his arms.

Callie's worst nightmare realized.

Melting to the edge of the dance floor, then farther back into the shadow cast by an oversize flower arrangement, she watched her sister and the man she loved waltz together.

They made a striking pair.

Reese's masculine build stood in stark contrast to Fanny's slight frame, his dark to her light, their steps flawlessly in sync with the music. The romantic waltz seemed to have been composed for this moment.

Callie sighed unhappily. Mrs. Singletary had commissioned entirely too many waltzes for this evening's ball. Why couldn't she have insisted upon quadrilles, where couples spent more time apart than together? Or, better yet, a scotch reel, where they didn't touch at all.

Reese and Fanny executed a well-timed series of turns. The action sent a fold in Fanny's skirt wrapping around his legs. He said something to her that made her laugh.

Callie had a peculiar feeling in her stomach, one of dread, as if her world was about to cave in around her.

A faint sigh slipped past her lips.

"You're frowning, Miss Mitchell. Please tell me I'm not the cause."

"Indeed not." She swung her gaze to meet Marshall Ferguson's. "I was merely caught up in the music."

"By the expression on your face I take it you don't like this particular arrangement."

She considered how best to answer the question. "If you must know, I find it a bit melancholy for my liking."

He shut his eyes a moment, as if attempting to listen to the music without any distraction. "The composer has relied too heavily on the minor chords," he said, opening his eyes. "That, I believe, is why the piece has a sad tone."

"You know your music, Mr. Ferguson."

"A bit." He gave her a sheepish grin. "Don't tell my mother, but I have been known to tap out a ditty now and then on the fiddle."

Picturing him with a fiddle beneath his chin, plucking out a jaunty tune, she laughed softly. "I should very much like to see that."

"One day, perhaps I shall satisfy your curiosity." Smiling, he gestured to the flurry of dancers. "Would you do me the honor?"

Her first impulse was to refuse, to lean back against the wall and retreat into the shadows she'd once worn as a protection from future heartache. She'd hidden from life itself, cloaking her true self behind ugly clothes and severe hairstyles. She'd allowed a false sense of shame to keep her trapped in the mistake of her past.

She was not that woman anymore.

"Why, thank you, Mr. Ferguson, I would love to take a turn around the floor with you."

Reese knew the exact moment Callie and Marshall Ferguson joined the whirl of dancers. He felt it in his gut, in the kick of possessiveness that hit him square in the heart. *Mine. She is mine.*

He had half a mind to cut in, to stake his claim in front of everyone assembled, as beastly as that sounded even in his own head.

Alas, he must finish this dance with Fanny first. A multitude of gazes were on them. Tongues wagged. Speculation abounded.

"Why did you come home, Fanny?"

He didn't ask the question for himself. They'd said everything that needed saying months ago. There was no point in rehashing the past, especially since matters were settled between them. But Fanny's ill-timed arrival had brought unkind speculation onto Callie.

That, he would not tolerate.

Her gaze not quite meeting his, Fanny lifted her chin and said, "I came home because I missed my family."

He believed that was partially true. The Mitchell brood was a tight-knit group. Fanny had always been close with her siblings. But her explanation brought up another, more significant question. "Why did you choose tonight, and this ball in particular, to make your return?"

"I…" She sighed delicately. "It's hard to explain."

"Try."

She fell silent.

Reese took the opportunity to eye her more closely. He dropped his gaze over her face, searching for the woman he'd thought he knew. The one with manners and grace, who would never think to cause a public spectacle as she'd done tonight.

"You must have known your entrance would create a resurgence of the gossip."

She remained silent.

"That isn't like you, Fanny." He spoke her name softly, hoping to instill her trust, at least enough to get the truth out of her. "You've never been one to draw unnecessary attention to yourself. Again, I have to ask why you chose to do so tonight?"

"Oh, Reese." She lowered her gaze to a spot near his left shoulder. "I guess I thought if I faced the gossip head-on, in a public setting, with half of Denver in attendance, my return would go…easier."

"Easier?" The muscles in his shoulders tensed. "You mean easier for you."

"Yes."

"It was selfish of you not to warn anyone of your arrival, especially your sister."

"I'm sorry, truly I am. I didn't mean to throw speculation in her direction. And I definitely didn't mean to hurt Callie."

Again, he believed her. Fanny was not inherently selfish. She would never do anything malicious. Nevertheless, her actions had hurt her sister. Not just tonight, but for months.

"Your absence has been hard on her." He steered around a slow-moving couple gawking at them. He chose to ignore their interest. "Despite how things were left between you and Callie, she's missed you."

"I've missed her, too. I hadn't realized how much until I saw her again tonight." Sighing, Fanny leaned her head to one side and scanned the dance floor. "She's changed since I left, for the better."

"She's come into her own." He caught Callie's eye across the dance floor. She smiled at him over Ferguson's shoulder.

The tautness in his chest lightened as he returned the gesture.

Fanny followed the direction of his gaze. "I hadn't realized you and my sister…" She broke off. "That is, I hadn't considered that you two would form an…an affection in my absence."

He rolled his gaze back to her. "We don't need your permission."

"No, you don't. I meant what I said the last time we spoke, Reese. I wish you nothing but the greatest happiness in life. If my sister makes you smile like that, more the better."

His feet paused, the barest of seconds, before sweeping them into a series of fast turns that left no opportunity for further conversation.

Fanny broke the silence between them as the music hit the final chords. "Reese?"

He guided her through a simple, three-step turn. "Yes?"

"I'm glad we never married." She angled her head and studied his face. "I believe you are equally relieved."

He nodded. "We would have had a comfortable life together. But I have recently discovered I want more out of marriage."

He glanced over at Callie and saw his future unfold, a future full of laughter and happiness, children and family, freshly baked cookies and battles with toy soldiers.

He turned his gaze back to his dance partner. "I should have never proposed to you, Fanny."

"I should have never said yes."

The waltz came to an end, as did the remaining threads of uneasiness between them. They'd needed this final confrontation. Had needed to meet again and say their proverbial farewells.

Reese could go forth into the future confident his relationship with Fanny was firmly in the past. He offered his ex-fiancée his arm.

She took it without hesitation. "Thank you for the dance."

"The pleasure was all mine."

Chapter Twenty-Two

"The evening is an unqualified success." Mrs. Singletary made this pronouncement from the edge of the dance floor.

Callie stood restlessly by her side, wondering when the ball would come to an end. Not for several hours at least. The clock had just struck midnight and the crowd showed no signs of thinning. In fact, the heavily populated dance floor seemed to have grown denser in the past half hour.

She stifled a sigh and struggled to arrange a pleasant look on her face. "Everyone seems to be having a marvelous time."

"Of course they are, dear, we left nothing to chance. The decorations are lovely, the food superb, the music divine." As if she were a queen and the party guests were her beloved subjects, the widow cast a fond smile over the room. "I am quite pleased with the turnout. I predict the new hospital wing will be fully funded by the end of the night."

A blessing, to be sure. Yet Callie couldn't shake the terrible sense of foreboding that tugged at her. She hadn't spoken with Reese since he'd danced with her sister. There'd been no real opportunity. Fanny's sudden arrival seemed to have sparked even more female interest in Reese. He was the most desired dance partner at the ball.

For the past hour he'd wound his way through hordes of smiling admirers. He barely took a step away from one woman when another appeared by his side. They each received a word or two, some a request to dance. He was so gallant, so handsome, so *sought after.*

"…and despite the brief scene your sister's arrival created." Mrs. Singletary continued the conversation, ignoring Callie's lack of response. "Or perhaps because of her ill-timed appearance, tonight's ball will be talked about for months to come."

Though Callie had missed most of the widow's words, she couldn't argue that last point. Fanny had made quite the memorable entrance. Hours later, people were still whispering about her return. Many openly wondered what the estranged couple had said to one another during their sole dance together.

Callie would like to know the answer to that question herself.

The widow clasped her hands together in glee. "I believe this year's ball has proven even more eventful than last year's, when your brother accomplished quite the coup d'état."

Callie's smile came easily as she remembered how Garrett had dropped to one knee right in the middle of the dance floor. A hush had fallen over the crowd as he'd taken his childhood sweetheart's hand and uttered seven simple heartfelt words. *Molly Taylor Scott, will you marry me?*

Of course, Molly's answer had been yes.

Wistfully, Callie wondered if Reese would utter similar words to her. *Callie Anne Mitchell, will you marry me?*

Perhaps he wouldn't propose at all now that Fanny had returned. There'd been no chance to discover how he really felt about her sister's appearance.

For the past hour, Callie had been relegated to watching him take a turn across the floor with seven different partners. She'd counted every one of them. Now he was dancing with Temperance Evans.

"Speaking of your family…" Mrs. Singletary turned her head to Callie, a question in her gaze. "Where is Fanny?"

Though her sister had danced nearly as many dances as Reese, with as many different partners, she'd gone missing in the past ten minutes.

"I'm not sure," Callie admitted. "Perhaps she's at one of the buffet tables."

"Perhaps." Something came and went in the widow's eye, something a little sneaky. "It would seem Mr. Hawkins has gone missing, as well."

Before Callie could respond, Reese's father appeared.

He greeted the widow first. Then turned and bent over Callie's hand next, giving her curled fingers a polite kiss. The gesture was very smooth and perfectly executed.

"Miss Mitchell." He straightened. "May I have the honor of this dance?"

"Oh, I… You wish to dance with me?" She'd assumed he'd come over to ask the widow.

"Other than your exquisite employer—" he winked at Mrs. Singletary "—you are the most beautiful woman in the room."

The compliment warmed her bruised heart. Until he'd uttered those kind words Callie hadn't known how much she needed to hear them.

Shielding her gratitude behind lowered lashes, she took his offered hand. As they pirouetted across the floor, Callie allowed herself to enjoy the dance, *another* waltz, with a partner she liked and admired a great deal. If Reese did ask her to marry him, if he truly loved her as Mrs. Singletary claimed, Callie would take great pleasure in having this man as her father-in-law.

He effortlessly took her through a series of turns then smiled into her eyes. "I trust you are enjoying yourself this evening?"

Her gaze caught hold of Reese and Miss Evans twirling

together just off to their left. Why did he have to look so...
pleased with his dance partner?

Callie forced a tremulous smile on her lips and focused
her full attention on her own partner. "While tonight has
had its special moments—" the loveliest when she'd danced
with Reese "—to say I'm enjoying myself might be a bit
of an overstatement."

"Ah." His eyes took on a sympathetic light. "Your sister
certainly caused a stir with her arrival."

"I believe that was her aim." Now that she'd had time to
consider Fanny's behavior, Callie thought she understood
her motives. "She probably assumed it would be best to
face the bulk of the gossip all at once."

Even as a child, Fanny had tackled the worst of any situation first, saving the less challenging tasks for last. Her
favorite saying had always been *Let's get this over with,
shall we?* The more Callie chewed on the notion, the more
she thought she understood why Fanny had arrived at the
ball unannounced.

Had her sister explained her actions to Reese? Callie's
gaze sought his. He wasn't looking at her. He was too busy
smiling at something Miss Evans said.

Sniffing in irritation, she swung her gaze back to her
partner.

Another gleam of sympathy sparked in Mr. Bennett's
eyes. "Do not despair, my dear. My son can be slow on the
uptake, but he's a very smart man. He will come around,
given time."

Did she want Reese to *come around?*

No, she wanted him to love her without reservation. She
wanted him to give her his heart freely. She wanted him
to ask her to marry him without having to "come around"
to the idea after the elimination of other potential brides.

If Reese continued to hold on to his determination not

to love again, they could never be happy together. One, or both of them, would grow to resent the other.

Hopelessness filled her very bones, but Callie refused to allow her misery to show on her face.

"Have faith, Miss Mitchell." Mr. Bennett gave her another kind smile. "The Lord has the particulars of your future already worked out. When the time is right, you and Reese will find your way to happiness."

"How can you be so certain?"

"I have prayed on the matter."

"You…have prayed for Reese and me?"

"I have, and I'm fully confident all will turn out well." The waltz ended. Mr. Bennett stepped back and dropped his hands to his sides. "Smile, Miss Mitchell. Here comes my son to claim the next dance."

The moment after she thanked him for his kindness, she was swept into strong arms and spun in time to the strains of yet another waltz. It was a glorious moment, one she never wanted to end.

Callie let the music pour over her as Reese skillfully guided her across the floor. Clutching breathlessly at his broad shoulders, she gazed into his eyes and simply allowed herself to enjoy this time with him.

He smiled down at her with a look of admiration, affection and something else. Something she didn't dare name.

Dimly, she heard someone mention how wonderful *they* looked together. Was the comment directed at her and Reese?

"You look happy." His deep voice was like a soft, warm caress across her cheek.

"I am. Oh, Reese." She opened her eyes and smiled up at him. "At this moment, here in your arms, I am very, very happy."

"You're beautiful, Callie. You take my breath away." He spoke the words reverently, with a look in his eyes that denoted deep emotion, the kind that would endure a lifetime. But was it love he felt for her? Or something closer to affection?

He pulled her close. "Before the night is over," he said near her ear, "I wish to speak with you alone."

Oh, my. She experienced a small flutter of anticipation. "What's stopping us from finding a private spot now?"

"What, indeed?" He spun her to the edge of the dance floor and released his hold. His eyes were filled with a question, and just the barest hint of nerves.

He'd never been more attractive to her than in that moment.

He took her hand.

She let him lead her out of the ballroom, through the attached drawing room and, eventually, into the main corridor. "Where are you taking me?"

"To the place where my bride search officially began and where I hope—" he smiled over at her "—it shall end."

The sweet pain of hope filled her heart. And she knew in that moment that not only did she adore this man, but she would also love him with all her heart for the rest of her life.

He stopped outside the blue parlor and peered inside. "Excellent. No one here but us." He pulled her into the room with him and shut the door behind them. "At last, I have you all to myself."

This was it, Callie realized. He was going to propose.

But would she say yes?

Now that he had Callie alone, Reese felt a roll of apprehension slide along the base of his spine. He'd planned for this moment. Had carefully considered the exact words he would use.

He wanted Callie for his wife—no one else would do—but he was no longer sure how to introduce the subject of marriage. His proposal would be something he and Callie would retell over and over again, sharing the particulars with their family and friends, their children and grand-children.

The list.

He should start with the bride list he'd tucked in his jacket before leaving his house earlier this evening.

He reached his hand inside the pocket. At the same moment, Callie turned to face him fully, and he balked at the look of vulnerability he saw in her gaze. "Will you tell me what you and Fanny discussed during your dance?"

Of course she would want to know. Moreover, she *deserved* to know.

He thought back over his conversation with her sister—it seemed a lifetime ago—and chose to give Callie a brief summary rather than a word-for-word retelling. "She explained why she showed up here tonight without warning."

"I think I can hazard a guess."

He lifted a brow.

"She decided it would be best to confront as many people as possible rather than suffer endless individual meetings over the coming weeks."

"You know your sister well."

She continued staring up at him. "Was that all you discussed?"

"Mostly that. We also both agreed we should have never become engaged."

"But, Reese, you were engaged." She sat on a nearby settee, her posture still and erect. "We both know you would have married Fanny had she not begged off."

Refusing to begin their life together with a lie, he made no attempt to disagree. "I won't deny that I once thought your sister and I would suit. We were well-matched in many ways."

Callie lowered her head. "Yes, you were."

He came to stand next to her. She didn't look at him, but

kept gazing down at her slippered toes. "That's not to say I would have been happily married to her."

"You once told me companionship in marriage was more important than happiness."

"I was wrong. Callie, because of you, because of our time together, I can no longer settle for a comfortable marriage with a suitable bride."

She lifted her head, hope shining in her gaze. "Truly?"

"I want more."

He wanted the dream he'd only glimpsed in his youth. A dream lost to him in a split-second riding accident.

Now that he'd put the past behind him, and the grief, Reese wanted something different for his future, something new and real and lasting. A deep, abiding relationship. With Callie, only her, no one else would do.

"The woman who meets these requirements is the one I hope to marry."

He retrieved his most recent bride list and thrust it toward her with a surprisingly shaky hand.

She drew back from the paper as if it was a poisonous viper.

"Go on, take it." When she continued to recoil, he placed the list gently in her hand. "Once you read what I've written, I believe you'll understand everything."

He hoped.

For the first time in years, he lifted up a prayer to the Lord. *Please, Lord, let her see the contents of my heart in the list I've created.*

"Oh, Reese, I can't go through this with you anymore." She spoke in a quiet, even voice that sent a chill up his spine. "I just can't."

She attempted to return the paper to him, unread. He clasped his hands behind his back. "Read the list, Callie."

She blew out a breath.

"Please."

Some of his desperation must have sounded in his voice, because she lowered her head and began to scan the paper in silence.

He waited as she perused the front of the page. Over half of the thirty-seven items were written there. The rest were on the back.

Some of his requirements were intentionally vague. *She should sing hymns in church with a clear, bold voice.* Others were incredibly specific. *She must have blond hair, green eyes and have worked as Beatrix Singletary's companion for at least two months.*

For levity, he'd even included a few items that bordered on the silly, yet would hopefully mean something to Callie. Items such as *her name must begin with the letter* C. And...*she must be prepared to battle with toy soldiers on a weekly basis.*

Eyebrows scrunched in concentration, she flipped over the page.

When her lips pressed into a grim line, Reese felt the first stirrings of concern. Callie should be smiling by now. Surely, she recognized that he'd made the list with her in mind.

He held his breath, fighting an urge to rush her.

Finally, she set the paper on her lap and lifted her head.

What he saw in her eyes made his throat burn. Her gaze was completely closed off. She looked numb, hurt.

Somehow he'd injured her.

"Did you read item number thirty-seven?" That had been the most specific of the bunch. *She must be Callie Anne Mitchell, no other woman will do for me.*

"I did." Her voice was hollow and distant and so full of pain he felt a similar sensation strike at his own heart.

Panic tightened in his chest. "Have you nothing else to say?"

She looked down again, read the last line aloud in a flat, pained tone that spoke of heartbreak. He felt something rip inside him.

Sighing, she lifted her head. "Tell me why you want to marry me, Reese."

Her question confused him. "It's right there, on the paper, all thirty-seven reasons. What more do you want me to say?"

She flinched as if he'd slapped her. "I need you to tell me why I should marry you, in your own words."

"Those *are* my own words."

When she didn't respond, he realized he'd made a mistake. Somehow he'd botched this and yet he couldn't pinpoint exactly how.

The silence between them grew. His heart lurched as he watched her eyes fill with tears.

He dropped in front of her and placed his palms flat on her knees.

"Don't cry, Callie." He took her hands and drew them to his lips. "Please, don't cry. I want you for my bride. Only you. There is no other woman for me. I will never want anyone but you."

Her wet, spiky lashes blinked at him. The sadness was still there in her gaze. *Why* was she still sad?

He rose, dragged her into his arms and kissed her on the mouth. After a moment, he pulled slightly away, looked her straight in the eyes and said, "Callie Anne Mitchell, will you marry me?"

"Oh, Reese. I've been waiting to hear those words for a very long time." She laid her head on his shoulder and whispered into his coat, "I love you."

His heart soared.

Then dipped. Something was wrong. Callie wasn't saying yes to his proposal. She was crying again. He could feel the tension thrumming through her.

She stepped out of his arms, lifted her chin and, after snuffling a little, placed steel in her spine. "Do you love me, too, Reese?"

For a moment he stood staring at her, speechless. Most of him wanted to answer yes. *Of course I love you,* his heart whispered.

He loved her more than he thought himself capable. But one small, stubborn part of him couldn't push out the words.

For an alarming moment, he was frozen between past and present, his very future at stake. And still, he couldn't seem to make his mouth work properly.

Callie's lower lip trembled. "Your hesitation is answer enough."

He reached for her, but she spun away from him and hurried out of the room.

Following hard on her heels, he called after her. "Callie, don't go. I love you. I—"

She couldn't hear him. She was already halfway down the corridor, slipping around the corner. He followed after her, but he was too far behind. She'd disappeared into the crowd before he could call to her again.

His heart turned to ice. His mind reeled. He knew this feeling. *This is what grief feels like. This is the agony that comes with loss.*

No different than a death.

He'd vowed never to experience this type of pain a second time in his life, only to have it become his reality once again.

Throat thick, Reese stared at the sea of bobbing heads, wondering how he would convince Callie he loved her with all his soul.

It wasn't going to be easy, but convince her he would. He couldn't lose Callie. He'd do whatever it took to keep her in his life forever. But he would not give her another list. No. More. Lists. He would win her over with words spoken from the deepest depths of his heart.

He prayed it would be enough. It *had* to be enough.

Chapter Twenty-Three

Still dressed in her ball gown, Callie lay on her bed, blinking up at the ornate, perfectly square ceiling tiles overhead. Tears leaked out of the corner of her eyes. She let them come, let them spill freely.

Let them blur her vision.

She was so tired. So scared and confused. Reese loved her. He *had* to love her. All the signs were in the list she held clutched against her heart. She had no doubt he'd put considerable thought into each and every item. She even understood what he'd been trying to tell her. The dear, sweet, wonderful man.

His marriage proposal had been simple, the exact words she'd dreamed of hearing from him. But there was still no guarantee he would give her his heart completely.

Without his full commitment to her, their life together would be nothing more than an empty shell of unrealized possibilities.

Why couldn't Reese embrace the gift they'd been given, a deep, abiding love that was meant to last forever?

Rolling onto her side, Callie crumpled the list tightly in her hand and continued to cry. Dawn's gray light cast its gloomy hue over the room. The quiet was unearthly, especially after the crushing din of the party that had only just concluded an hour ago.

Callie was going to lose Reese. The prospect was so awful that she squeezed her eyes tightly shut and begged the Lord for relief from the pain in her heart. All she wanted was for Reese to admit he loved her. Why couldn't he say three simple words? *I love you.*

Perhaps she was asking too much of him. Perhaps he'd expressed his feelings in the only way he knew how, in a list of thirty-seven requirements that only she could meet.

"Callie?" A light scratching came from the other side of her door. "Are you in there?"

She pressed her face into her pillow.

The knocking increased, growing louder with each blow of fist to wood.

"Go away, Fanny."

"I'm afraid I can't do that." The door creaked on its hinges. Light footsteps sounded on the wood floor. And then, her sister stood next to the bed.

Callie rolled to her other side. "I don't wish to speak with you right now."

"But you're crying."

"I'm fine."

"You've never lied to me before, Cal, don't start now."

At the disapproval she heard in her sister's voice, something inside Callie snapped. "Go. Away. Fanny." She swiped at her eyes. "It's an easy enough request for you to follow. You're good at leaving."

As soon as she said the words, she regretted them. But before she could offer an apology, Fanny laughed softly. "A valiant effort, but you won't run me off that easily."

Callie swiveled her head to meet her sister's gaze. "I didn't mean to criticize you for leaving town."

"Yes, you did." Fanny smiled affectionately down at her. "I can't say I blame you."

"You did what you thought was best at the time."

"Very true." Fanny came around to the other side of the bed and sat down beside Callie. "But that doesn't take away the fact that I was impossible to live with during those initial days following my broken engagement."

"You weren't *that* bad."

"Oh, I was. I was surly, short-tempered, about as inflexible as a wood plank. I only thought of myself. When I made my plans to leave Denver, escape was all I cared about. I know that's no excuse for my behavior, but I couldn't stand the gossip another day, or—" she gave Callie a meaningful gaze "—the censure."

"You mean the censure from me."

"I mean from everyone. You. Garrett. Even our parents." Fanny twisted around and stretched out on the bed beside her. "I knew I was letting everyone down, but there was nothing I could say, no explanation I could express that seemed to satisfy any of you."

Callie squeezed her sister's hand. "I'm sorry I was so hard on you."

"I understand why you were." Fanny turned her head. "You thought I was making a mistake, the biggest of my life."

Callie frowned at the memory of that difficult time. She'd said a lot of things to her sister, all of them true, none of them tactful. Looking back, she wished she would have spoken with more grace, less disapproval.

"I'm sorry," she said again. "I could have chosen my words better."

"Apology accepted."

They fell silent, each staring up at the ceiling.

"Callie, do you still believe all the things you said about Reese?"

"I—" She cut off the rest of her words and considered the question seriously, trying to remember exactly what she'd said about Reese back then. The same she would say about him now. "Yes, I believe he's a good man, decent and loyal, the best I've ever known."

"You're in love with him."

She kept her gaze focused on the ceiling. "I am."

Fanny laughed delightedly. "That's terrific, Callie."

"It doesn't bother you that I'm in love with the man you once planned to marry?"

"Not in the least. What Reese and I shared would not have sustained a marriage in the long run. You two are far better suited. I wish you nothing but happiness together."

Callie had needed to hear those words from her sister, she realized. Yet her heart remained locked in despair. "Reese and I will never be truly happy if he continues to hold a portion of himself back from me. It's not that I want him to forget his first wife. I just want him to—"

"His first wife?" Fanny hopped off the bed and spun around to gape at her in open-mouthed shock. "What are you talking about? Reese has never been married."

Mind reeling, Callie sat up and swung her feet to the ground. "You don't know about Miranda?"

"Who's Miranda?"

"The woman Reese married when he was eighteen. She died a month later in a tragic riding accident. He never told you about her?"

Fanny's eyebrows drew together. "In the entire time we were engaged, not once did he mention that he'd been married before."

"And yet he told me the whole story." Callie processed this new twist in her relationship with Reese, felt a spark of hope ignite.

"You do realize what this means?" Fanny sat down on the bed beside her. "Reese loves you, Callie. Why else would he trust you with the secret of his past?"

The secret of his past. Yes, Reese had shared much with

Callie, including the pain and grief he'd experienced after Miranda's death.

He claimed he'd loved once and once was enough. Yet, he continued to love deeply. He loved his father. He loved the children at Charity House.

He loved Callie.

He'd tried to tell her as much with his bride list. His feelings for her were written in that bold, looping script of his, the truth all but glaring at her from every item. He'd done so much more than speak three simple words. He'd spelled out his love thirty-seven unique, individual times.

She must find him and tell him she understood. She would tell him she loved him and convince him that she didn't need him to say the words back. She would—

"What's that you're twisting around in your fingers?" Not waiting for an answer, Fanny took Reese's list and began reading it aloud. "'My bride must meet the following requirements. Number one, she must—'"

"Give me that back." Callie snatched the paper out of her sister's hands. "It's for my eyes only."

"What is it? Something Reese gave you, I can tell. I recognize his handwriting."

Callie's heart slammed hard against her ribs. Of course Fanny would recognize Reese's handwriting. There were a lot of things her sister knew about Reese. It would take Callie a while to get used to Fanny knowing him so well.

Not as well as you. He never shared himself with her as he has with you.

The peace that flowed through her brought another wave of tears.

"Thank you, Fanny." Callie pulled her sister into her arms and gave her a tight, heartfelt hug. "Thank you so very much."

"You're so very welcome. But, Callie, what are you thanking me for?"

"For breaking your engagement with Reese."

"Ah, that." Fanny stepped back and grinned. "You're most welcome, dear sister, most welcome indeed."

They shared a laugh.

"Oh, Fanny." Callie's heart swelled with sisterly love. "I pray you find happiness one day with the man of your dreams."

"I pray that, as well. I even think I know the man already." A turbulent expression fell over her face. "But I may have already ruined my chances with him."

For the first time since her sister's return, Callie realized Fanny had changed. Not outwardly. She was still as beautiful as ever, perhaps even more so. But there was a sadness in eyes, one that denoted heartache. Callie recognized the look. She'd worn it herself for years. "Has someone hurt you, Fanny? A man, perhaps?"

"Yes and no."

"That's an interesting answer that tells me absolutely nothing."

"It's complicated, Callie. Suffice it to say I misunderstood someone's intentions and now I must either move on with my life or wallow in self-pity."

Callie gripped her hands. "If you need to talk…"

"I know I can come to you." She firmed her chin. "Yes, yes, but enough about me. What about you. What are *you* going to do about Reese?"

"I'm going to take the biggest leap of faith in my life. And leave the rest up to the Lord."

"Now that's the fighting Mitchell spirit. But before you approach Reese, I highly recommend you consider changing that dress." Fanny's gaze narrowed over her. "You may also wish to splash cool water on your face."

"Is that your tactful way of telling me my gown is wrinkled and my eyes are puffy?"

Fanny pursed her lips. "You'll also want to rethink your hair."

* * *

The first thing Reese did the next morning was return to Mrs. Singletary's, back to the place where he began his search for a suitable bride.

Callie had been with him every step of the way. It seemed fitting she was where his journey ended. He would not leave the widow's mansion until he secured Callie's hand in marriage.

A bleary-eyed Winston let him in. "Good morning, Mr. Bennett."

"A fine good morning to you, Winston."

The butler blinked, his brows pulling together in obvious confusion. "I wasn't aware you had an appointment with Mrs. Singletary this morning."

"I've come for Miss Mitchell."

The confusion dug deeper across the man's forehead. "That presents a problem, sir. Miss Mitchell left the house nearly thirty minutes ago."

Reese's heart took a plunge. Of all the scenarios he'd taken into account, he hadn't expected Callie to be out when he returned this morning.

He forced down the thread of panic weaving through him and made himself speak slowly. "Do you know where she went?"

The butler's gaze shifted around the entryway, then fell back on Reese. "I believe Miss Mitchell mentioned she was heading to your house, sir."

Callie had gone in search of him? Joy wound through his apprehension, the sensation so profound Reese nearly lost his footing. "Thank you, Winston."

A renewed urgency in his steps, he exited the house, his sole intent to find Callie as quickly as possible.

Halfway home, he caught sight of her across the street. His heart slammed against his chest, as it always did whenever she was near.

She hadn't seen him yet. That didn't stop Reese from cataloguing her every feature. The tall, lithe frame. The exquisite face and sea-green eyes. The pale blond hair pinned beneath a jaunty, feathered hat, her loose curls hanging down her back in pretty waves.

Callie. His Callie.

For too many years, she'd stood on the edges of life, content to observe rather than participate. She'd hid her true self behind drab clothes and severe hair. Never again. He would make sure she had no reason to camouflage her true nature. She was a beautiful, kind-hearted woman meant to live each moment to the fullest. With him by her side.

Pulse roaring in his ears, he crossed the street. "Callie."

Her gaze connected with his and her feet ground to a stop. For a moment, neither of them spoke. Neither of them moved.

Reese swallowed.

The pretty speech he had planned vanished from him mind. Everything he'd been, everything he was, everything he desperately wanted to become, pinpointed to this one moment. To this declaration of his heart. "I love you."

"Oh, Reese." She leaped into his arms. It was more a collision than an embrace and defined their relationship perfectly. No half measures for them.

He held her tightly to him and simply breathed her in for several long moments.

"I love you, too," she whispered in his ear. "So very much."

They kissed, right there, in the middle of the neighborhood, for entirely too long to be considered proper.

Reese loved every scandalous, reckless second.

When he pulled back and looked into her eyes, he saw his whole future staring back at him. With their combined love and commitment to one another, they would raise their children in a happy, somewhat messy, boisterous home.

He had much to say to her, but first...

He pulled her close again and whispered the contents of his heart another time. "I love you."

"I don't think I'll ever get tired of hearing that." She sighed into his neck. "I came looking for you this morning, but you weren't home. I was on my way to your office."

He set her at arm's length. "Winston kindly told me where to find you."

"You went to Mrs. Singletary's in search of me?"

"I came to give you the words you deserve to hear." He took her hands, placed them next to his heart. "I love you, Callie Mitchell."

"That's the third time you've said that."

"I plan to tell you every day for the rest of my life, three, four, five times a day, even more on special occasions."

She laughed. "What a pair we make. I went to your house to tell you I already know how you feel about me. You don't have to say the words, Reese."

"Callie, my love, I want to say them. I *need* to say them." He drew her hands away from his heart and kissed each set of knuckles. "After Miranda died I foolishly vowed never to love again, at least not with the careless abandon that had led to my unspeakable grief. I was wrong to close myself off from the possibility of loving again."

"It was an understandable response to your loss. I don't want to replace Miranda in your heart." She smoothed her fingertips over his face, flattened her palm against his chest. "I believe there's room in there for both of us."

This woman understood him in a way no one ever had before. "Miranda was the love of my youth, but you, Callie." He dropped his head and placed a kiss on her palm. "*You* are the love of my life."

"Oh, Reese."

"Callie Anne Mitchell." He bent to one knee. "Will you marry me?"

"Yes. Oh, yes, Reese." Tears filled her eyes, spilled down her cheeks. "Of course I'll marry you."

"Don't cry, Callie." He rose, wiped at her tears with the pad of his thumb. "You're supposed to be happy."

"I am. I'm ecstatic." She turned her head slightly away. "But I've never been a pretty crier. I must look a mess."

He cupped her face in his hands. "You've never looked more beautiful in my eyes."

"Oh, Reese, stop. Stop being so wonderful. You're going to make me cry harder."

"I love you, Callie." He pulled her into his arms, rested his chin on her head. "I'll love you until the day I die."

This time, she pulled back. "I'll love you just as long, Reese, until there's no more breath in my lungs."

His heart stilled, and his mind clouded over with abject terror. No. He would not allow fear to prevent him from reaching for a lifetime of happiness with this woman.

"Whether you live one day, fifty years, or a hundred and fifty, my life will be richer for having you in it."

She lifted on her toes and kissed him on the mouth. "I'll do my very best not to die on you anytime soon."

He knew it was a promise that came straight from her heart, but there were no guarantees in life. "We'll live each day to the fullest and face every moment, whether good or bad, together."

"That sounds like a wedding vow."

"All that's left is the ceremony." He kissed her forehead. "How do you feel about short engagements?"

"I think they're the very best possible kind."

He kissed her temple. "We're in agreement."

She laughed.

He kissed her nose. "One month from today you will become Mrs. Reese Bennett, Jr. and I'll become the happiest man on earth."

"I love you, Reese."

He kissed her mouth. "I love you, too, Callie. I will love you for the rest of my life, with all my heart."

It was a pledge he would never grow tired of giving.

Epilogue

Exactly one month after the day he'd proposed, Reese stood at the front of the church. His father was on his left, Pastor Beau on his right. All three men were really very handsome, but the most attractive in Callie's eyes was Reese.

He looked magnificent in his gray morning suit.

In a matter of minutes he would become her husband.

Fanny gripped both her shoulders and kissed her on the cheek. "Ready to get married?"

If asked, Callie would say a month engagement was twenty-nine and a half days too long. "I'm more than ready."

"Then you better follow me." Fanny spun around, winked at Callie over her shoulder then waltzed down the aisle.

Not a single whisper rose up in her wake, not one comment about the maid of honor having once been engaged to the groom. Reese and Callie had invited only family and close friends to their wedding, as much for Fanny's sake as theirs.

The dress Callie wore had been a gift from Mrs. Singletary. The widow had spared no expense on the gown. The yards of cream-colored satin overlaid with imported lace was the finest Callie had ever owned.

Mrs. Singletary had been with her at every fitting, and had helped her plan every detail in the short time between

Reese's proposal and today's ceremony. Through it all, she'd gloated over her role in making what she called "the match of the season."

Callie would miss the woman dearly. She took great comfort in knowing that Reese was still Mrs. Singletary's personal attorney and Callie was still a member of the Ladies League for Destitute Widows and Orphans. She would have chance upon chance to socialize with the widow, especially if Reese's father would take the hint and start pursing her with more enthusiasm.

Once Fanny took her place at the front of the church, the organist switched her sheet music and began playing the wedding march.

The guests rose to their feet and swung their gazes in Callie's direction.

"That's our cue." Her father kissed her on the forehead. "This is where I would normally give you one final chance to change your mind. But there's no need for such silliness here."

Callie laughed softly. "No, sir. No need at all."

He offered her his arm. "Shall we?"

"We shall."

Head high, shoulders square, Callie began her march down the aisle on her father's arm.

Gabriella and Daniel waved from the pew they shared with the other Charity House children. Of course, she waved back. Their big, happy smiles were proof the children were finally settling into life at the orphanage.

At the end of the aisle, Callie caught sight of her mother's eyes filling with tears of joy. She had to look away or risk crying herself.

Her father kissed her one last time, and then passed her off to her groom.

Smiling broadly, Reese leaned over and whispered her

three favorite words in her ear, low enough that only she could hear.

Her heart lifted, sighed.

Pastor Beau cleared his throat. "Shall we begin?"

As one, they turned to face the altar.

After they recited the traditional vows, and the rings were exchanged, Reese took Callie's hand in his.

"I love you," he said simply.

She made the same pledge from the depths of her soul. "I love you."

"With the Lord as my guide," he continued in a gruff voice, "I'll stand by your side, Callie. I'll stick with you through the joys and sorrows of life, through every first and every last, through births and deaths and everything in between."

"And I'll stand by your side, Reese, I'll never waver, never question your devotion. I will be your helpmate and honor you always."

Pastor Beau concluded the ceremony with a few words. "Reese and Callie, may your love always be sincere, full of kindness, grace and mercy. Make it your mission to esteem one another above yourselves. Be joyful in hope, patient in affliction and faithful in prayer. Live in harmony with one another and your neighbors." He paused, smiled, then finished with, "I now pronounce you man and wife."

A loud cheer rose up from the Charity House pew. Not to be outdone, Callie's brothers added their own hoots and hollers of approval.

"On that joyful sound." The preacher gave a hearty laugh. "You may kiss your bride."

"Gladly." Reese pulled her into his arms and gave her a long, drawn-out, soul-searing kiss.

When he eventually stepped back, Callie smiled up at her husband. "We're going to have a lovely life together."

"While we're at it—" he pulled her back into his arms "—let's have a little fun, too."

She eagerly agreed. "That's a splendid idea."

With their family and friends shouting to *kiss her again,* Reese touched his mouth to hers.

It was a perfect start to their marriage. A moment Callie would cherish all the rest of her days.

* * * * *

Dear Reader,

Thank you for purchasing Reese and Callie's story. I hope you enjoyed reading about their journey to love and happiness as much as I enjoyed writing it.

His Most Suitable Bride is Book 8 in my Charity House series, with more still to come. I never expected to have so many stories to tell, or that I would be able to create so many characters, or have the opportunity to explore so many wonderful themes. As I look back over all eight books I realize several themes have become staples in the various storylines: the joy that can be found in nontraditional families, the difficulty of overcoming past mistakes and letting go of the resulting shame. The dangers of false pride, false humility and, of course, inaccurate first impressions.

We live in a culture that glorifies outer beauty. Yet, as *1 Samuel* 16:7 reminds us, *the Lord does not see as man sees…but the Lord looks at the heart.* I loved digging deeper into Callie, a woman who hid her beauty for fear of being noticed. I wonder how many of us can relate? How many times do we hide our true natures for fear of being sought after for the wrong reasons? From the beginning, Reese recognized there was more to Callie than drab clothes and severe hairstyles. He eventually sees her as the most beautiful woman of his acquaintance, as much for her inner beauty as her outer appeal. We could all use someone like that in our life. Don't you agree?

I always love hearing from readers. Please feel free to contact me on Facebook or Twitter @ReneeRyanBooks or at my website www.reneeryan.com

In the meantime, happy reading!

Renee

Questions for Discussion

1. The opening scene introduces the heroine, Callie Mitchell. She's a woman who sees herself far differently than the world sees her. Why do you think Callie has this particular self-image? How does Reese see her and why does this present a problem for him?

2. Why does Reese dislike this particular opera in the opening scene? What does the storyline bring to mind? Do you avoid certain plays, movies or storylines because they bring back bad memories? Why or why not?

3. What reasoning does Mrs. Singletary use when she insists Callie change her outer appearance? How does Callie react? Why does changing the way she dresses bring on a state of panic for her?

4. Mrs. Singletary informs Reese he is considered by some in town to be stern and overly rigid. Why does this cause her concern? What does she propose will help his image? How does he react?

5. Why does Reese agree to Mrs. Singletary's plan to find him a bride? What twist does the widow throw into the mix that makes him question his original agreement?

6. Why is Callie upset to see Jonathon Hawkins at Mrs. Singletary's dinner party? What does he give her at the dinner party that makes her reassess her original opinion of him?

7. Reese shows up at Charity House while Callie is teaching some girls how to bake pies. How is this encounter

different than others before? What do Reese and Callie discuss on the way home? How does this discussion draw them closer?

8. What happens when Reese invites Callie and Mrs. Singletary to join him at the theater? What play is being performed and who is the lead actor of the play? Why does this upset Callie?

9. How does Reese handle Callie's revelation about her shameful act back in Boston? Have you ever carried shame over a past mistake? Did you accept God's grace? Why or why not?

10. Reese finally attends church with his father, but doesn't make it through the entire sermon. Why did he leave the service? What does he reveal to Callie when she finds him in the cemetery beside Miranda's grave?

11. How does Reese's bride search actually bring Callie and Reese closer together? What does he do to sabotage the process? What does Callie do?

12. Who shows up at Mrs. Singletary's charity ball? How do Reese and Callie react?

13. How does Reese propose to Callie? Why does she reject his offer? What does Fanny tell Callie later that morning that helps her see Reese really does love her?

14. How does Reese propose to Callie the second time around? What is her response this time?

REQUEST YOUR FREE BOOKS!

2 FREE INSPIRATIONAL NOVELS
PLUS 2
FREE
MYSTERY GIFTS

Love Inspired.
HISTORICAL
INSPIRATIONAL HISTORICAL ROMANCE

YES! Please send me 2 FREE Love Inspired® Historical novels and my 2 FREE mystery gifts (gifts are worth about $10). After receiving them, if I don't wish to receive any more books, I can return the shipping statement marked "cancel." If I don't cancel, I will receive 4 brand-new novels every month and be billed just $4.74 per book in the U.S. or $5.24 per book in Canada. That's a saving of at least 21% off the cover price. It's quite a bargain! Shipping and handling is just 50¢ per book in the U.S. and 75¢ per book in Canada.* I understand that accepting the 2 free books and gifts places me under no obligation to buy anything. I can always return a shipment and cancel at any time. Even if I never buy another book, the two free books and gifts are mine to keep forever.

102/302 IDN F5CN

Name _____ (PLEASE PRINT)

Address _____ Apt. #

City _____ State/Prov. _____ Zip/Postal Code

Signature (if under 18, a parent or guardian must sign)

Mail to the Harlequin® Reader Service:
IN U.S.A.: P.O. Box 1867, Buffalo, NY 14240-1867
IN CANADA: P.O. Box 609, Fort Erie, Ontario L2A 5X3

Want to try two free books from another series?
Call 1-800-873-8635 or visit www.ReaderService.com.

* Terms and prices subject to change without notice. Prices do not include applicable taxes. Sales tax applicable in N.Y. Canadian residents will be charged applicable taxes. Offer not valid in Quebec. This offer is limited to one order per household. Not valid for current subscribers to Love Inspired Historical books. All orders subject to credit approval. Credit or debit balances in a customer's account(s) may be offset by any other outstanding balance owed by or to the customer. Please allow 4 to 6 weeks for delivery. Offer available while quantities last.

Your Privacy—The Harlequin® Reader Service is committed to protecting your privacy. Our Privacy Policy is available online at www.ReaderService.com or upon request from the Harlequin Reader Service.

We make a portion of our mailing list available to reputable third parties that offer products we believe may interest you. If you prefer that we not exchange your name with third parties, or if you wish to clarify or modify your communication preferences, please visit us at www.ReaderService.com/consumerschoice or write to us at Harlequin Reader Service Preference Service, P.O. Box 9062, Buffalo, NY 14269. Include your complete name and address.

LIH13R

SPECIAL EXCERPT FROM

Love Inspired

*Get ready for a Big Sky wedding…or fifty! Here's a
sneak peek at
HIS MONTANA BRIDE by Brenda Minton,
part of the BIG SKY CENTENNIAL miniseries:*

"Bad news," Cord said. "That was the wedding coordinator. She's quitting."

"Ouch. So now what?"

"I'm not sure."

"With no coordinator to help, will you call off the wedding?" Katie asked.

"No." There was too much at stake. The town needed this wedding and the money it would bring in. They had a bridge in need of repairs and a museum they couldn't finish without more funds. "I'll just figure out how to pull off a wedding for fifty couples, maybe get some media attention for Jasper Gulch and hopefully not mess up anyone's life."

"I think you'll do just fine. Remember, it's all about the dress."

"How long are you going to be in town, Katie?" He placed a hand on her back and guided her up the sidewalk.

"I'm not sure. I'm supposed to be helping my sister, but she seems to have escaped and left me here." She sighed and glanced at him.

"Do you think that as long as you're here…"

They were standing in front of the massive wooden doors that led to the church. She had a slightly red nose from the cool morning air and her lips were tinted with pink gloss. As long as she was there, she could be a friend. That wasn't what he'd planned to say, but the thought framed itself as a question in his mind.

She was studying his face, waiting for him to finish.

"Maybe you could help me with this wedding?"

"I thought maybe you wanted me to run interference and keep the single women at bay. 'Hands off Cord Shaw,' that kind of thing." As she said it, somehow her palm came to rest on his shoulder as if they'd been friends forever.

It was the strangest and maybe one of the best feelings. It tangled him up and made him lose track of the reality that he was standing in front of the church. The door could open at any moment. And for the first time in years, a woman had made him feel at ease.

Can rancher Cord Shaw and Katie Archer pull off Jasper Gulch's latest centennial event without getting their hearts involved? Find out in HIS MONTANA BRIDE by Brenda Minton, available October 2014 from Love Inspired.

Danger and love go hand in hand in the small town
of Wrangler's Corner. Read on for a sneak preview of
THE LAWMAN RETURNS by Lynette Eason,
the first book in this exciting new series from
Love Inspired Suspense.

Sheriff's deputy Clay Starke wheeled to a stop in front of
the beat-up trailer. He heard the sharp crack, and the side
of the trailer spit metal.

A shooter.

The woman on the porch careened down the steps and
bolted toward him. Terror radiated from her. He shoved
open the door to the passenger side. "Get in!"

Breathless, she landed in the passenger seat and slammed
the door. Eyes wide, she lifted shaking hands to push her
blond hair out of her eyes.

Clay got on his radio and reported shots fired.

He cranked the car and started to back out of the drive.

"No! We can't leave!"

"What?" He stepped on the brake. "Lady, if someone's
shooting, I'm getting you out of here."

"But I think Jordan's in there, and I can't leave without
him."

"Jordan?"

"A boy I work with. He called me for help. I'm worried
he might be hurt."

Clay put the car back in Park. "Then stay down and let
me check it out."

"But if you get out, he might shoot you."

He waited. No more shots. "Stay put. I think he might be gone."

"Or waiting for one of us to get out of the car."

True. He could feel her gaze on him, studying him, dissecting him. He frowned. "What is it?"

"You."

He shot a glance behind them, then let his gaze rove the area until he'd gone in a full circle and was once again looking into her pretty face. "What about me?"

Red crept into her cheeks. "You look so much like Steven. Are you related?"

He stilled, focusing in on her. "I'm Clay Starke. You knew my brother?"

"Clay? I'm Sabrina Mayfield."

Oh, wow. Sabrina Mayfield. "Are you saying the kid in there knows something about Steven's death?"

"I don't know what he's doing here, but he called me and said he thought he knew who killed Steven and he needed me to come get him."

A tingle of shock raced through Clay. Finally. After weeks with nothing, this could be the break he'd been looking for. "Then I want to know what he knows."

Pick up THE LAWMAN RETURNS, available October 2014 wherever Love Inspired Suspense books are sold.

Big Sky Cowboy

by LINDA FORD

JUST THE COWBOY SHE NEEDED?

The last thing Cora Bell wants is a distracting cowboy showing up on her family's farm seeking temporary shelter. Especially one she is sure has something to hide. But she'll accept Wyatt Williams's help rebuilding her family's barn— and try not to fall once again for a man whose plans don't include staying around.

Since leaving his troubled past behind, Wyatt avoids personal entanglements. He just wants to make a new start with his younger brother. But there's something about Cora that he's instinctively drawn to. Dare this solitary cowboy risk revealing his secrets for a chance at redemption and a bright new future with Cora by his side?

Montana Marriages

Three sisters discover a legacy
of love beneath the Western sky

*Available October 2014 wherever
Love Inspired books and ebooks are sold.*

Hunter Jacobson wants no part of his grandfather's matchmaking. The lone cowboy is certain that's what the old man is doing when he trades part of their Montana ranch for Scarlett Murphy's shares of an old Alaska gold mine. Or is he running one of his legendary scams on the sweet single mom? A trip to Dry Creek, Alaska, reveals the truth—and brings Hunter and Scarlett face-to-face with a past family feud and a vulnerable present. But surprisingly it's the future that intrigues Hunter most…if he can get Scarlett to make him her groom.

✦ NORTH *to* DRY CREEK ✦

The road to Alaska is paved with love

Alaskan Sweethearts

by

Janet Tronstad

Available October 2014
wherever Love Inspired books
and ebooks are sold.

LI87914